SUMMER'S FALL

CAMILLA OCHLAN
CAROL E. LEEVER

OF CATS AND DRAGONS BOOK 3

Copyright

Summer's Fall

Dedication

To our fathers, who — in their own ways — taught us that in an infinite multiverse, anything is possible.

CONTENTS

Timeline of Books

Counted from the year of the last Covenant, 14,000 years ago.

❖

14,021 *Autumn:* Night's Gift (Book 1)
14,021 *Winter:* Winter Tithe (Novella)

❖

14,022 *Spring:* Radiation (Book 2)
14,022 *Summer:* Summer's Fall (Book 3)
14,022 *Summer:* Hollow Season (Book 4)
14,022 *Summer:* Autumn King (Book 5)
14,022 *Summer:* Solstice Thyme (short story)

❖

You can get Night's Gift (Book 1 e-book) for free when you sign up for the Of Cats And Dragons Newsletter.

Radiation (Book 2 e-book) is also available for free when you sign up for the Of Cats And Dragons Newsletter.

We offer Winter Tithe as a seasonal gift for our newsletter subscribers.

Solstice Thyme will soon be available on our website at OfCatsAndDragons.com

Chapter 1: Monsters

OMEN

Even through the heavy mist rolling in off the ocean, Omen could see the dragon watching them from the far cliff. The rumble of crashing waves mingled with the soft voices of Omen's little brother Kyr and their two cats as they climbed effortlessly down the stone steps carved into the side of the cliff near their home.

"Moffles!" Tyrin, the smaller of the two orange cats, squeaked. "I love &$@# moffles!"

Kyr and the cats paid little heed to the golden dragon perched upon the high cliffs or the gathering fog that spread rapidly over the white sand below.

The day had been sunny only an hour ago when Omen had promised the noisy trio that he'd take them down to the beach to look for sand urchins. But before they'd even reached the cliffs, the sky had grown overcast. And while the dragon had been completely visible mere moments before, now fingers of cold mist wrapped around its form, leaving only the occasional glint of dragonscales flashing in the muted light to betray the great winged creature's presence.

Strange weather, Omen mused to himself. *Early summer in Melia is normally sunny and warm.*

"You is trying moffles, Kyr," Tyrin proclaimed loudly from his perch on Kyr's shoulder. The little cat fluffed his orange fur against the crisp breeze, wrapped his tail neatly around the skinny half-elvin boy's neck, and snuggled up against his pointed ear.

Tormy, identical in coloring to the tiny Tyrin, but not in size, gently brushed up against Kyr's side, as if to assure himself that the boy was safely on the inside of the cliff's edge. Nearly the size of a horse, Tormy dwarfed the young boy and set each white-tipped paw down cautiously on the stone steps, taking great care not to knock Kyr over.

Kyr kept one pale hand braced against the large cat's shoulder, his thin fingers buried in Tormy's long orange fur to steady himself.

"Yes, you is trying moffles after Omy is making them for us," Tormy agreed happily, his rumbling voice vibrating with a low purr at the thought of meals to come.

"I'll make you waffles," Omen called down to the two cats, "but I'm not putting mice in them!"

"But moffles is the bestest, Omy," Tormy whined.

"Yes, moffles is the bestest," Tyrin agreed. "But you is making mouse-cakes instead maybe?" The little cat looked back over his shoulder at Omen, ears perked forward eagerly.

Omen's lips twitched as he shook his head in firm denial. His mother was remarkably indulgent when it came to the two cats and their odd requests, but she drew the line at adding mice to any meal. "No, mouse-cakes," he insisted. "You want mice, go catch them yourselves."

"But Kyr is never having moffles before," Tormy argued as he reached the bottom of the stone steps and hopped forward onto the white sand.

Suddenly suspicious, Omen placed his hand on his little brother's shoulder. "They haven't given you any mice to eat? Have they, Kyr?"

The boy, who had spent most of his life starving, would eat pretty much anything put in front of him. *And he trusts the cats completely.*

The cold wind blew Kyr's golden hair back from his face as he solemnly shook his head. "No mice," he assured Omen. "The ocean has eyes."

Only partially relieved, Omen patted his brother's shoulder. "Waves, Kyr," he corrected the boy's vocabulary. "The ocean has waves, you mean." In the five months Kyr had lived with Omen's family, the boy had learned a smattering of three languages, but he still frequently mixed up words.

A glint of red on the sand at his feet grabbed Omen's attention. He shifted the greatsword strapped across his back as he bent over to retrieve the broken piece of shell. "A rosehead crab shell," he noted out loud, surprised to see it. "Rosehead crabs never appear until midautumn." His words caught the wholehearted attention of both cats.

"Is we having crab cakes?" The cats' ears perked straight up, all thought of mouse-waffles gone at the mention of another favorite treat.

Omen tossed aside the broken piece of shell, briefly noticing a few others scattered amid long ropy tangles of dark green seaweed washed ashore at last tide. "No. It's far too early for rosehead crabs," he replied. "These shells must be from last season. We're looking for sand urchins, remember? We can buy fish at the market later if you want."

Few things made the cats as happy as promised fish, and Tormy spun in the sand, whacking Omen with his great plume of a tail with each turn.

Omen steered Kyr around the large cat and toward the water's edge where the wet sand was hard-packed and easier to walk upon.

"Sand urchins look like small sandy cookies, Kyr," Omen told his brother. "They're pretty, but don't eat them. We should find some on the shoreline."

Kyr hesitated as they reached the wet sand. He stared down at the ocean foam surrounding his booted feet.

Concerned, Omen also paused, wondering what was bothering the boy. "Come on, Kyr," he urged gently. "Sand urchins aren't dangerous."

"What about the people in the sand?" the boy asked, blinking uncertainly at Omen.

Turning full circle, Omen looked up and down the deserted beach. The day was overcast and cold, the out-of-season weather likely the cause for the absence of beachgoers. "We're the only ones here, Kyr," he told his brother. "There's no one in the—"

Tormy's growling hiss was the only warning Omen got as the sand at his feet exploded upward in a shower of salt water and grasping claws. Tormy pounced, the heavy cat coming down hard on a flailing, multi-segmented limb emerging from the sand.

Omen leaped back, grabbing ahold of Kyr and dragging him away from the snapping claws. The long ropy strands he'd mistaken for dark green seaweed were all moving as spidery shapes emerged all around them. Crawling out of the sand along the shoreline, creatures lifted themselves up on hard-jointed legs and pulled themselves across the ground with lethal purpose.

"Sandlures!" Omen yelled as he unslung the greatsword from his back and drew the weapon from the scabbard. He swung the blade and sliced through the nearest dark green limb, severing it at the first joint. Several more sandlures reached for him, but one curved pincer clamped around his left ankle and pulled him hard toward the water's edge. Yanked off center, Omen hit the ground and nearly lost his grip on the sword.

He heard Kyr shriek in fear, followed by the voice of tiny Tyrin shouting, "I'll bite the &!%@* monster!"

Bracing, Omen pushed himself upright and brought the full weight of his sword down upon the limb that had captured him. The heavy blade cut through the segment.

Omen spun, leaping to his feet as he turned toward his brother. Kyr too was lying in the sand, prying at a claw wrapped around both his legs, while the tiny orange fluffy bundle that was Tyrin scratched and bit at the green limb trying to drag the boy into the water.

Like a flea trying to eat a stalk of celery!

Before Tyrin could get hurt, Omen severed the spindly limb holding his brother.

Two more claws reached for him, and several bulky spider shapes skittered across the sand, swiftly approaching.

"Tormy, get Kyr!" Omen shouted to the large cat.

Tormy, ears flat against his head, looked up from where he'd been ripping apart one of the claws, the wiggling appendage still locked firmly between his teeth. The cat leaped with one great bound and landed over Kyr, enormous furry paws surrounding the child like a protective cage.

"Climb on Tormy's back, Kyr!" Omen shouted and deftly cut away another grasping limb.

The boy scrambled through the sand, reaching for little Tyrin in a panic, more worried about his tiny cat than about himself. Realizing that his brother wasn't going to flee without the kitten, Omen hummed a bar of music. Instantly, a familiar psionic pattern formed in his mind, triggering vibrant, pulsing power as energy sparked through him. The power came easily to him these days, and he reached effortlessly out with his thoughts and lifted the little cat into the air, floating him across the sand and dropping him neatly into Kyr's outstretched hands. Then Omen spun and slammed his sword down on another snapping claw.

Kyr stuffed the kitten down the front of his tunic and then scrambled monkey-like onto Tormy's back.

A multitude of claws reached for them, the segmented limbs closing around them like a trap. Desperately, Omen tried to remember everything he knew about sandlures. *These claws are just the end of the creature — a tail with a hand attached to it!*

He recalled seeing an ink drawing of a sandlure in a book. *Like a spider on a ball and rope.* The book had depicted large, twelve-legged spiders attached to a single long tail which ran back out to sea and connected to the actual body of the creature floating on the surface of the water and watching for prey upon the shore.

He scanned the sand. Just below the surface he could see something moving. He leaped high in the air and brought his sword down with a powerful overhand strike, cutting into the wet sand and severing the long tail leading back out to the water. Instantly the claws around them spasmed and went limp, cut off from the main creature.

"More &$#@! monsters!" Tyrin chirped at the top of his lungs.

Dark green shapes moved across the sand in ripples, clicking and crawling spider-like toward them, uprooting their trailing tails from the ground.

"Back to the staircase!" Omen shouted to Tormy. "They

can't get farther inland!"

The nearest set of claws reached them, and Omen swung his sword, guarding Tormy's retreat.

With Kyr clinging to his ruff, Tormy stumbled across the dunes, the dry sand slowing his progress considerably. One of the clawed clusters had already cut him off, barring the way as two more approached from behind.

Omen rushed forward, his feet sinking into the sand as he hacked at the creature blocking Tormy's path. The cat spun and clawed at the sandlures coming up behind him.

"There's too many! We have to get to the stairs, Tormy!" Omen gasped.

And then a great shadow arced over them, and a rush of wind from unfurled wings threw sand into the air. A thundering boom reverberated as the enormous scaled form of the glittering dragon dropped from the sky and closed merciless claws over the nearest crawling spiders, crushing them utterly.

Omen and Tormy backed away as the dragon raised another deadly claw and crushed two more sandlures. The rest skittered swiftly away, long tails exploding upward along the shoreline as they were instantly retracted and pulled out to sea, leaving the beach empty once more.

Breathing heavily, Omen stared as the mighty Sundragon turned his huge, horn-tipped head and fixed his azure gaze upon him. Despite the muted cloudy light, the dragon gleamed golden and bright, his shimmering scales glinting with the underscales' vibrant blue as if a piece of the sun and sky had landed upon the beach.

"Thank you, Lord Amar." Omen inclined his head to the Sundragon respectfully, mindful of the dagger-sized teeth in the dragon's jaws. "I've never seen sandlures in Melia."

He still held his sword in his right hand, blade pointed downward and away from the dragon.

"Nor have I," Sundragon Amar replied, his voice low and deep, resonating in the musical tones of the Melian language.

Omen's eyes widened. *Amar is hundreds of years old. If he hasn't seen sandlures here—*

"They are sometimes found up north in Nelminor," Amar continued, "but they never enter the warmer waters of Melia. And even in Nelminor they are only seen in mid or late autumn." The dragon glanced at the bedraggled cat still carrying an equally bedraggled Kyr. "Are you and your companions injured, Prince Armand?"

Omen flinched at the use of the formal name but knew better than to correct a Sundragon. He glanced over his shoulder at Tormy. Kyr was still clinging fiercely to the cat's back. Tyrin, who had wormed his way out of Kyr's tunic and was perched on top of Tormy's head, opened his mouth to answer.

"We're fine!" Omen spoke before the cat could. *Can't have that little pottymouth blabber to a Sundragon.*

"Do you hear the singing?" Kyr asked breathlessly from Tormy's back, seeming mesmerized by the crashing ocean waves.

"What singing?" Omen stared at his brother. *Does he hear singing from the Temple of the Untouchables? The wind is blowing the wrong direction for that.*

"Coming from the water," the boy explained. "Thousands of voices singing the song of Urgolath."

"Urgo—" Omen began only to be cut off by a low hum from the Sundragon. He turned. Lord Amar's draconic eyes were fixed on Kyr. "Do you know that name?"

"Urgolath, the Widow Maker, is the name of an ancient leviathan," Amar explained. "But it only appears in the western Luminal Sea on the night of the autumnal equinox. It is said that those doomed to death can hear its song. You had best keep your brother away from the ocean until we can figure out what these strange occurrences mean. The Widow Maker devours the souls of drowned sailors, and it is attracted to mystics."

"My brother is not—" Omen cut off his own protest at the dragon's sharp stare. *My brother is not a mystic,* he thought to himself instead of speaking the words out loud. But every time he tried to insist that was true, Kyr did something to prove him wrong. "I'll keep him away from the ocean," Omen promised.

"Go and tell the Untouchables to keep people off the beach," Amar said. "I will search for more sandlures." The dragon turned, sand spraying up as his long tail slithered behind him.

Omen watched in silence as Amar moved farther down the beach, his claws sinking deep into the sand with each step. More sandlures reared up as he neared them, all scampering back out to sea as the dragon approached. Several of the fleeing creatures were horse-sized — more than capable of dragging a grown man out to sea.

"That's not good," Omen said quietly through his teeth.

The dragon too seemed startled at the sandlures' size and after a few moments, he opened his great jaws and roared. Fire bright as the sun rushed from those jaws, an enormous flare shooting out across the sand and heating it. The salt water instantly turned to steam as the sand glowed red hot.

Tormy brushed up against him, and Omen reached out to steady Kyr who was balanced on the cat's back. "Did Tyrin say a naughty word?" the large cat asked sincerely as they watched the dragon scorch the sand with his fiery breath.

"I is cursing the &!%@* monsters!" Tyrin scolded loudly. "You is allowed to curse when there is being monsters!"

"Yes, yes," Omen replied, distracted. He reached out to pat the little kitten's head. "You were very brave, Tyrin."

Spying his sword sheath near the surf's edge, Omen hummed the familiar tune again in his mind, summoning his power. He reached out with his thoughts and grasped the sheath, lifting it silently into the air and floating it across the dunes toward his outstretched hand. Carefully sheathing his blade, his eyes still fixed on Amar and the far-too-numerous creatures fleeing the dragon's wrath, Omen felt an ice-cold shiver splash down his spine.

Kyr was right, the ocean did have eyes, he thought. *Melia is the safest place I know, but this is the second time we've been attacked on this beach.*

"They sound sad." Kyr gave a heavy sigh.

"The sandlures?" Omen asked. As far as he knew sandlures didn't actually make any sort of sound.

"The singers," Kyr explained, looking toward the water. "Sad and frightened."

"Let's go tell the Untouchables." Puzzled, Omen patted Tormy's flank to get him moving toward the staircase once again. "And then I think it's time I teach you how to use a sword, Kyr."

Chapter 2: Teaching Kyr

OMEN

The thin sword hissed past Omen's left ear. He swerved just in time to avoid a blow to the shoulder.

Rat's teeth! That was close! he thought as a strand of his thick copper hair flicked to the ground. Omen narrowed his eyes and shot a dark look at his sparring partner. "Templar! Burning night!" he cursed. "I said no live blades!"

Templar circled Omen, sword held before him, yellow eyes flashing with mischief. "Where's the fun in that?"

"What did you do?" Omen asked, feeling belligerent. He'd supplied the swords himself, and had made certain the edges were unsharpened. "We agreed. No offensive spells." Omen slashed his blade toward Templar's shoulder.

"Temporary sharpening spells are not offensive." Templar leaped away. "I believe they're categorized as domestic."

"Cheat!" Omen closed in with two long strides.

"Nobody ever fights fair." Templar knocked him back with a hard kick to the chest. "You said we're teaching Kyr how to fight, not knit."

Omen twisted like a cat as he fell, catching himself before he struck the ground. He shot a quick glance over his shoulder toward the grassy clearing, checking on his little brother.

Kyr sat on a dark green cloak spread beneath the shade of a willow tree. The fragile boy stared with the rapt atten-

11

tion of any ten-year-old at a glittering beetle in the palm of
his hand, heedless of the sword battle playing out for his
benefit. Tormy and Tyrin snored loudly beside him, lulled
to sleep by a group of bards rehearsing in the park's central
gazebo. Tormy's large form curled protectively around both
Kyr and the small kitten Tyrin.

"Leave the bugs alone, Kyr!" Omen called. After the
sandlure attack on the beach the day before, he didn't want
to delay teaching his brother to defend himself. "Pay attention!" Omen gestured to his weapon. "When fighting you
have to maintain your balance — keep your weight over
your feet."

Obediently, Kyr dropped the shiny beetle and shifted the
entirety of his attention back to the practice bout. The summer breeze swirled around them, rustling the trees. "The
flowers can fly," Kyr mused and gave Omen a brilliant
smile.

There he goes, Omen thought, concerned. *The ocean has
eyes, the flowers can fly. What next? Though at least the
weather is much nicer than yesterday. More like summer.*

"What were you saying about crazy not running in your
family?" Templar snorted.

The small hairs on the back of Omen's neck stood up,
and he let out an irritated growl. "You're the crazed Night-
blood who sharpened the practice swords," Omen snapped.
He rotated away from Templar to focus on his little brother.
"So, Kyr, if you can get your opponent's weight off his feet
—" Omen twisted his sword, trapping Templar's blade,
pushed and sent him stumbling backward.

Templar should have gone down, but ever contrary,
Omen's friend did a theatrical backflip out of the stumble
and landed with nimble grace on both feet. Trained at his

12

father's court of Terizkand, Templar excelled at a dual-s-word method, which relied on speed and agility and frustrated Omen greatly.

Burning night! Omen glared. "We're supposed to be teaching Kyr the basics — not carnival flips!"

Templar looked unrepentant. "There are people watching," he excused his own behavior offhand.

Of course. Defiantly, Omen ran a familiar piece of music through his mind — the notes, a mnemonic device, instantly awakened a psionic pattern which triggered his mental powers. He felt the rising buzz of energy at the base of his skull as he extended the psionic force in a sweeping motion that caught Templar unaware. He knocked both feet out from under his friend, and Templar went sprawling to the ground.

But Omen's triumph was short-lived. A second later blazing tendrils, crackling with wild magic, wrapped like vines around his ankles and yanked him into the dirt as well.

Omen spat the dust from his lips. "Let me guess, rope spell." *Can't really complain since I just broke the rules myself.*

"Still domestic," Templar quipped, rising to his feet. "If you want to teach Kyr how to fight, why don't we just go down to the beach and see if any of those critters are still there? What did you call them?"

"Sandlures." Omen dusted himself off as he stood. "And I'm not taking Kyr back down there — you didn't see those things. They could have dragged him out to sea. Besides, the dragons don't want anyone getting in the way while they search for more."

"Killjoys," Templar snapped quickly, but then his face

13

turned thoughtful. "Sandlures," he repeated. "I don't think we have those in Terizkand. You've always said that Melia was peaceful, safe. Sandlures don't sound very safe. Are they common here?"

Omen shook his head. Everybody he'd talked to had been shocked at the presence of the sandlures. "They're cold-weather creatures, and don't like warm water."

Templar flicked his dark hair back from his face. "Melia's waters are really warm. What are they doing here?"

"I don't know," Omen said. Unease stirred in him again; he remembered the dark, silent looks his parents had exchanged the night before when he'd told them about the attack. And after learning about the singing Kyr had heard coming from the ocean, his mother had warned him to keep the boy away from the shoreline.

Determined, he motioned toward his brother. "Come on, Kyr, your turn with the blade."

Kyr rose dutifully, flashing Omen a mercurial smile. Pale and skinny, with wind-blown hair and large sunset violet eyes in a fragile face, Kyr looked almost too frail to hold any blade, let alone a sword.

Still too skinny, Omen noted worriedly even though Kyr's current health was vastly improved from the bone-starved, fleshless, feral child he had been five months ago. When Omen had rescued Kyr from the burnt-out wasteland that had been his home for far too long, he and the rest of the Daenoth family hadn't even been certain Kyr would survive, let alone become the much adored little brother they all cherished. *He could have just as easily fallen asleep with the cats instead of watching. Glad he paid attention.*

"That was great Omen! It's just like the song!" Kyr exclaimed with innocent enthusiasm.

"Which song?" Omen asked, glancing through the trees where he could still hear the group of bards rehearsing, hoping Kyr was talking about them. *He can't be talking about the song of Urgolath again — we're nowhere near the beach.*

"The Maiden and the White Rose," Kyr answered. "I don't know how you remember all those verses."

"The ballad about the first Melian Festival? You remember that?" Omen asked, relieved to hear it was a different song this time. *But what does that song and the number of verses have to do with sword fighting?* He motioned to Templar. "Take the spell off the blades now. It's Kyr's turn."

"More fun this way," Templar evaded at first, but then relented under Omen's glare. He touched both blades briefly, pausing to inspect the weapons. "Aren't most Lydonian long swords made of silverleaf?" he asked.

Omen handed the newly dulled blade to Kyr, hilt first. "These are just practice weapons. I'll get him something proper later." He'd specifically picked this make of sword because it was smaller than many others, and would be more suited to Kyr's thin frame — at least once he grew a bit more.

Kyr gripped the sword, his knuckles turning white with the effort. "We should take flowers to the lady," he said, struggling to hold the blade steady.

"Those ladies?" Omen asked, motioning toward a nearby group of women and their chaperones strolling along one of the park's shady footpaths. Templar grinned and waved to them. The ladies giggled at the attention but made no effort to stop, their chaperones pausing to glare darkly at the foreign prince.

Kyr shook his head emphatically. "No, the sister."

"What's this about flowers?" Templar asked, turning his attention away from the ladies.

"Kyr thinks you should take flowers to Lilyth," Omen half-joked, guessing at Kyr's meaning.

Templar's eyes flashed amber in the sunlight. "Your sister scares me. I gave her a compliment the other day, and she punched me."

"You called her adorable, you pignut," Omen pointed out while supervising Kyr's blundering attempts to mimic a fighting stance. The boy swung the sword experimentally through the air a few times, biting his lip in concentration.

Templar frowned. "So?" He stepped back from Kyr's wild swing.

"She was covered in mud," Omen clarified. He placed his hands on his brother's shoulders and physically turned Kyr so that he wouldn't accidentally step on the sleeping cats.

"And it was adorable," Templar insisted. "She punched hard. It hurt!"

"She's ten," Omen stated, familiar with his sister's violent temper.

Templar gingerly touched the bridge of his nose, faking injury. "It still hurts!" he whined. "She used some of your weird Daenoth psionics behind the punch."

That caught Omen's attention, and he lifted his eyebrows, incredulous. "She knows how to do that?" He shifted his weight from foot to foot. "She's not any good at it, is she?"

"Better than you!" Templar scoffed.

"My dad is always giving her extra training!" Omen kicked at some pebbles on the ground, annoyed. Even though he was five years older than his sister, there was still a great deal of competition between the two of them, and he often felt on the losing end of things. Lilyth had a conniving nature that Omen just couldn't seem to second-guess.

"Didn't your father tell you to meet him for your psionic lessons four hours ago?" Templar asked innocently. "And didn't you decide to go to the park with me instead? When I came through the portal, you had me sneak out a back window."

Omen scratched the back of his neck. "That's different."

"Not that I'm judging your choices," Templar said, laughter in his words. "I applaud them."

"We're not just wasting time, you know," Omen insisted, feeling a twinge of guilt he refused to acknowledge. "We're teaching Kyr how to sword fight. That's important. We were attacked on the beach — who knows when it might happen again." He moved around his brother and placed his hand over Kyr's on the hilt of the blade. "Come on Kyr, hold the sword like this." The moment he touched his hand, however, Kyr dropped the blade as if it had burned him.

The boy turned toward Omen with a wide, earnest look on his face. "We're supposed to put all the iron in the chest, Omen. They don't like it. It burns."

Omen exhaled slowly and bent down to pick up the sword. He then reached out to take hold of his brother's wrist. He knew there was little point in asking Kyr what he was talking about — no doubt the explanation would make no more sense than anything else the boy said. *Kyr lives in his own world. Sometimes I wonder if I'll ever understand him.* "The dragons don't mind the iron, Kyr. So it's fine." Omen forced an encouraging smile and put the sword back in Kyr's hand.

17

Kyr nodded and accepted the iron weapon without argument. "But I wish the boat would stop going up and down. It's hard to sleep. When are we getting off the ship?"

Templar, inexplicably amused by Kyr's bizarre behavior, grinned and clapped the boy on the shoulder. "Right now!" he exclaimed, humoring the child. "There! You see, we're off the ship, back on dry land — and look at that, we're in the park. You like the park."

Kyr mimicked Templar's grin. "I like the park. It's green." He looked to Omen for further instruction.

Omen stayed silent but adjusted Kyr's stance and his grip on the sword.

"Now you have to make the blade flame," Templar suggested, motioning to the weapon.

I didn't grab firebrands. Templar just can't help himself, Omen thought, but a quick double-check of the blade's surface showed that Kyr's practice sword now had runes etched into the metal, courtesy of Templar's magic, no doubt placed there when he'd altered the sharp edges. *I recognize those marks. With the right incantation and a little bit of magical force, they're going to light right up.*

"Don't you think teaching him the long sword and magic at the same time is a bit too much?" he asked Templar sharply.

Templar shrugged, unimpressed. "Kyr's a demigod and a Venedrine elf. Of course it's not too much. I've done the hard part for him — all he has to do is trigger it. Doesn't even have to memorize a pattern. Besides, it looks much more impressive on fire."

All good points, Omen had to concede. He knew the only reason Kyr was even still alive was the extraordinary blood flowing through his veins — but certainly his colorful heritage had to have given him more gifts than mere survival. Omen's varied bloodlines had given him great strength and easy access to the magic surrounding them. *Certainly not out of Kyr's reach. He should be able to ignite the runes.* "All right then, Kyr. Let's make the sword flame too," he said, turning his attention back to his brother.

"Is it night?" Kyr asked, befuddled, and looked around the sun-drenched park. "It's dark. The shadows are watching me."

"Which is why we need a flaming sword," Templar told him, looking more entertained by the minute.

Kyr grimaced. "The autumn wind is very cold. Someone should really close the door."

"It's still summer, Kyr," Omen said, feeling compelled to correct his brother. *Probably pointless.* "But we'll close all the doors you want when we get back home. Now, to make the blade flame, all you have to do is concentrate on the magical energy around you and say the incantation — it's written here on the blade." He indicated the marks newly etched, though he knew Kyr's reading skills were poor at best.

"The incantation is—"

But before Omen could speak the command word or instruct Kyr how to channel the magical energy around him, bright blue flames erupted from the metal and ran up and down the edge of the sword.

Kyr shrieked in shock and tossed the weapon away from him. The flames extinguished the moment the sword struck the ground.

"Sun and scales, Templar! You scared him!" Omen exclaimed.

Templar threw his hands up in protest. "I didn't do anything. That was all him."

Startled, Omen looked at his frightened brother, his heart clenching in alarm. "Tha . . . that was amazing, Kyr," Omen stammered.

"What did I do?" Kyr asked, his voice quivering.

"You activated the spell," Omen said. *It takes months to learn how to manipulate magical energy — sometimes years depending on your gifts.*

Kyr turned eagerly toward him, looking somewhat breathless. "Does that mean I won the game?"

Templar laughed out loud. "Yes, you won!"

"I'm hungry!" the boy told them both with vigor.

Instantly little Tyrin lifted his furry head, ears perking forward.

Tormy jerked swiftly awake, rolling over as he shouted, "Fish, fish, fish!" He was either announcing what he had been dreaming about or, alternatively, his lunch order.

Omen regarded his giant cat fondly. He'd been certain Tormy had been sound asleep. *Mere mention of food and he's awake. How does he do that?*

"That's really amazinglynessness!" Tyrin exclaimed as he stretched his tiny furry body, paws extended forward. "On account of the fact I is being hungry too, Kyr! It's like you is reading our minds!" Despite the cats' strange grammatical choices and their bizarre habit of conjugating inventively, their desire for lunch was unmistakable.

Kyr beamed at the two cats.

Omen pinched the bridge of his nose and gave Templar a look of resignation. *Now that the cats are awake and demanding food, sword lessons are over.* "Fine, we'll go to lunch," he acquiesced. *They'd run off to get food even if I said no.*

20

Omen retrieved the extinguished sword from the ground, pausing to study the magical sigil Templar had cast upon the blade. An uneasy thought passed through his mind. "Kyr's not going to go around lighting things on fire accidentally, is he?" he asked Templar. While Omen had studied rudimentary magic, he'd concentrated the majority of his studies on the art and craft of psionic manipulation.

"No, he won't." Templar shook his head dismissively as he retrieved his own sword belt from the ground and fixed the two bone blades he typically wore at his side. "It takes years to learn the magical patterns to cast a fire emblem like that. All Kyr did was channel raw magic into the already existing emblem — which is impressive enough. That usually doesn't come easy. You're going to have to train him before too long."

There was a long list of things Omen needed to teach Kyr and it never felt as if there was enough time in the day. "Psionically too," he added forlornly. The boy currently wore a shielding bracelet around his right wrist similar to the one Omen had worn through most of his childhood — it would protect his mind from stray psionic attacks. But Omen knew from experience that was only a temporary measure. While Kyr did not possess the stronger mind powers of Omen's family, he had ability enough to prove dangerous if left untrained. "Never enough time."

Omen sheathed the practice swords, before retrieving his own enormous two-handed greatsword from where it lay in the grass. Strapping the large sword across his back and latching the quick-release fastener on the belt, Omen then attempted to pull his leather jerkin out from under Tormy. "Nice pillow?" He tried to make it sound like a scold.

Tormy nodded, the tip of his tongue sticking out through

21

his front teeth in a sweet cat smile.

Kyr grabbed Omen's hand as he passed, catching his attention. "Thank you for teaching me!" the boy said sincerely.

A smile stretched across Omen's face. *That's the thing about Kyr. His honest gratitude more than makes up for anything else.*

"You're welcome, Kyr," he said, pleased.

Kyr nodded. "I liked shooting a bow." He headed after the cats, making whizzing arrow sounds as he walked away.

Templar practically snorted with laughter. "Good going, sword master. He thinks we were practicing archery." He playfully punched Omen's shoulder.

Utter bewilderment swamped over Omen. "Is Kyr getting better?" he asked Templar plainly. "Or is he getting worse? Some days I can't tell."

Templar's eyes followed Kyr and the cats. "We spent the entire morning with him and not once did he stop to talk to imaginary dead people." Templar mustered a supportive smile. "I'd call that a win."

Omen considered. They fell into step, side-by-side, and hurried to catch up. Kyr chatted happily with Tormy and Tyrin, oblivious to Omen's worry.

"Remember last week when he got into that huge argument in the street — rambling on about flour and eggs?" Templar reminded Omen.

"Well, to be fair, I had just taught him how to bake cookies, and he was arguing with a group of dead bakers," Omen cast about, knowing he was making excuses. *Kyr was so upset. I should have pretended they were real.*

"Imaginary dead bakers," Templar corrected, emphasizing *imaginary.*

Omen frowned. "We don't actually know if they're imaginary or not," he admitted hesitantly. More and more he felt it difficult to argue against it. "Kyr might actually be a mystic." *As my mother stresses constantly.* Kyr's habit of muttering in Kahdess, the Language of the Dead, didn't help matters either.

Templar looked skeptical. "A mystic who talks to dead bakers? Why?"

"Maybe they have something important to say." Omen bit his lip, wondering if he should mention the incident on the beach yesterday. "You never know. Maybe there's some ancient prophecy about bread that we don't know about."

"By that argument anyone could be a mystic," Templar told him. "Maybe I'm a mystic. I predict that tomorrow the sky will be blue, it will be summer, and somewhere some Melian will start singing."

Omen sniffed and was about to reply when, to his surprise, Kyr looked over his shoulder at the two of them and gravely shook his head. "You're wrong about summer," he said, indicating that despite having carried on the conversation with the cats, he had been listening to Omen and Templar. Luckily he didn't seem bothered by anything they had said.

Templar reached out to ruffle the boy's hair. "Actually Kyr, that's the one part of my prediction I'm pretty certain about. It could technically rain tomorrow, in which case the sky won't be blue, and for all I know the Sundragons may have declared tomorrow some sort of national day of silence in which case there might be no singing. But it will still be summer no matter what we do."

Kyr thought about that a moment and then went perfectly still. "The ocean will still sing, and the darkness will still stare," he said finally. "Even if you don't look at it." Then he turned his attention back to the cats.

Templar threw Omen an "I told you so" look. Omen winced.

They veered north along a stone path and emerged near the shore of the small lake in the center of the park. Up ahead, they spied Omen's cousin Bryenth Deldano and their friend Liethan Corsair approaching from the market. Liethan, golden-haired and blue-eyed, with the deeply tanned skin of the island-dwelling Corsair clan, called out to them. "There you guys are! How did the lessons go?"

Omen mockingly raised an eyebrow when he noticed that, unlike Bryenth who was dressed like a proper Melian nobleman complete with a starched undershirt, brocade doublet, finely stitched breeches, and well-polished boots, the younger Liethan was barefoot and windblown as if he'd come from the beach, despite the dragons' warnings to stay clear of the shore.

"Archery practice went great!" Templar quipped enthusiastically.

Bryenth brushed his ink-black hair away from his eyes. "I thought you were teaching Kyr the sword?"

"Swords are good when the wyverns attack," Kyr said sagely. "They bite, bite, bite."

"At least the bakers stayed out of it," Templar snorted.

Omen ignored him. "Sword practice went fine. Kyr did great!"

"HUNGRY!" Tormy shouted with a snap of his tail.

"Ah, lunch again," Liethan remarked. "I'm in."

Omen grinned as Tormy hopped forward, skipping and dancing awkwardly before them like a clumsy kitten. The large cat made his way around the small lake and beelined to the nearest tavern, The Harps. *Guess that's where we're eating. Tormy does love the way they fawn over him.*

The Harps was also one of the few taverns where Tormy could come and go with ease as the entire southern wall of the building had been designed to swing open wide like barn doors so that the evening crowds who came to hear the bards performing inside could spill over into the park itself. *Also makes it easier for the dragons to hear the music when they're not in their human forms.* Some of the Melian dragons preferred to appear as human, walking among their people as if one of them. Others rarely transformed, far preferring their golden draconic bodies.

Omen's eyes fell on one such dragon, Lady Frey. The enormous golden-scaled, winged creature slept under the willows by the lake, her great wings folded around her body and her long tail trailing.

Omen could recall only ever seeing Frey in her human form once. He'd accidentally interrupted her tutoring Bryenth at the Deldano Hold.

Mathematical analysis. Yuck.

More used to Frey in her dragon shape, at first Omen hadn't recognized her as the fine-featured, stunning human woman inviting him to join the lesson. But her melodious voice, her telltale sunlight-golden hair and the faint trace of scales highlighting the sides of her cheeks had given away her draconic nature.

But Frey typically preferred her dragon form, and was now resting at the edge of the grass near the very stone path they were walking upon. Omen swallowed a yelp as he realized that his large, furry orange and white companion was blithely skipping toward the outstretched reptilian tail and the sharp bone-spikes that ridged it. Gamboling happily, Tormy could be a veritable whirlwind of destruction. The great plume of his silky tail alone had destroyed more than one of Omen's mother's prized antiques. *Should probably warn Tormy to tread lightly, before he—*

"Watch out! You'll wake the dragon and she'll squash the stuffin' out of the &^$@^#% squirrels!" tiny Tyrin called out from his roost on Kyr's shoulder.

Foulmouthed little stinker!

Omen made a grab for the pint-sized cat.

The skinny orange kitten leaped from Kyr's shoulder and raced straight toward the sleeping dragon and the dozen squirrels frolicking near her glittering form as if bewitched by the glint of gold in her scales.

"Hey, Dragon! Frey, wake up! You is smooshing the furbags if you is rolling over!" Tyrin shouted as he raced across the grounds. "I is not being allowed to eat them, Kyr is saying so! So you is not smooshing them!"

A startled squirrel abandoned a treasure it had discovered between the dragon's toes and dashed away, chittering wildly.

"Tyrin!" Omen hissed, not certain who looked more surprised, his brother or the Melians strolling through the park. *Poor Bryenth looks mortified!*

"Now you've done it," Templar, ever helpful, remarked gleefully and dropped back several steps so that he would not be included in any potential fallout. He waved a hand, adorned with numerous flashing rings, as if saluting Omen's imminent demise.

"Oops," Kyr exclaimed, turning wide-eyed toward Omen. "Waking dragons is bad, isn't it?" The boy looked panic-stricken, and Omen placed his hand upon his brother's bony shoulder to calm him.

Tyrin paused in his charge toward the dragon to glance back. "I is not waking her. Tormy is. I is helping!" Satisfied that his motives were understood, he headed forward again. "Hey, Frey! Frey! Frey!"

Omen cringed. "It's Lady Frey!" he called to the cat, figuring it was too late to tell him not to disturb the dragon. Even he, a prince of the Kingdom of Lydon, didn't address a Sundragon without some sign of respect. *I might not be a Melian, but I know better than to approach a dragon without invitation.*

"Lady! Lady! Lady!" Tyrin shouted, which sounded even worse to Omen than the kitten merely yawping her name.

This time the dragon's eyes opened, dark blue sapphire glinting in the sunlight as she turned her gaze on the small tangerine-colored kitten approaching. Frey's enormous claws dug deep furrows in the grass as she pushed herself upward. She was large enough to swat even the giant Tormy cat aside with one swipe, a possibility little Tyrin seemed oblivious to.

The dragon raised her head, the golden swept-back horns crowning her brow glinting in the sunlight. She turned with a serpentine sway to focus on Omen, the cats, and his companions.

Templar and Liethan moved surreptitiously away from Omen, abandoning him to his fate. But Omen's cousin, Bryenth, son of a Melian Hold Lord, stepped swiftly forward, one hand held over his heart as he bowed to the dragon.

"My apologies for disturbing you, Lady Frey," Bryenth proclaimed, looking like a child about to be chastised.

27

Omen knew that Frey was, in fact, Bryenth's Hold Dragon; he'd grown up with her as his tutor for all things Melian, and the mortification on his face was most genuine. Bryenth wasn't like Templar, capable of faking emotion when it suited him.

Tyrin turned, outrage burning in his amber eyes, tail fluffing up twice its normal size. "I is not disturbing her!" he yowled. "I is saving the @#$$%&! squirrels!"

There were gasps of shock from those nearby who heard the terrible word — Terizkandian if Omen had heard correctly — spill from the kitten's mouth.

Templar! Templar and Liethan, still moving away, could both barely hold back snickers. *No doubt, we have Templar to thank for the cat's improved vocabulary. Why that kitten loves to swear, I don't know! And Templar encourages it!*

Omen took several swift strides forward, snatched the kitten off the ground, and gave him back to Kyr. Hands trembling, the boy accepted the tiny creature and gripped him close to his chest.

Frey tilted her enormous scaled head, her golden wings shifting and drawing in tightly to her body as she prepared to leap into the air and abandon the no longer peaceful park.

"I'm sorry, Lady Frey," Omen said with a respectful bow of his head. He saw the chagrin on Bryenth's face and sweat started to form on the nape of his neck. "We really didn't mean to bother you. Please don't leave on our account. We're just going to have lunch in the tavern, and Tyrin is—"

"No longer speaking Sul'eldrine," the dragon finished for him, her tone soft and low, like a deep, musical purr. The Sundragons' greatest magic lay in their music, and there was not one of them who did not have a hypnotic voice.

Omen cringed inwardly. When both Tormy and Tyrin had first joined their family, they had spoken only Sul'eldrine, the Holy Language of the Gods. Since then they had learned to speak both Merchant's Common and the musical tongue of Melia. *And obviously some Terizkandian.* "Yes, well, they're terribly clever," he said self-consciously.

"We is learning Melian!" Tyrin agreed eagerly. "On account of the fact that we is teaching Kyr to speak."

Everyone within earshot, the dragon included, stared at the large-eyed elvin child clutching the orange kitten.

"Is she awake?" the boy whispered to Omen, disoriented and distressed.

Omen smiled encouragingly, hiding his worry. "She's speaking to us, Kyr, that's usually a good indication that someone is awake."

Kyr shook his head, his white-gold hair falling into his eyes. "Not always. Sometimes they speak and they're not even there, remember? Did I upset a dragon? I'm not supposed to do that. Your mother told me not to."

Imagining there were all sorts of things his mother had told the boy not to do, Omen moved protectively in front of his brother. He glared at the gathered crowd, daring anyone to mock Kyr's aberrant behavior. *Kyr's mind doesn't work like everyone else's. I'll punch the first person who says anything.*

But it was Tormy who smoothed things over. Tormy, who'd paused in his prance toward the tavern when he realized there was some disturbance behind him, came galumphing back to their side with a happy chirp and a purr. "This is being Lady Frey, Kyr," Tormy exclaimed.

"And she is being really real on account of the fact that I can see her. She is waking up because of the squirrels. Squirrels is being naughty, because they is being so noisy-nessness, and we is not being allowed to eat them because they is having little squirrel fists that they is shaking at us. But that is being fair and fine because we is going to eat lunch — right Omy, we is going to eat lunch, and you is going to sing, so the dragon is being happy."

A bright gleam sparked deep in Frey's eyes by the time Tormy had finished speaking, and Omen realized with intense relief that, far from being truly annoyed, the dragon was amused. "You're going to sing?" She lifted her great reptilian head and turned her gleaming sapphire orbs toward Omen.

Unable to answer right away, Omen cleared his throat. "I would be honored, my lady." He bowed again, glad that his cat's sweet nature had charmed the Sundragon so swiftly. "Any song you desire."

"Are you up to the Deldano standards?" Frey asked curiously. "You are no Beren Deldano, but they say you have his blood. Are you as good as him?"

"Better." Omen smirked. "You forget, 7 is my father."

"Ah yes, you and your strange mixed-breed history," Frey remarked. "So impossible to keep your ridiculous bloodlines straight. S'van Daenoth is indeed a sublime musician."

Omen bit back the response to that. *It's 7, not S'van. Mother hates it when people call him S'van.* But he caught himself before making the mistake of correcting a Sundragon.

Frey sighed and settled back down into the grass, laying her head upon her front claws and closing her sapphire eyes. "Very well," she commanded, seemingly content to fall back asleep. "Go into the tavern, feed your cats and the boy, and then sing to me 'The Ballad of the Maiden and the White Rose' and all will be forgiven."

Omen blanched at that. *Wasn't that the song Kyr just mentioned?* The song requested had over fifty verses, and as it was currently in high favor in the city of Melia, a bard was expected to sing it in its entirety without error. *Creepy. Kyr mentioned the verses too.* Omen glanced over at Templar who was now also giving Kyr a curious look.

"Oh, that is being my absolutelynessness favoritest song!" Tormy proclaimed — the same proclamation he made about every song Omen had ever sung.

Already numerous eavesdropping Melians had scrambled to their feet and headed into the tavern, eagerly discussing the promised performance: "I don't think he'll get past the part with the mermaid." "I've only heard him sing the chorus." "I think Prince Armand is so gallant."

Omen blushed, wondering if he could talk himself into something a little easier than "The Maiden and the White Rose."

"I like 'The Turning Wheel' too," Omen began, but Bryenth's sharp elbow to his ribs stifled his attempt to dissemble. "Of course, my lady," he amended immediately.

Omen began to follow his cat to the tavern, pausing only briefly to throw a dramatic disappointed look at Templar and Liethan. *Snickering at a safe distance . . . Just you wait,* he thought as he ushered Kyr past the tranquil Sundragon.

31

Chapter 3: Clear as Fog

OMEN

When they arrived at The Harps, innkeeper Jarlen enthusiastically hurried them all inside. The man's eager hand-wringing gave away his joy at Omen's command performance. *He probably sent out runners to gather up more customers.*

Jarlen showed them straight to their usual table near the hearth. The corner was lit with glowing magical lamps which illuminated the shadowed spaces that the sunlight coming in through the great opening in the tavern's wall failed to reach.

"If it pleases you, my lords," Jarlen chatted away as his wife began setting bottles of wine — the lush variety Templar favored — upon the table. Templar, spoiled by the sumptuous bounty of his father's court, had extravagant tastes and always ordered one of the more expensive vintages. "Your table is already prepared," Jarlen continued cheerfully. "And here's your pillow, Master Tormy." He plumped up a large blue pillow with a flourish. "Your appetizers are on their way now. Please enjoy fresh peaches with clotted cream and a drizzle of dragon-bee honey." He looked pleased with himself.

"That sounds wonderful, Jarlen." Omen patted the man's arm. "Thank you for your kind consideration."

The table itself was one that Omen knew Jarlen had purchased especially for him and his cat. The legs of this table were nearly a foot thick, the tabletop an enormous polished

slab of wood that could take any weight placed upon it, including Tormy's overly large form.

When Omen had first brought Tormy to the tavern, the
cat had been small enough to sit in one of the chairs. But as
he'd grown from kitten to beast, Tormy had begun sitting
on the floor, resting his front paws on the table.

Jarlen's daughters had diligently sewn together the special pillow that now lay at the foot of the table. Tormy had
oohed and *ahhed* the first time he'd seen it, knowing immediately it had been made for him.

Now Tormy happily sat down on his pillow, folding his
fluffy orange tail around his body. He ran his long tongue
over his cheeks hungrily in anticipation of the coming
meal.

"And here, my lad," Jarlen said to Kyr, holding out the
chair next to Tormy's pillow. The tavern owner smiled
benevolently at the boy.

Far cry from the first time I brought Kyr to the tavern.

During that first visit, Kyr had cheerfully grabbed a
knife and begun scoring the surface of the table. Far too polite to say anything critical to such august company, Jarlen's
distress over the ruined table had been obvious. That
evening Omen had included an extra bag of gold when he'd
paid his tab, apologizing for Kyr's behavior and paying for
the table many times over.

Jarlen had of course graciously accepted the apology,
and the incident had been mostly forgotten until Jarlen had
later tried to return the money. The man had explained that
far from damaging the surface of the table, Kyr had transformed it from the purely functional into an object of beauty. The boy had carved the guardian figure of Sundragon
Amar Lir Drathos with breathtaking detail. Kyr's skill as an

artist was undeniable, and it wasn't the first time Omen had witnessed his remarkable abilities. When Omen had found his feral, starving brother in a dead and empty city, Kyr had been carving an army of faces and figures into the crumbling stones of old buildings in an effort to keep his lonely soul company.

The boy continued his carving every time they visited the tavern — adding more reliefs so that nearly a third of the surface of the tabletop was covered with some recognizable figure. The table was now considered a prized work of art.

And true to form, Kyr grabbed a knife the moment he sat down and leaned over the table, his skinny fingers already working the blade against the wood as he carved some new contour that haunted his mind.

"And you, my lord." Jarlen motioned toward the raised stage. One of Jarlen's daughters had already placed a lute upon the chair for Omen's performance. The instrument was one of a dozen that normally hung on the walls of the tavern.

I miss my *lute.* His favorite lute had been the victim of an unfortunate accident involving Tormy, fueled by Templar's announcement that there was a trout inside the instrument. *Still haven't forgiven Templar for that!*

"And don't skip any of the verses," Bryenth warned Omen as he stepped onto the stage. "It's Lady Frey's favorite song. She'll know if you skip even a syllable."

"Don't worry, Omy!" Tormy exclaimed happily. "I is reminding you if you is forgettingness of the words. I is knowing all the words."

"Thanks, Tormy." Omen smiled, knowing it was highly unlikely that Tormy could even remember the name of the song he was supposed to be singing, let alone all the words. Nonetheless, Tormy was his most ardent fan and would likely sing tunelessly along with him, making up the words if necessary. But there were a dozen other gifted singers in the tavern who would no doubt join in with the chorus, their perfect harmonies more than drowning out the cat's musical deficiencies.

The tavern filled quickly, and by the time Omen began to sing, he had quite an audience gathered to listen to his rendition of "The Maiden and the White Rose." Singing, in this case, was not the challenge. Remembering the verses in their proper order was the true challenge, as the lyrics were complex and told a long story — and that was the point. He knew he'd never hear the end of it if he made even the slightest mistake. But despite that, he was eager to show his skill with the lute. He could hardly take credit for his voice — his bizarre magically mixed bloodline had assured that his voice was flawless. But his skill with the lute was something he had to work hard at, and he was anxious to see how his rendition of the main melody line would be received. He took care to add his own flair and twist to the beat and measure, adding in some complicated harmonies that he'd been practicing with his father. He started the first verse.

"The rolling of rivers and crashing of sea
fell silent one summer day.
The people of Lir found their Maiden asleep
her head on a seabed of whey.
Wake up our dear Lady, they called through the waters
for we fear where your mind came to rest.
She woke with a sigh, wiped a tear from her eye
and held a white rose to her breast.

I ate of the curds of a Maiden above
and the whey is just tears from my eyes
I saw through her eyes to the world of man
and discovered my love is despised
They chained him in irons, took the crown from his head
and I fear he is lost, nearly dead.
Can we save him, my people, or must I face all my woes
a Maiden alone with a rose?"

He need not have worried. By the end of the song, even his companions joined in on the chorus. All seemed well-entertained and content. The round of applause was gratifying, as was the call for another song. Smiling, Omen agreed — though the first had been exhausting. *Fifty-three verses are a bit much.* He started a song he was certain everyone knew by heart, and sure enough the entire tavern sang along. Two fairly well-known bards joined him on the stage with a set of pipes and a sheepskin drum. Innately talented and trained as Dragonbards, the two Melian musicians had flawless voices which harmonized perfectly with Omen's tenor, their instruments blending with his lute.

Halfway through the second encore, Omen noticed that Tormy had moved, abandoning his spot at the table to sit in the back of the tavern away from the others. Curious what might have drawn the large cat away — the table laden with copious amounts of exotic dishes — Omen kept a close eye on him. *Tormy doesn't readily abandon food, and he always pays attention when I perform.*

He shot a quick glance toward his little brother, worried Kyr might grow frantic if he noticed Tormy's absence. Luckily Kyr's head was still bent over the table, his attention held entirely by the figures he was carving into the tabletop. Tyrin, perched mere inches away, watched his boy intently.

It had only been five months since Omen had rescued Kyr from his cursed imprisonment in a long-devastated realm, and the child still grew frightened when he found himself alone. Though Templar, Bryenth, and Liethan were seated beside the boy, Omen wasn't entirely certain Kyr believed any of them to be real. *Sometimes I think he only believes the cats and I are real. And everyone else is one of his shades.*

Omen watched Tormy from the stage, unable to see what had the cat's attention until a shift in the crowd opened up a clearer view. Sitting on a smaller table in the back was another cat — this one no larger than Tyrin, but with fur as grey as the evening fog. Omen's eyes widened, and he nearly missed a beat when he realized that Tormy was talking to the cat. Their two heads, one enormous, one tiny, were bowed together as they whispered words only a cat could hear over the noise of the music-filled tavern.

When the song had ended, Omen pleaded a dry throat to excuse himself from the stage. He spared a glance out the open tavern wall and spied the glittering Sundragon still sleeping beside the lake. *Guess my performance was acceptable.* A wave of pride crested over him when he saw a flick of the golden wings and imagined it a sign of approval from the dragon. He shot a smile at his cousin Bryenth who nodded happily, satisfied that they'd properly apologized to his Hold Dragon for Tyrin's mischief.

Omen rejoined his companions at the table, sitting down next to Kyr who was still intently carving, wood shavings piling near his fingers. *That looks like he's carving Shalonie.* The delicate curves of the girl's face appearing beneath the blade of Kyr's knife certainly looked like his

37

young friend, Lady Shalonie.

Templar handed Omen a heavy tankard filled not with the expensive wine, but fresh spring water. Omen drank it down greedily.

"You remembered all the words," Templar said, genuinely impressed. "I was hoping Tormy would have to finish for you."

With an indulgent smile, Omen nodded toward his cat. "Speaking of Tormy — is that Fog?"

"Indee's cat?" Templar asked, showing as much curiosity as Omen. "Must be."

"Indee's here?" Liethan eagerly looked around the room.

"Indee is eight months pregnant, of course she's not here," Bryenth told him.

The blond Corsair boy sighed a heavy sigh. "She's beautiful!" he said dreamily. "If I were just ten years older—"

"Lord Sylvan would bite your head off, literally," Bryenth insisted and took a gulp of wine. Melian through and through, Bryenth would be the first in line to defend Indee's honor and the dignity of her draconic husband Sylvan Lir Drathos.

"And you'd have to fight my father for her too, Liethan." Templar smirked and shook his head with an exaggerated shudder. "For a short while there, we all thought she'd become the queen of Terizkand."

Omen considered the possibility. Cut from the same conqueror's cloth, Indee and Templar's father, King Antares, would not have stopped until the whole world lay at their feet. As it was, separately, each had conquered more than their fair share of four lands.

Omen had never seen much of Indee, though he knew his mother had been one of the wild queen's companions.

He'd never gotten a full accounting of how a group of low-born adventurers had gained their outrageous fortunes and titles. His mother spoke of timing, but his mother was a consummate liar. Omen knew there were secrets woven into secrets when it came to his parents' generation, but he tried not to wonder out loud.

Omen did however question why Queen Indee's small cat might be in the tavern alone, locked in what appeared to be an intense conversation with Tormy.

"Ever met Fog before?" Templar asked.

Omen shook his head. He'd heard of Fog's arrival a few months ago, shortly after Tyrin's arrival in Melia, but had yet to meet the cat. Now more than ever, he wondered what governed the cats, and what had drawn them out into the world. *What makes them pick one person over another? I thought it was all about me when Tormy and Tyrin joined my household. But I have no connection to Indee. Why did she get a cat? My sister is still furious about that.*

Fortunately, his curiosity didn't have long to burn, for a few moments later Tormy came prancing back through the tavern to join them.

Following in Tormy's wake, Fog raced across the floor, slipping between legs while avoiding stomping feet. The dusky kitten took a mighty leap, grabbed the edge of their wooden table, and pulled himself up with tiny claws. He shook himself, blinked round jade green eyes at the company, and settled next to Omen's plate. Then the miniature feline folded his tail around his tiny paws with purpose.

"This is being Fog," Tormy informed Omen.

"I is being Fog," the little grey cat repeated. "That's with an 'oooooggg', and no silent letters."

Amused by the cat, Omen chuckled warmly. Tormy and

39

Tyrin had also taken great pains to explain the proper pro-
nunciation of their names when he'd first met them. He suspected in the cats' land it was considered rude to mispro-
nounce a name. *Doesn't explain why he calls me Omy instead of Omen. At least he doesn't call me Armand like my
grandmother does.*

"Hello, Fog," Omen greeted. "Pleased to meet you."

"I is pleased as well," the little cat agreed, speaking with
a diction more refined and clipped than the rolling tone natural to Tormy and Tyrin. "On account of the fact that I is in
need of a great hero for a grand adventure, so I is thinking
of the great hero Prince Tormy of the Cat Lands. He is going to go on my secret mission which will be grandness."

"Prince Tormy, huh?" Omen smiled broadly at the way
his cat puffed up at the pronouncement. *Cat Lands? With a
cat monarchy? I'll believe it when I see it.*

"What grand adventure?" Templar asked in perplexed
fascination.

The little grey cat flicked his tail sharply, drawing his
ears back against his head. "I is just saying it is a secret
mission, so you is not listening to my conversation on account of the fact that it is a secret."

Surprised by the cat's rebuff, Templar gave Omen a
pointed look. "A secret?" he said shrewdly. "You're absolutely right then. We're not hearing anything at all."

Satisfied, the little cat relaxed his ears and nodded.

"I is going to rescue the losted king," Tormy explained.

"On account of the fact that he is missing," Fog added.
"He is supposed to be ruling Kharakhan, but now he is kidnappeded and Indee is not knowing what to do."

"Wait a minute . . . are you saying King Khylar . . ."
Bryenth choked on a cream-covered strawberry, prompting

Templar to pound on his back. "Of Kharakhan? Indee's son? Has been kidnapped?" Bryenth's voice rose with incredulity.

"We're not listening, remember?" Templar told him. "It's a secret."

"Yes, you is not hearing us on account of the fact that it is a secret mission that only Tormy knows about," Fog agreed. "I is hearing from Indee, and I is thinking that I is fixing it on account of the fact that I is a Finder of Great Things. Except I is going to be finding a baby dragon soon, so I is not having time to find a losted king as well."

"So I," Tormy said happily, "is going to find the losted king instead."

"I is finding Tormy, you see," Fog explained. "Because I is good at finding stuff."

"Fog is the bestest at finding stuff," Tyrin piped up, his mouth full of whitefish stolen from Kyr's plate.

"The bestest," Tormy agreed.

Suddenly concerned that Tormy might have committed himself to something a bit more complicated than finding a good place to eat dinner, Omen frowned. "Wait a minute, who was Khylar kidnapped by? Was he visiting Melia when this happened?" If the king of the distant land of Kharakhan had indeed been kidnapped, it would be an international incident of dangerous proportions, not at all something he wanted his cat getting into the middle of.

"He is kidnappeded in Kharakhan by the Autumn Dwellers," little Fog announced, and Liethan, Bryenth and Templar stopped pretending not to listen and leaned in closer to hear the cat's words. Luckily none of them said anything, and Fog took no notice of their attention.

"Autumn Dwellers?" Omen had never heard of such

41

creatures. "Black night's curses, what are the Autumn Dwellers?"

"I is not knowing that," Fog explained. "On account of the fact that I is not reading that in my book of Great Things that I is writing."

"Autumn Dwellers describes anyone from the Autumn Lands, like the faerie folk," Templar informed him with a quiet murmur. "One of the Gated Lands separated by the Covenant from the mortal world."

"It's summer," Omen said lamely. He didn't really know much about the Gated Lands. All he knew was that in summer, the Summer Lands held sway over the world. Stories said that at midseason, the Gate of the land in ascension briefly opened, allowing anyone from beyond to pass into the mortal world for one night. People all over the world participated in festivals to honor such visitations or to ward off evil they believed could escape into the land during that time.

Omen was aware that he possessed faerie blood through the Deldano side of the family, but he had never had any connection to the other worlds beyond the yarns told by Beren Deldano.

"Didn't you say those things on the beach were Autumn creatures?" Templar reminded him.

"There's also rumors down on the docks that the Widow Maker has been spotted out at sea," Liethan added.

Omen guessed that Liethan, coming from a family of sailors, would be far more likely to have heard any seaport gossip.

"I didn't pay much attention to the stories," Liethan continued, "because sailors are always telling tales. But the Widow Maker supposedly only appears at the autumnal equinox. Maybe there is something to the stories?"

"They sing, and they cry, and nobody listens." Kyr's soft voice caught all their attention though he never looked up from his carving. "The shadows are frightened, and they're howling at the Autumn Gate."

Omen winced as his friends all stared at the boy. It was times like this when Omen really wished he knew if Kyr were truly mystical, or just plain crazy. *He said something about the seasons earlier as well.*

"The shadows, Kyr?" he asked gently. *I distinctly remember he mentioned autumn in the park.*

Kyr looked up at the sound of his name, his white-blond hair glinting in the magical lamplight. "I don't like shadows, Omen," he said solemnly. Then he spied Fog sitting on the table, and his face lit up in delight, all solemnity gone. "Look, Omen, it's a little grey kitten! Is he a twin too?"

"Fog and me is not twins!" Tyrin pronounced, seemingly astonished. "We is looking nothing alike. Not like me and Tormy who are identicallyness so that you is barely telling us apart."

"That is being true," Fog agreed sagely. "I is getting you two confused all the time."

"I is having freckles on my nose," Tormy offered, ever helpful. "That is how I is telling us apart."

"Can we get back to the bit about the Autumn Dwellers and Khylar?" Omen interrupted. "Are you sure he's been kidnapped?"

"I is telling you, Indee is saying it, and I is fixing it by finding Tormy to find Khylar so that I can find the baby dragon," Fog explained.

"Maybe we should talk to Indee?" Templar suggested,

the look on his face confirming to Omen that Fog's revelation sounded alarming.

"Tormy is talking to Indee about this," Fog corrected. "On account of the fact that you is not knowing anything because it is a secret that I is only telling Tormy."

Wondering if his cat was about to leave him behind to go off on some secret mission, Omen glanced at Tormy, concerned. Already the cat was on all four paws, ready to leave; Tyrin and Kyr rose as well.

"Come on, Omy." Tormy hurried him along. "Let's go find out about my secret mission."

The giant cat headed toward the open tavern wall with Tyrin and Kyr in tow, Fog following along behind as if the inclusion of Tyrin, Kyr and Omen were perfectly acceptable to him.

Mystified, Omen looked at his other friends. "Wait here. I'll tell you later." He waved them off.

They all watched in silence as Omen followed his brother and the cats out of the tavern and back into the sun-drenched park.

Chapter 4: Temple

OMEN

The euphonious tones of the temple choir practicing the Twilight Greeting in the nave floated through the early afternoon air as Omen, Kyr, Tormy and Tyrin followed their tiny feline guide down the stone path toward the gated entrance of the Temple of the Sundragons. The temple beyond the gate rose with grace and majesty. Resplendent dragon reliefs curled around the tallest spire, shapes etched into the gold-flecked marble depicting Melia's long and colorful history.

At a row of white flowering shrubs, Fog took a sharp turn, abandoning the main path. He fluffed his grey ruff as a dusting of pollen brushed onto his shoulders from the low-hanging blooms.

"Everyone is always going in the front," Fog said with a chirpy purr, "but I is liking to go through the garden gate."

As they veered from the path and wound around the side of the glorious structure, Omen wondered, not for the first time, where the Melian ancestors had acquired so much gold-flecked marble. *Wonder if those quarries still exist.*

"Is you sure the Untouchables want us to just wander in?" Tyrin asked, looking concerned. "They is usually pretty cranky. Like when I is trying to conduct a scientific poll about the deliciousnessness of hamsters."

"You interrupted one of their special ceremonies," Kyr said solemnly, "to ask if they prefer hamster candied or pickled."

45

Omen cringed as he remembered how an infuriated Ryael, Speaker of the Untouchables, had arrived at the Daenoth Manor, carrying Tyrin on an outstretched palm. The Melian cleric had threatened to cast Tyrin from the kingdom if the cat ever dared to interrupt another Sundragon ceremony. *"The Sundragons are disappointed in you, Omen Daenoth."* Ryael had scolded. Omen shook off the chill of the icy memory.

"It is being a quandary, because I is interrupting lots of them," Tyrin bragged out loud, "on account of the fact that they is ceremonizing so very often. I is being very good at interrupting."

Omen's lip quirked involuntarily. *One thing's for sure, he keeps things lively.*

"That's correctedness," Tormy agreed. "I 'member 'member the Bring Tyrin Cookies ceremony. That's almost being as greatnessness as the Great White Winter Cat celebration."

"Neither of those are dragon celebrations, Tormy," Omen interrupted. *Obviously made up.*

They had arrived at a large conservatory discreetly set to the side of the temple. The conservatory's crystal dome sparkled in the afternoon sun. For a distracted moment, Omen noticed how the last notes of the choir's music mirrored the glints of light spraying from the cupola.

Song and nature in harmony. In Melia, music was the magic that fueled the spells of protection all over the kingdom.

"The Great White Winter Cat ceremony is being an everybody celebration," Tyrin supplied. "The Great White Winter Cat is bringing presents to all the cats on Great White Winter Cat Day."

As Omen swept a billowy curtain aside and held it for Tormy to duck inside the temple, he tittered at the little cat's comment. *Pretty certain there is no Great White Winter Cat, but I'm not going to tell the cats that.*

"And everybody is celebrating cats getting presents and me getting cookies. So they infactedness is both dragon ceremonies, even if they is not knowing about it." Tyrin finished unwinding his logic and took a mighty leap onto Kyr's shoulder.

"Yes. And—" Tormy cut himself off, his large ears swiveling forward, his nose twitching. "Ooh. Ahh," the cat loudly admired the summer garden sprawling all over the inside of the conservatory. Then he raised his nose in the air to catch a scent.

The sweet aromas of thousands of exotic flowers mingled together could hardly compete with the exquisite sight of the cosseted indoor garden in full bloom.

"You like it?" Omen asked his little brother.

Kyr stood still, enchanted by the sight, his mesmerized gaze underscoring how enamored with the green and growing world the boy always seemed.

If I had lived centuries in a burnt up, dead world, I'd be the same.

Omen detected faint strands of magic in the air, and his skin tingled with the caress of the venerable ley lines that ran beneath the temple. He knew that the music constantly performed in the temple invoked powerful spells that carried their energies down those ley lines to all parts of the city.

"Some plants is liking to be eaten—" Tyrin started to say, but Kyr reached up and stuffed the little cat into his pocket unceremoniously.

47

"Don't," he warned the squirming creature, "or I'll button the button."

Omen raised an eyebrow at what — for Kyr — had been forceful words. The guilty look on Kyr's face said everything.

There's no hope of him ever disciplining that little monster, Omen thought and looked over at his giant orange companion, who at that moment was happily batting away at a large frond. *Good thing Tormy's perfect.* Omen knew the cats didn't mean any true mischief, they just saw the world differently — as something to be played with or perhaps eaten.

"Pot, meet kettle," he murmured.

"Is you going to cook, Omy?" Tormy asked, happy hope unchecked.

"This way," little Fog advised and strode down a line of pink lavender bushes.

Remembering that they were here to meet Indee, Omen raked his tangled hair out of his face and tugged on the laces of his sleeves.

Left my jerkin at The Harps, he thought with a twinge of annoyance.

"Right here." Fog twitched his whiskers toward a curtained opening camouflaged behind the greenery. "It is being a secret passage."

"Why are we going through a secret door?" Omen stepped through cautiously.

"The dragons is guarding the main entrance on account of the fact that nobodies is being allowed to visit Indee," the little grey cat said as he hopped ahead.

Omen stumbled forward. *Great. Then what are we doing here?*

"You have to understand," Indee's unmistakable cadence reached a sharp cord, and Omen put a hand on Kyr's shoulder to regain his balance, "it is imperative that no one find out!"

"That is just like you!" a second female voice rang out.

Omen could feel Kyr shaking and guessed that the women's loud, heated words scared the boy. "Don't worry, Kyr. We'll just say hello and leave. Whatever is going on isn't our problem."

Kyr smiled wearily.

"Your concern over appearances outweighs your concern for your son!" the other voice continued.

Omen recognized the quick staccato as belonging to Indee's daughter. *Caythla! I had no idea she was in town.* He'd always liked Caythla and looked forward to greeting her, but when he stepped further into the room, he saw only Indee.

Indee'athra Lir Drathos was not a Sundragon. But Indee'athra was much more than a noble from a foreign land. In the known kingdoms, she was a creature of legend and rumor.

Nelminorians whispered of her low birth and her faerie lineage. Kharakhians, superstitious and cautious by nature, refrained from comment and looked slyly over their shoulders at the mention of her name. Melians treated her with the same deferential respect they showed her husband — Sylvan Lir Drathos, youngest of the Elder Sundragons and beloved ruler of Solara, a kingdom far from the shores of Melia. Solarans, of course, called Indee'athra Lir Drathos their queen. But at the Daenoth Manor and among the close-knit circle of friends, she was referred to as "her" or, on less belligerent occasions, simply as "Indee."

In the not so distant past, Indee had been the ruler of Kharakhan, widow of their late king Charaathalar and queen mother of King Khylar Set-Manasan.

Officially sanctioned and approved history proclaimed that she had united the kingdom, brought the people through a bloody civil war and fought off the scourge of Nelminorian invaders. She'd then smashed Nelminor with her wrath, her magics and with the help of her powerful allies — allies who included Omen's parents.

Self-proclaimed Empress Indee'athra had gone on to punish the Nelminorian royalty until all that remained of them was a memory. And then she'd swiftly reorganized borders and neatly arranged her enemies and supporters into manageable camps.

As Nelminor lay broken and conquered, Indee had bestowed the country onto her daughter Caythla, as if that vast land were a pet or a bauble. And Indee had joined Sylvan, her new husband, in his kingdom of Solara, at the edge of the known world.

Now the fabled ruler stood in front of a large picture window in a chamber of the Temple of the Sundragons in the capital of Melia, pregnant and alone.

Tall and beautiful, with skin as pale as snow, Indee wore her knee-length ebony hair loose. Flickering white lights danced around her lithe body like a swarm of glow bugs orbiting a flame. Clad in a simple, high-waisted summer gown of sea blue, Indee hardly seemed pregnant, though Omen knew she was eight months along. Everyone in Melia knew exactly when she was due — the birth of a baby Sundragon was an event that would be celebrated across the land.

To Omen's surprise, Indee was barefoot. He wondered if

she'd picked up the carefree habit from the Corsairs — his friend Liethan Corsair hardly ever wore shoes. According to Omen's mother, Indee and Liethan's aunt, the Corsair sorceress Arra, were close friends.

Her back to Omen, Indee held her ivory hand pressed to the enormous glass windowpane. The tiny lights ebbed and flowed against Indee's form, crowding around her — never touching. In the glass, behind the glowing sparks, Omen saw the lick of flame, but no fire burned in the chamber. *Must be an unusually cold summer day on the other side.*

"Khylar is missing!" Caythla's voice rang out again, though he still saw no sign of her.

Kyr stared at the shimmering window and shifted uncomfortably. "Is the voice trapped in the glass?" he whispered with grave concern.

"No, I think it's a communication spell. Like scrying," Omen whispered back.

Tormy curled his front paws underneath his chest with a little *murr*. He pushed into Omen's leg just enough to let Omen know exactly where he'd settled down.

"You will tell your husband to travel to Kharakhan," Indee directed her command toward the glass. "You will tell him to rule in my stead, in Khylar's stead until such time—"

Caythla let out an annoyed yelp. "You are not listening, Mother!" A tapping sound emanated from the glass as if a bird were pecking at the pane. "You find someone to rescue Khylar, or nothing else happens. I'd go find him myself, if it weren't for the double-cursed Nelminorian summer festival."

"Double-cursed," Tyrin's awed whisper came from inside Kyr's pocket. "That is being more than cursed one

51

times."

"Shh," Omen scolded Kyr's pocket.

"I remember well how draining that festival can be." Indee seemed to consider something. "You should—"

"The one and only time you presided over the summer festival, you didn't even stay the whole three weeks," Caythla barked back. "You made me do the last fourteen days, Mother. And we had to start over three times because my Nelminorian accent wasn't quite right, and I kept saying 'Torkash' instead of 'Tarkash.'"

"Languages were never your strong suit," Indee commented casually.

"I is here to fix everything," Fog trumpeted. "I is brought heroes."

Indee spun to face Omen and his fluffy entourage.

"Fog?" Her eyes, black as the night sky, narrowed with displeasure, but then almost instantly sparkled with disconcerting shrewdness. She smiled like a satisfied cat and turned back to her daughter.

"There, you see. Everything is solved." Indee's voice hit a majestic note of studied superiority. The cortege of glowing lights whirled around their own axis and circled Indee's head like a spinning wreath. She swiped her hand at them, shooing them away.

"Omen!" Caythla squealed in delight.

Beyond the shimmering gleam of magic, Omen could now clearly distinguish the form of Queen Caythla Set-Manasan of Nelminor — apparently locked inside the glass.

"Is the lady trapped—"

"Nobody is trapped, Kyr." Omen hoped he could keep the boy from worrying. "That's Caythla. She's in Nelminor right now. Speaking through the mirror."

"Is she—"

"She's not a ghost." He patted Kyr's arm. "She's alive. She's just in another country."

"Green," Kyr muttered sagely.

The last time Omen had seen Caythla, they had been sledding down the hills of Melia in the winter snow. Though several years older than him, Caythla had fit in well with Omen and his friends. His extraordinary strength and stamina had made Omen a worthy playmate for Caythla, who had the fierceness of a grizzly bear. None of her ladies-in-waiting had been able to keep pace with her.

Caythla was married now and Queen of Nelminor, clad regally in a gown of pure white, a golden headdress with the symbol of the Nelminorian sun god upon her brow. Omen had to smile at her untamed tangle of black hair — a sign that the wild, leather-clad, mud-covered girl he'd known remained within the trappings of the queen.

"Hello, Cay," Omen greeted, his awe of meeting Indee assuaged at the pleasure of seeing his old friend in the scrying glass.

"Are you helping my mother?" Caythla sounded relieved. "Hey, is that your new brother?"

"Yes, obviously!" Indee snapped before Omen could utter a syllable. "The child lost in time. But that's not important. What is important is that Omen came to help! He'll take care of Khylar and you'll send Fel'torin to Kharakhan at once."

"Wait a minute!" Omen protested, wondering how the mission Fog had recruited Tormy for had suddenly become his quest. "I don't even know what's going on. Fog said something about Khylar being kidnapped."

Caythla's eyes narrowed. "Mother," she said in a low, warning tone. "If Omen isn't going, I'll send Fel'torin after Khylar and one of the Set-Manasans can rule Kharakhan."

"No!" Indee shouted, her dark eyes flashing with raw anger. The little lights sprayed out across the room like tiny flaming arrows shot out by a company of archers.

Omen stepped to the side, shielding Kyr with his body. Tormy seemed to take no interest, which Omen found odd. *Can he not see those lights? That's exactly the kind of thing cats love to chase.*

"I will not allow it!" Indee slammed her open palm against the glass. "No Set-Manasans!"

Set-Manasans. The remaining family of the former king of Kharakhan. Indee's former in-laws. I can see why she'd prefer Fel'torin on the throne instead of one of that lot. She'd never wrestle the kingdom back from them, but shouldn't she be more worried about her son?

"Omen will rescue Khylar," Indee stated emphatically, closing both fists tightly. The little lights returned and hovered around her shoulders like a stole.

That sounds more like a royal decree than a request. Indee didn't have any actual authority over him, but he found himself starting to sweat. "You still haven't told me what happened to Khylar," he pushed out each word with difficulty. "How can a king get kidnapped? Doesn't he have guards?"

Indee's obsidian eyes bored into him as if she were looking right into his brain.

"Yes, Mother," Caythla threw out quickly. "You still haven't explained that to me either. Exactly what happened to my brother?"

Indee's eyes flashed again. The lights vibrated, letting

off low hums, and then zipped through the room like miniature shooting stars. Indee took a deep breath to calm herself. "Your brother, Cay, has been abducted by Autumn Dwellers, and taken into the Autumn Lands."

A small jolt coursed through Omen. *That's impossible.*

A hard silence fell and lingered while Omen tried to collect his thoughts. *Why would she make up such a ridiculous story? But if it's true—*

A minute scratching sound tore through the quiet. Despite the tension, Omen turned his head toward the origin of the scraping.

Tiny Tyrin scrambled up and down a nearby, no-doubt priceless, tapestry in an effort to trap one of Indee's little lights.

"Get him!" Omen hissed and elbowed Kyr, who stood still as if nailed to the floor.

"Absurd!" Caythla finally burst out. "Mother, you are not being rational. Is this baby brain talking?"

"Hold your tongue, Caythla. There is no need for insults. I am in complete control."

"You are? What about the wyrding lights all around you? Your spells are breaking loose. And you know it!"

"My spells are doing exactly what I want them to do."

"Really? Then why don't you bring them back to you? From what I see they are just flying around the room, and the little cat is about to eat one."

Kyr bolted forward to grab Tyrin. Nearly tripping in his effort, he scooped the grumbling creature up from the floor where the kitten had corralled a glowing light between his front paws.

"Let me lay out the facts, Mother." Caythla's voice had turned dark. "The Autumn Gate is closed. No one can cross in or out until the fall equinox. And even if they could, the Autumn Dwellers would have little interest in kidnapping the king of a human kingdom."

"Not any human kingdom," Indee replied, glaring at Caythla. "And not a human king. Your grandmother's blood runs strong in both you and your brother. Your grandmother is a very powerful Autumn sorceress. She could have enemies moving against her." Indee pressed her lips together as if attempting to stem the flow of words, but a few slipped out quietly. "Of course she has enemies moving against her. She always has enemies moving against her. My mother—" Indee managed to finally cut herself off.

"You are speaking of a grandmother we've never had any contact with," Caythla said sharply. "And as far as I know, you've also had no contact with anyone from the Autumn Kingdom since you were a child. How would Autumn Dwellers even know that Khylar exists?"

Omen felt his head spinning. *Indee is of Autumn? Do my parents know?*

"Is this why there are sandlures on the beach?" Omen spoke up. He knew very little about the Gated Lands, but he knew the Gates controlled the movement of all sorts of creatures. "They don't belong here."

"Sandlure . . . I don't . . . " Indee shook her head, sending the little lights spinning through the room. "The Gates are more metaphorical than physical," she said with a sniff. "There are always secret ways in and out of these lands if you know where to look."

"If that's true . . ." Caythla paused momentarily.

"The door is open," Kyr whispered to Omen. "All we have to do is step through it."

"We'll leave in a minute, Kyr." Omen waved his hand toward the curtain that led to the garden.

"How do you know Autumn Dwellers took him?" Caythla's voice shook. "Have they asked a ransom?"

"Tylith told me," Indee said through her teeth.

This is getting interesting. Tylith Corsair had acted as King Khylar's personal bodyguard since they were both children. She was a highly trained warrior and the daughter of Lady Arra.

"Tylith!" Caythla looked even more astonished. "I had assumed Tylith was missing as well. If she's still around, why isn't she looking for Khylar? I would think that she'd stop at nothing to find him."

"She can't. She's looking for Tara," Indee replied stiffly.

"What happened to Tara?" Caythla shouted, obviously growing angrier with each of Indee's answers. "Mother, the whole story!"

Tara Corsair was Tylith's sister, and King Khylar's future wife and queen. *If something has happened to both of Lady Arra's daughters, news would have spread. The Corsairs are not a quiet lot. Liethan didn't say anything about his cousins earlier.*

"I don't know what's happened to Tara," Indee stated with annoyance. "All I know is that Ty just showed up here and told me that Khylar had been kidnapped by the Autumn Dwellers, and that Tara is gone."

The little lights gathered in what seemed like the shape of a fist.

"The dragons is being none too happy with Tylith's news," Fog explained. "They is afraid for Indee's dragon baby. They is telling her she has to go live in the Dragon-lands."

"I am not getting locked up in another realm for any reason or by anybody." Indee picked up a vase and threw it across the room. The little lights swooped forward, caught the ceramic container and gently floated it to the ground.

Indee ignored her own outburst. "Ty has gone after Tara, and someone trustworthy has to rule Kharakhan while Khylar is missing."

"You mean to say that someone has to go rescue Khylar, don't you?" Caythla insisted.

Indee pointed a sharp finger at Omen. "That's what he's here for!"

"I don't know anything about rescue missions or Autumn Dwellers," Omen protested. "I don't even know where the Autumn Lands are, or how to get there." *That sounded whiney. Am I being whiney?*

Indee glared at him with venomous annoyance. "The Mountain of Shadow, obviously. Haven't you ever listened to your mother's old stories? You can get anywhere from there, into any realm, any world. Under the right circumstances, even the Gated Lands."

Caythla let out a screech. "Secrets upon secrets upon secrets. Is nothing ever what we've been told it is? The Gated Lands are supposed to be—"

"Not just anyone can access the Mountain of Shadow." Indee turned to Omen. "But you may be able to."

"The Mountain of Shadow!" Omen sputtered. *This is way bigger than I thought.* He'd grown up hearing stories about that mountain, adventures and nightmarish tales occasionally told by his mother about her early days of roaming the world. "But that place is cursed! And it's in Kharakhan across the Luminal Sea." *Definitely whiney.*

"What of it?" Indee demanded. "You're the son of a god, if I'm to believe your mother's crazy stories about all the curses and blessings placed upon your birth. What could you possibly be afraid of?"

Omen flushed, not sure he'd liked the idea that Indee thought he was frightened. "I didn't say I was afraid," he insisted.

Indee waved her hand at Omen in satisfaction and turned to Caythla. "There you see, he's promised to rescue Khylar."

"Wait a minute!" Omen protested. "I didn't say—"

Indee turned swiftly toward him, her eyes flashing with renewed anger. Her magic lights flared around her like a halo. "Omen Daenoth! Are you going to stand there and tell a pregnant woman that you're not going to help her?"

"What? NO!" Omen took a step back. "Of course I'll help you. I only . . ."

A look of triumph blazed in Indee's stormy eyes, and in an instant the magic lights flurried and lashed toward Omen. But, as if he'd been expecting an attack all along, Kyr stepped in front of Omen. The flare wrapped itself like a tendril around Kyr's left wrist, and then vanished in a flash, leaving only shadows.

"Kyr!" Omen bellowed.

"What was that?" Caythla demanded.

"My magic was just reacting to Omen's promise." Indee sighed heavily. "It wasn't intentional, but now it's binding." She frowned down at the boy and pursed her lips. "Not what I had in mind, but what's done is done."

"What did you do to him?" Omen felt fury gathering as his throat tightened.

Kyr simply stared at Indee with an accusing expression. Tyrin had scaled Kyr's shoulder and licked his ear with quick, nervous swipes.

Omen knew that Kyr had an incredibly high pain tolerance, so even if he had been injured by the flash of magic,
it was unlikely he'd give any indication.

Tormy sat perfectly still, watching, back muscles tense.
Only Fog seemed completely at ease.

"I'm eight months pregnant!" Indee waved her hand dismissively. "You should all know better than to make me upset. My magic is unpredictable at best."

"Unpredictable?" Caythla spat out a harsh-sounding
Nelminorian word.

"Caythla!" Indee's voice whipped at the glass, sharp with
reprimand. "I do not condone that kind of language in my
presence, not even from my daughter."

Caythla's jaw tightened. She struggled to say words of
apology through clenched teeth. "Will the boy be all right?"
she finished, glaring at her mother.

Indee nodded graciously. "In time . . . Are you content
now?"

Caythla sneered. "Fine! I'll send Fel'torin to Kharakhan.
But don't think you've heard the end of this." A second later
the fire in the glass swelled and then vanished entirely,
leaving only the warm afternoon sunlight to dance on the
colored tiles.

Indee scooped up Fog, who'd climbed onto the window
ledge. "Now I'm very tired, and I want to rest," she said.
"You, Omen, have a rescue to plan. Talk to your mother if
you need any further information."

"My mother?" Omen stammered, wondering what his
mother had to do with any of this. "What did you do to
Kyr?" He started to move toward Indee, but Tormy's large
front paw snaked around his ankle and held him in place.

"We must go, Fog." Indee headed toward the back door

of the chamber. "Sylvan will be wondering what's keeping us."

"Did I fix everything?" Fog asked hopefully. "On account of the fact that I found the great hero Tormy to rescue Khylar?"

"Yes, my dear." Indee smiled, completely ignoring Omen's sputtering protests behind her. "You're a brilliant little cat."

"Did Caythla say a bad word?" Tyrin asked hopefully. He sat on Kyr's shoulder, head tilted to the side.

"When's dinner?" Kyr wondered out loud.

At a loss, Omen put an arm around his brother. "Let's go home and figure out what just happened."

"The tide is coming in," Kyr said, as if answering back. "It is the will of the stars in the firmament. One goes along."

Omen's insides felt as if they'd crumbled to ash. *Hope dad knows what to do because I think I just let a bad thing happen.*

Tyrin loudly repeated Caythla's Nelminorian swearword.

"Couldn't have said it better myself," Omen grumbled under his breath as they headed back toward the garden.

Chapter 5: Home

OMEN

By the time Omen got home, cold unease had spread through his body. He worried about traveling to Kharakhan to do Indee's will. He worried about leaving Kyr behind in Melia. He worried about what Amar had said about the Widow Maker. *"You had best keep your brother away from the ocean until we can figure out what these strange occurrences mean. The Widow Maker devours the souls of drowned sailors, and it is attracted to mystics."*

He sifted through options but could find no good solution to this thorny dilemma.

Kyr never leaves my side . . . Keep him away from the ocean. How? Taking him to Kharakhan is too dangerous . . . But he's terrified of being abandoned . . . But I can't risk Urgolath finding him. The creature comes after mystics . . . If Kyr is a mystic . . . But I promised I would never leave him . . . I promised . . . But I promised Indee . . .

Contradictory thoughts somersaulting in his mind, Omen entered the Daenoth Manor. He waved off the footman and watched the cats cross over the threshold into the great hall. The enchantments wreathed around the large door's frame hummed faintly as they passed.

As the domestic spells washed over them, the cats' matching orange-and-white coats suddenly gleamed as if combed and brushed with impeccable care. His mother's tangled household spells stretched like veins throughout the gold marble of the manor, keeping Tormy and Tyrin clean and, he suspected, minor irritants — mosquitoes, fleas, houseflies, spiders, creeping curses, and mild poisons — at bay.

Like soldiers on the march, the cat duo trotted ahead with purpose, heading, he guessed, to the kitchens where a never-ending supply of cookies and treats awaited them.

A crinkling sound bored into Omen's ear with the speed and annoyance of a gnat on a damp summer day.

That was his only warning.

A wave of power hit him, lifted him off his feet and smashed him against the closest marble pillar. Omen felt his teeth grind as he bit down in frustration. *I forgot again!* He clamped his eyes shut, a brief piece of music filling his mind as he recalled a familiar psionic pattern, and threw up an energy shield large enough to encompass both himself and Kyr, who'd been trailing behind him through the door-way. A tall crystal vase exploded on the other side of the room, the lavender stalks it had held catapulting through the air in an indigo blast.

"Dad!" Omen yelled. He crouched down and covered Kyr who cowered in a heap on the floor. The scrawny boy whimpered like a scared dog.

The psionic assault cut off abruptly.

Omen shook his head. Long copper strands of his hair veiled his eyes like a curtain.

A gallop of padded paws thundered from down the long hall as Tormy and Tyrin rushed back to help. "Oooomy!" Tormy shouted. "I is coming!"

"Dad!" Omen yelled again, more petulantly than he had intended, and raked the hair out of his eyes.

7 stepped from the shadows of the far hallway; sunlight streaming through the window caught in his platinum mane of hair. Dressed in fine Lydonian leathers, 7 was every inch the lord of the manor despite his youthful appearance. He looked at Kyr, concern wrinkling his forehead. "You're fine, lad," Omen's father told the boy in a low, soothing tone he seemed to have reserved for Kyr. "Nothing happened. Get up."

The cats crowded Kyr, sniffed at his face and poked their noses at his shoulders.

Kyr folded Tyrin into the crook of his arm and then spied the scattered flowers strewn across the golden marble entryway. The fear melted away from his face. "Look what Omen made! It's so pretty — purple patterns."

7 raised an eyebrow at his son. "Omen, I told you I was going to test your psionics when you returned home." 7 sounded as if he'd grown tired of his own words. "I told you I was going to attack you the moment you walked through the door. Your enemies won't give you a warning ahead of time. You've got to keep your shield up, Omen. Keep your shield up . . . all. . . the . . . time. You have to build up your stamina. Even your ten-year-old sister—"

"I know. I know." Omen picked Kyr up by the arm. "I think I'm done with lessons for today. Besides it's not like I have a whole lot of enemies here in Melia. Who's going to attack me here?"

He swallowed hard remembering the grasp of the sand-lure on his ankle only hours before. *That was an anomaly.*

"I want to sculpt the flowers." Kyr's eyes shone with ex-citement. "A giant-sized metal flower. For the garden. It would be so beautiful, Omen."

"Later, Kyr." Omen nodded, trying to get Kyr to mimic

the agreement. *How can he get so distracted so quickly?*

"Pot, meet kettle," 7 murmured.

Omen frowned at hearing the phrase he'd uttered so recently. He looked up at his father in surprise and saw both annoyance and amusement. *Attacked me and read my mind all at once. How does he do that?*

"Unlike you, I actually practice." 7 blew out an exasperated sigh, and Omen realized his father was still reading his thoughts right through his hastily constructed mental shield. "You have to train, Omen. You have to. Forget about protecting yourself. What about Kyr? What about the cats?"

I got it. Omen sent prickly jabs along with the words.

7's mouth twitched. "Nice. The prickles are a good touch."

"I'm hungry." Tormy sighed dramatically. The cats clearly had gotten over their fright and were back to their single-minded focus on snacks.

"Come on, you," Omen said and patted Tormy's flank. "I'll make you something to eat."

"Stop! You've been hexed!" The shrill words lashed from the second-floor railing; Omen's mother stood at the top of the stairwell, staring down at all of them.

Oh, great! Mom's attacking now too?

Omen tensed, braced for whatever challenge his mother might have for him. Unlike his father, however, his mother would use magic — she lacked the devastating Daenoth psionics. Unfortunately, despite his failure with his father, Omen actually felt more confident in his psionics defensive abilities than he did his magical skills.

His eyes swept up toward his mother who stood at the top of the grand staircase like a statue from a dark temple. Her sable black hair spilled over her blue gown and down

65

past her knees like a mantle. Her eyes gleamed silver in the light.

"Hexed," she repeated. "It already has you. Where is it?"

"What?" Omen jumped back a few steps and patted his arms as if driving away a legion of tiny spiders. He'd been uneasy already, and his mother's words had made it worse. He felt the hairs on his arms stand on end.

His mother's people were fiercely superstitious, so much so that they even chose "hex" names to ward off ill luck and dark curses. The Machelli clan's peculiar superstitions about the warding power of their unconventional nick-names held sway in the Daenoth household, and woe to the fool who called her Ava instead of Avarice.

While Omen felt no spell, no hex upon his skin, he knew his mother was rarely wrong about such things. He cursed under his breath.

"The boy brought home a hex," Omen's mother announced, directing her words toward 7.

Omen didn't know if she was complaining about him, or blaming 7, and it worried him that his mother sounded uncharacteristically troubled.

She stalked down the stairs with animal grace, her silver gaze studying him with unnerving intensity.

"Avarice?" 7 spoke her name like a caress, though Omen could hear the worry in his voice.

Avarice mumbled foreign-sounding words and knotted her fingers in a fluid sequence.

"Hexed? What? How?" Omen shook, a full body shake this time like a sopping wet cat.

Creepy. Creepy. Creepy.

Avarice took more measured steps down the last section of stairs. The whisper of her slippered feet crushing down on the soft center rug was barely discernible. *That's practically stomping for her. She's angry — at me? It's not fair.*

"Omen Armand Locheden Machelli Daenoth," Avarice murmured his full name over and over as if possessed, and he shivered uncontrollably as he realized she was casting some sort of spell upon him, seeking out whatever hex she'd sensed when he'd passed through her domestic enchantments.

He felt the cool wash of her magic move lightly over the surface of his skin, so different from the driving force of his father's psionic blast.

Avarice stood in front of him and gently ran her hands over his shoulders and arms, all the while searching his face. "Touched by a hex," she murmured as if to herself, "but it didn't settle on you." Her words had an edge of dread. "Not the cats. No." She cast a wary eye to Kyr. "My poor lamb." She took the boy's left hand in hers, pushing up the sleeve of his shirt and revealing his painfully thin wrist. "Have you ever noticed this mark before?"

Omen stared at a coin-sized spiderweb on the back of his brother's left hand. The lines pulsed sluggishly, their black-as-ink knits weaving into a tiny design.

"Pretty," Kyr exclaimed and put his hand right up to his nose. "It's moving! Is it alive?"

"It's a growing hex," Avarice spoke slowly, perhaps trying not to frighten the boy.

Kyr seemed more delighted than scared. "It's really, really beautiful. All those colors!" Kyr turned his hand as if to see if the mark had reached his palm.

There are no colors. Just black, Omen thought.

"Where would he have picked up something like that?" 7 stepped closer and examined the boy's hand.

"'Member, 'member the light," Tyrin announced.

"Indee," Tormy blurted out. "We is just with Queen Indee . . . She is giving us our grand hero's quest."

"You is . . . were . . . What? Omen?" Avarice spun on her son. "You met with Indee?"

"Fog is saying . . ." Tyrin started to explain, but quieted down when Avarice gave him a sharp look.

Kyr placed little Tyrin in his pocket. The kitten squirmed but didn't try to escape. He poked his fuzzy head out and watched with great curiosity.

"Indee asked us to look for Khylar, who's apparently gone missing," Omen said, at a loss. "I don't really want to help, but she said—" A loud yelp from his brother silenced his words, and he spun toward Kyr in alarm.

Kyr stared down at his hand with a look of profound confusion. He waved his hand through the air several times before he started to blow on it as if to cool it off.

"Serpent's Scales!" Avarice exclaimed. "You've triggered the hex. Take it back! Take it back!"

"Take what back?" Omen asked in alarm.

"Say you want to help — say you'll do it! Now!"

"I want to help! I'll rescue Khylar!" Omen proclaimed.

Avarice snatched up Kyr's flailing hand and turned it over to reveal the pulsing mark. "Good, it's stopped growing, but look at this, it's burned him. That blasted witch!"

Omen pushed past his mother and took Kyr's arm. Tiny blisters circled the strange markings, Kyr's skin turning an angry red. "Kyr!" Shock ricocheted through Omen like chain lightning.

My fault. He felt as if his blood had turned to sand. *My fault. I didn't protect Kyr.*

The boy looked from Omen to Avarice, searching, not

certain what to say. "Ouch?" he pressed the word out hesitantly, and Omen's heart clenched as he realized his little brother still didn't understand how to react to pain, his tolerance so high Omen suspected he'd say nothing at all if he thought that was what they wanted.

Seeing the look on Omen's face, Kyr hid his hand behind his back. "It's fine, Omen."

"No, it's not, Kyr." Omen bit the inside of his lip until he tasted blood. He felt the touch of his father's mind brushing past him, though this time he knew no amount of shielding would keep that presence from skimming his thoughts. He looked up to see both of his parents exchanging intense looks, and he realized that an entire conversation had passed between them in the second or two that ticked by.

"Indee said something about the Mountain of Shadow," Omen began, uncertain what he could say safely. "But that's in Kharakhan — across the Luminal Sea. . ." He trailed off, knowing his parents understood the geography better than he did, and he'd told them what Sundragon Amar had said about the Widow Maker. "I mean . . . Kyr can't—"

"Stop!" Avarice raised her hand. "Kyr is the one hexed — but you're both bound by it. You both have to do what you promised, or Kyr suffers. Do you understand?"

He understood. Leaving Kyr behind, safely tucked away in Melia, was not an option. Despite himself, he felt relieved. "We don't actually know if he's really a mystic," Omen tried to reason. He looked from his father to his mother. His father was less likely to believe in supernatural bonds between sea monsters and mystics, but 7 looked worried. Avarice looked furious.

"Can't you just get Indee to remove the hex?" Omen asked.

"I can try," Avarice bit out. "But don't count on it. I know how she works — most likely the hex is tied to the completion of her goal. She plans these things out very carefully."

"She said it was an accident!" Omen added quickly, feeling more uncomfortable by the moment. *What if she lied? What if it was planned out? What if she meant to hex Kyr? How can I trust one word she says?* He hoped that it had been an accident. He hoped it wasn't unbreakable.

If anything Avarice looked more irritated than she had a moment ago. "Indee never does things by accident!" She wrapped an arm around Kyr's shoulder. "Let's get some salve on your burn, Kyr." Avarice hustled the boy out of the hall. She cast a molten glance toward Omen. "You are a stupid, stupid boy. Tell him, 7. I'm too aggravated. Meet me in my office later, Omen. After I've taken care of this poor, poor lamb."

7 cleared his throat. "So, you've been had."

"Indee . . . I didn't mean . . ." Omen broke off, not certain what was safe for him to say. *If talking about the quest triggers the mark on Kyr's hand, what am I allowed to say?*

"Why would she do that to Kyr?" Omen felt his anger rising. He burst out, "Fine! If she's going to hex my brother, then I'm not going—"

"Stop!" 7 cut him off immediately with a sharp probe to Omen's mind — like a quick jab. "Saying you refuse the quest, or even implying it, will trigger the hex again."

Stifling a scream, Omen burned with rage. "Then I'll get the hex removed, and I'll hex her back!"

"You're going to hex a pregnant woman?" 7 asked mildly.

Omen felt himself deflating. "I'll wait until after the

baby is born, and then I'll hex her."

"She'd serve your head to you on a platter," 7 informed him. "And then her dragon husband would eat what was left."

"I thought she was your friend!" Omen protested. "I grew up playing with her daughter. Why would she do something like this?"

"Ally not friend," 7 replied. "There's a difference."

The growing feeling of betrayal in his gut was sharp and cutting. He remembered the instant the hex had struck. "Kyr saw the hex coming. He intercepted it. It was supposed to hit me, not him."

7 nodded his head. "You know your brother sees things others do not."

The weight of Kyr's sacrifice settled over him. *I'm supposed to protect Kyr, and he protected me. I have to keep him safe.* "Sundragon Amar said the Widow Maker was attracted to mystics. And Liethan Corsair said the Widow Maker has been spotted recently. If I take Kyr to sea . . . " He broke off again, not certain how much he could say.

"There is a chance the Widow Maker will find you," 7 finished for him.

I can't let that happen! "Is there some other way into the Autumn Lands besides the Mountain of Shadow?" Omen pressed.

"You could try going into Nvrel," 7 suggested. "It is riddled with openings into the Night Lands, and from there you might be able to find a way into the Autumn Lands. But Night Dwellers are far more dangerous than Autumn Dwellers. And Nvrel is twice as far away as Kharakhan. It will take longer. And you'd still have to cross the Luminal Sea."

71

Omen's shoulders sunk. "Can't you make a portal to Kharakhan?" he asked his father. "We have a portal to Lydon and Terizkand. Can't you just make one to Kharakhan?"

"The portal has to be made on the other side. I can't open a portal from Melia," 7 explained. "I'd need to go to Kharakhan, make a portal there, and then link it back to the one here. I'd have to cross the Luminal Sea, and you would have to wait."

Omen's stomach dropped. *There's no other way. We have to go to sea.*

7 closed his eyes for a second and bit together his lips. "I'll see if Kadana's ship is still at port," he said finally. "She was heading back to Kharakhan, and her ship is fast. If anyone can get you safely there, it's Kadana."

"Maybe mother will convince Indee to remove the hex, and then I won't have—" Omen cut himself off before he could refuse the quest again.

"But Omy, is you forgetting? Who else can save the losteded king?" Tormy blinked his giant amber eyes, seeming bewildered. "We is being the heroes. And there is being savings to be done."

"No matter how rotten it was of Indee to hex you and Kyr, Tormy has a solid point." 7 put an arm around his son's shoulders. "Not to mention, you'd be hard-pressed to find anyone who can remove Indee's hex." He pointed him toward the entryway. "You're going on this quest. And you should avoid saying anything that might trigger the hex, or Kyr gets burned. And you can't take too much time; these sorts of hexes grow. That's what your mother wanted me to tell you."

7 stopped outside into the courtyard and looked up at the

clear sky. "I can go with you to Kharakhan, and then build a portal home once we arrive. But building the portal is going to take weeks, so you'll need to investigate Khylar's disappearance on your own while I'm busy."

Omen stared at his father. Hope and embarrassment warred inside of him. "You're coming to Kharakhan with me?" he asked, uncertain.

"If the Widow Maker is out there, I'm going to have to," 7 replied. "But you should take some friends as well — they can help you once we arrive in Kharakhan."

Omen knew that his father wasn't happy about leaving Melia. And he knew his mother would be even less pleased. *Which may have been why she was so angry. She knew Dad was going to come with me.*

Guilt gnawed at Omen. He took a deep breath and squared his shoulders. "I'll be fine alone," he said with false bravado. "Or mostly alone — Templar and Liethan will come. Maybe Bryenth too. And if the Widow Maker finds us, we can fight it off. Between my psionics and Templar's magic—"

"No!" 7 cut him off harshly. "That's why I'm coming with you. If the Widow Maker shows up, you'll leave the fighting to me and hide below deck."

Omen felt as if he'd been punched.

"Hopefully it won't come to that," 7 continued quickly. "Kadana knows to steer clear of the creature's hunting grounds. Our best options are to avoid it or else — outrun it."

"You want me to hide below deck?" Omen sputtered. "I've never run from a fight!"

"This isn't a fight you can win." 7's voice was low and stern, filled with warning. "The Widow Maker is an ancient leviathan — it subjugates the minds of its victims. You've never been in a true psionic battle, and—"

"What are you talking about!" Omen snapped. "You and I duel all the time. Just now when I came home —"

"Listen!" 7 clasped Omen's shoulder tightly, his gaze so intense that Omen shrank back a little.

"That isn't a psionic duel," 7 spoke quickly, relentlessly. "I've never hurt you; I've never even tried to hurt you. Those are just simple exercises to teach you to keep your shield up. Even the other things I have taught you — levitation and other psionic manipulation — are useless when it comes to a true psionic duel. A battle between two psionicists takes place in a matter of seconds, and there are no flashy tricks. One person wins, and the other person ends up utterly mindless — brain-dead. Most psionicists never risk touching a stranger's mind for fear of attack. You only touch the mind of someone you trust absolutely."

Omen flushed, imagining the reality of such a battle. His tongue felt dry and too thick. There were stories of terrible magical duels that left the loser stripped of all magic, but he'd never heard much about psionic duels. The possibility of losing the ability to think struck a deep terror in him. *Complete helplessness.* "But my shield is strong," he said uncertainly. "And aren't the Daenoth psionics stronger than everyone else's?"

"Yes, we're stronger," 7 agreed more gently. "And your shield is excellent — when you remember to keep it active. Against a human psionicist, I wouldn't be worried. But the Widow Maker isn't human — it's ancient, and powerful, beyond anything you can imagine. It controls the minds of tens of thousands of dead souls it has devoured. It steals their power. You're no match for it."

"But if—" Omen's words were cut off by a sharp cry. His mother's voice called out to both of them. Without another word, they rushed back into the manor, Tormy capering behind them.

Avarice stood in the foyer with Kyr, a white bandage wrapped around his left hand. The boy clamped both hands over his ears and shook his head back and forth violently. Tyrin, still in Kyr's pocket, stood up on his hind legs, front paws stretching upward toward the boy's thin chest as if wanting to pull himself up to the boy's face.

"They sing and they cry and the people are marching into the sea!" Kyr blurted out, his expression twisted. His words rang out like a death knell in Kahdess. "You cannot sing and swim! Their mouths are open and they claw for breath!"

"No, Kyr! Not the Language of the Dead!" Avarice slipped her hands around the boy's thin shoulders, trying to keep him from twisting back and forth. "Stop! Stop!"

"Kyr!" Omen ran forward and caught hold of his brother's face. "Kyr, it's all right!"

Kyr's eyes, wide and frightened, locked onto his. "Do not leave me all alone with the screams. I like Omen's music, not the song of death, not the cries and the wails of the water."

"7, can you—" Avarice began.

Abruptly, 7 turned away from all of them. "Something's wrong!" he hissed.

Omen's eyes went to 7, but his father gazed around sightlessly, searching.

Off in the distance, the bells in the Temple of the Sundragons began sounding in warning.

Chapter 6: Song

OMEN

O men knew the various patterns that rang regularly from the bell tower of the Temple of the Sundragons, but this agitated blare screaming
through the city diverged drastically from anything he had
heard before. The heavy undertones — *From the largest
bell,* he guessed — colored the loud *clang, clang* and unde-
niably warned of danger.

His heart racing, Omen hurried after his father who returned to the courtyard, searching heedfully. The bright sky
had dimmed with evening, and a heavy band of unseasonal
clouds had rolled in.

Dark shadows passed overhead. *Dragons!* In a matter of
moments, five of the great creatures flew by. Omen caught
glints of their uniquely colorful underscales. "Hold Dragons," Omen murmured with reverence.

While it wasn't unusual to see one or two of the Hold
Dragons throughout the city, the sight of five of them in the
sky all at once was breathtaking. And troubling.

"They're headed for the shore." 7 motioned Omen back
inside, pushing past Tormy who pranced nervously around
the foyer, tail twitching wildly.

Racing through the manor, 7 flung open the double
doors to the back gardens with a precise psionic burst.

Perched high on the western cliffs of Melia, Daenoth
Manor was surrounded by several lush, tiered gardens,
which led to a large rocky outcropping and the stone stair-

case that wound down the cliffside to the beach.

Omen wrapped his fingers around the cold marble of the top garden banister and set his sights on the vast ocean before them. He breathed in the salty air and scanned from the water to the cliffs that rose north and south of the city.

Avarice, Tormy, and Kyr had followed after them, the boy having fallen silent once the warning bells had begun. Tyrin had climbed up Kyr's body and perched on his shoulder. Behind the family, several servants had made their way outside. All looked frightened. Omen spotted his little sister Lilyth racing from one of the lower gardens up a wide side staircase.

"What's happening?" Lilyth called out, her long dark hair flying behind her as she raced to her mother's side.

High in the sky, the glittering shapes of dragons circled far out over the ocean. They skimmed over the crests of the waves, then rose high on the air currents only to turn and circle back again as they searched for something beneath the surface. Omen's eyes tracked four Sundragons as they glided mere feet above the water. Along the cliffs, six more dragons perched on rocky outcroppings, intently focusing on the shoreline, great claws digging into the hard rocks, wings spread wide — ready to launch into the air at any moment. As one, they turned westward, gleaming jeweled eyes locking onto their dragon brothers who zipped over the turbulent ocean waves.

"Ten Hold Dragons!" Omen exclaimed. Even growing up in Melia, he'd never seen so many dragons all at once.

This means trouble.

"Where are the other two?" Lilyth asked, awe in her voice. She turned a full circle, scanning the sky for the remaining two Hold Dragons.

"If the threat is real, they wouldn't leave the city," Avarice replied. "One dragon always has to stay in Lord Darshawn's Hold." Her angular brows furrowed. "The other would be scouting the city."

"Is they being hungry?" Tormy asked as he placed his front paws on the marble banister and stood on his hind legs to watch the dragons going in circles over the water. The wind blew his fur back against his face. His white ruff shimmered in the stormy light as he gazed excitedly out to sea. "Maybe they is fishing?"

"I don't think they're fishing, Tormy." Omen shivered with anticipation. *Something is really wrong!*

"What's that strange music?"

Omen turned to see Conley, the footman, standing behind him, his head cocked to one side, a bemused expression on his face. "It's rather melancholy, isn't it?" the man continued. Several of the maids crowded together beside Conley. They too stared off into the distance, listening to something Omen couldn't hear.

"Shield your minds. Now!" 7 ordered. He reached out for Lilyth and Omen.

Omen didn't hesitate — the familiar tune of the strongest shielding pattern he knew played through his head. The pattern formed clearly and brightly, triggering his power as he closed off his thoughts from intrusion.

Powerful magic brushed over his skull. Along with his own shielding pattern, he felt the touch of his father's psionics surrounding him and reinforcing his mental shield. That power linked immediately with Lilyth and then his mother, the cats, and Kyr. 7 shielded them, supported them, and for one brief moment Omen stood under the cloudy sky linked in perfect harmony with his family.

Unlike magical patterns that could be learned from a book or a scroll, psionic patterns could only be taught mind-to-mind. Everything Omen knew about psionics he'd learned from his father. The patterns had to be internalized — for Omen they took the form of music, loud and clear and brilliant in their harmonies. For his mother and Lilyth, they took the form of movement, like dance steps rooted deep in muscle memory. He could feel their minds awash with the patterns, moving forms and swirling currents unique to each of them.

Tormy and Tyrin had no psionic abilities, but Omen sensed his father's shield encompassing them as well — their feline minds gleaming like bright beams of pure emotion. And beside them, the raw, unformed chaos of his little brother Kyr — whose abilities were utterly untrained, unprotected, exposed. Without the shielding bracelet he wore on his right wrist, he'd be vulnerable to any random attack.

Since he'd rescued Kyr from the deserted city, there had hardly been time to teach Kyr basic skills, let alone teach him the first thing about psionics. The few attempts Omen had made had left him engulfed in swirling confusion and given him brutal headaches. Kyr's grasp on reality was tentative, containing no solid fixture, no point of origin, and thus his mind produced nothing but chaos.

He might not ever learn to use psionics.

Omen couldn't guess how his father navigated the snarls of Kyr's mind enough to shield the boy, layering his protections over that of the bracelet. 7's mind was powerful, unbreakable, familiar. Omen understood the mnemonic devices his sister and his mother used to hold their patterns in place, but he had never been able to understand his father's. 7's mind was filled with layers and layers of sharp angles and edges, points and vectors that seemed more chaotic than even the psionic patterns themselves. Everything in 7's mind moved at a speed Omen could barely comprehend.

Eerie music flared. Deafening, it surrounded them — spilling forth the agonies of loss and terror and longing. The song had words, but Omen could not make out the language. There were harmonies, but he could not distinguish individual voices. Percussion throbbed as if from a heartbeat, but he could not follow the uneven rhythm.

It's in my mind! he realized. *Not my ears.* He wasn't hearing the song — he could feel it vibrate through his bones, pulse through his blood. It reached out to him, trying to grab him, trying to overwhelm the steady melody he used to keep his shield in place. But each time it tried to latch on to his thoughts, the dreadful sounds slid off the surface of his shield, unable to truly touch him.

"I is hearing singing!" Tormy exclaimed, ears perked forward.

"I is hearing it too!" Tyrin chirped from his perch on Kyr's shoulder.

"Dark words and dark waters," Kyr shook his head, still speaking Kahdess. "It cries and sings, and they listen. And now they all march away, all gone, all lost."

"What is it?" Omen asked, troubled and jumpy. He could only guess that this awful music was what Kyr had been hearing all along. It was the first time Omen had heard the imaginary things Kyr claimed to hear all the time. *He's not making it up!* "Is this what you've been hearing, Kyr? Do you know what it's saying?"

"Omy!" Tormy's voice cracked with alarm. With a great bound, the cat leaped away from the banister toward the stairs leading down to the lower garden. He barred the way down with his body.

The five servants who had followed them from the house shambled toward the stairs, all staring ahead blankly — so lost, they seemed oblivious to the drop before them. Meanwhile, the cook and two of the upstairs maids had stepped from the manor and were moving toward the trail as well, faces expressionless, eyes locked on the distant waters.

"Stop them!" Avarice hollered. She blocked several scullery maids before they could move past Tormy and make their way down the stairwell. Lilyth grabbed one of the cooks by the arm, and Omen ran down the balcony staircase to stop the two young gardener's assistants from taking the cliffside stairs.

"What's happening?" Omen bellowed up to his father, catching each of the boys by their wrists. While both tried to continue walking away, they didn't struggle against him. Movements slow and stilted, they seemed unaware of Omen's grip.

Above, on the upper balcony, Tormy had knocked down Conley, the footman, and had placed one heavy paw on his back, holding him pinned to the ground. Lilyth had a firm grip on the back of the cook's tunic, keeping her in place. 7 cut off the remaining servants who were trying to walk down the staircase and shooed them back up toward the house.

"It's the music," 7 shouted back, answering Omen. "It's calling to them."

They are being controlled. Omen shuddered with disgust.

One of the dragons on the cliff roared and leaped forward, wings catching the wind as he dove down toward the beach.

Omen stared in disbelief as people on the beach, men and women alike, walked as if in a trance toward the water. They had come from the city, wandering down the northern path to the far trail and the white sand beach.

The dragon — Sundragon Amar, Omen noted — landed in the crashing surf, placed his great body between the ocean and the townsfolk, wings still unfurled as he barred their way.

"He's going to jump!" Lilyth shrilled. Omen spun — northward along the cliff he could see a man heading toward the ocean. Unlike the people who had at least sought out the trail, this man marched straight toward the edge.

Another dragon launched — Sundragon Geryon. Omen recognized the amethyst sparkle of his underscales. The man on the cliff took a step into nothing and fell — no scream echoing from his mouth. Geryon swirled in the sky, banking sharply, one enormous claw reached down and caught the man straight out of the air.

But along the cliff's edge, more people started to appear. One more dragon hovered just over the cliffs and beat his wings furiously; the force of the wind pummeled the people and sent them backward to the ground. Another dragon launched into the air, tilting northward toward the city's docks.

There's nothing to stop people from leaping from the docks! Omen realized with a start. *If this music is reaching all the way into the city, there will be hundreds of people swarming the docks.*

"Omen! Grab that man!" Avarice shouted down to him.

A young red-haired man had slipped past Omen and was heading toward the garden railing. *That's Rinlan from the stables.* Omen hesitated. *If I let the gardeners go, they'll disappear down the stairs.*

"Sorry!" he said to both, releasing one and punching him hard across the jaw. The youth went down like a sack of potatoes, hitting the ground with a hard *oomph.*

Omen knocked his second charge to the ground before turning and running toward the stable boy, who had climbed up the banister. Omen reached out and caught Rinlan's arm just as he fell. Despite dangling over a deadly drop, Rinlan never made a sound, nor did he take hold of Omen's hand. Omen hefted the young man to safety, but the moment Omen released him, Rinlan stood again and turned to climb on the banister once more. Omen grabbed the back of Rinlan's belt and pulled him roughly away from the edge.

"Stop that!"

A moment later Omen felt a crackle of energy all around him as his mother's magic washed past him to encompass Rinlan. From one instant to the next, Rinlan stiffened and collapsed to the ground, Avarice's spell sending him into a deep slumber.

Glancing back up at the upper garden, Omen saw other servants dropping to the ground as well, all forced into a deep sleep by Avarice's magic.

Omen felt a little queasy but realized his mother had just saved their lives.

He turned his gaze toward the cliffs where the dragons still fought to keep people from jumping over the edge. The dragons had resorted to similar tactics as his mother, using magic to put people to sleep. Melian after Melian dropped to the ground, unconscious.

There are far too many of them. More are coming! He

worried about the lure of the haunting song.

Omen spied an old woman coming from the house. *That's mother's seamstress!* He ran toward the patio doors, and roughly shoved the woman back inside, pushing the doors shut. Through the glass, he could see several other servants heading for the outside. *This isn't the only way out of the house! There's nothing stopping them from going out the front doors!* He agonized over the two side doors to the lower garden and the servants' entrance by the kitchen.

Holding the doors, Omen turned to see the beach below filled with people — more were appearing on the cliffs. Omen tried not to imagine what was happening down by the docks.

The haunting music had to have reached all of them, calling out to the citizens, calling them toward the sea. "We can't hold back the entire city!" he shouted to his parents, frantic.

Melia is my home, these are my neighbors.

Along the cliffs, another dragon leaped into the air, catching people who'd managed to reach the cliffs' edge before they could fall to their deaths.

Sundragon Andrade, the youngest and smallest of the Hold Dragons, plucked drenched Melians from the surf and carried them to the beach. But once he'd dropped them into the sand, they just got back up and continued their relentless march toward self-destruction.

A new song, bright and clear, vibrated through the air, real and powerful. It enveloped them all.

The dragons near the cliffs had started to sing. Their voices echoed with deep, powerful harmonies that rang through the air, carried through the earth and overwhelmed the terrible dark music creeping through everyone's mind.

The physical sound was impossible to tune out, low and mellow, inhuman in tone, but beautiful in the way of a flawlessly played instrument.

All around him, Omen felt the air vibrating, energy rising and pulsing through his bones.

The dragons had all lifted their heads to the cloud-filled sky, great jaws open as pure harmonies burst from their throats.

Omen felt a sizzle in the air and sensed pulses of power running through the ground. *They're using the ley lines,* Omen realized in awe. *They're invoking the spells of protection on the city.* Though Omen had never seen it, he'd heard that shortly before his parents had arrived in Melia, the entire country had been shrouded by a magical shield that had kept the rest of the world from seeing the land. Melia had been lost to the world for many centuries.

For reasons of their own, the dragons had chosen to remove the shield, allowing foreigners to their shores — for better or worse.

Though the shield was gone, Omen had always been told that those protections still surrounded Melia, awaiting the moment the dragons reawakened them.

The crowds of people who had been pressing toward the cliffs stopped. Men and women on the beach ceased their mindless march toward the water's edge. They stood blinking in confusion and looking around them in alarm. Their eyes widened, awestruck as they saw all the dragons surrounding them.

The dragon song is blocking out the haunting music. They're free!

"Omy!" Tormy cried out. "Miss Penelope is not stopping!"

85

Omen turned toward his cat — Tormy had snagged the apron strings of an old woman who'd come from around the side of the house. Omen recognized her immediately as the Scaalian cook who regularly made treats for the cats and Kyr. But unlike the Melians around them who had awakened from the strange stupor caused by the terrible song, Old Penelope was still blank-faced and lost, still trying to walk down the stairs toward the ocean waters.

"The dragon song is only affecting the Melians," Lilyth cried out, catching on immediately. Lilyth pointed toward the far cliff again.

While groups of people stood upon the cliffs, milling about in confusion, freed of the spell that had consumed them, Omen saw a few stragglers still walking forward, still heading toward the deadly drop below. The dragon song had only awakened the native Melians — the foreign population was still walking toward their death.

"Omen, I need you to shield your brother," 7 called out. His father stood at the edge, hands braced on the banister as he stared out to sea. Four distant dragons still circled the waves, searching for something in the water.

"What?" Omen had released his hold on the door, letting the Melian servants inside free. Though bewildered, they immediately ran forward to grab hold of Miss Penelope. Others had caught a young Nelminorian maid still trying to escape the house.

"Take over shielding Kyr for me," 7 commanded. "And Avarice and Lilyth — you're going to need to shield the cats. I don't think they're actually affected by the song, but I can't be certain."

"What are you going to do?" Avarice demanded. Omen could see fear in her eyes.

7 threw a sharp glance at each of them. "The dragons can't reach the creature causing this." He pointed toward the circling dragons out at sea. "It's too far below the water. If I don't stop it, it will kill all non-natives in the city — and the dragons can't keep singing indefinitely. We don't have time to argue — do as I say!"

His father rarely raised his voice, but Omen knew better than to disobey, despite burning to protest. *Didn't he say not to fight the Widow Maker? Didn't he say it was a fight I couldn't win — that it was too powerful!*

He felt the shift in his mind, felt 7's protective shield pulling away as his father turned his attention elsewhere. Frantically, Omen shifted the song in his mind, increasing the tempo, taking the melody line up a step. *Too much music!* he thought in despair. Between the Widow Maker's eerie song, the dragon song, and his own mnemonic melodies, he was having a hard time concentrating on his own defenses. *Block it all out — tune everything out except the pattern!*

His shield expanded, and he pushed his thoughts outward toward Kyr, surrounding his little brother's mind with his own shield, keeping it just outside the layer of protection created by the bracelet. He held back the creeping, grasping claws of the Widow Maker's music.

Omen felt the shift in Lilyth and his mother — felt them both reaching to modify their own shields to encompass the cats. His mother lacked the powerful psionics of the Daenoth line, but she'd had years of psionic practice with 7. Her mind did not waver. And for once Omen was grateful that his little sister continuously surpassed him psionically — her shield was strong and steady.

Without the buffering force of his father's mind, Omen

could feel the malignant power behind the Widow Maker's song. It crept over him, dark and insidious, eating away at the edges of his shield. There were thousands of voices mixed in with the song — thousands of cries of lament and sorrow that pulsed endlessly and beat at him with the force of the ocean's tides.

Vicious light blasted through his senses. A shockwave of deafening thunder struck at the same instant, assaulting his mind so suddenly that no amount of shielding could lessen the crushing pain. Omen fell to the ground. Beside him he heard his sister and mother crying out, both stumbling back and falling. Kyr shrieked and crouched in terror, wrapping his arms around his head as he curled into a tight ball. From the cliffs, the dragons roared with alarm — deep, blaring voices that screamed defiance, their song utterly broken by the ear-shattering noise.

Then silence settled over the garden — pure, still, simple. Through the ringing in his ears, Omen heard the dull crash of waves from the beach below. Overhead, seagulls called out, riding on wind currents.

A soft brush of fur against his neck startled Omen, and he pushed himself up. Tormy was leaning over him, nuzzling his face, furry whiskers tickling his neck. He caught hold of the cat's ruff and pulled himself upright. His father was still leaning hard on the banister, breathing heavily. Omen realized with utter shock that the terrible noise had originated from 7. It had been the sound of 7 striking out at the Widow Maker with his mind — deafening all of them, even through their shields.

The Widow Maker's song was gone.

Omen scrambled to his feet. Lilyth was already standing, so Omen hurried to help his mother up. When she waved him off, he picked up Kyr instead. The boy was trembling but seemed unhurt. He stared up at Omen, silent and pale.

Omen turned to his father. "Dad?" Omen heard the tremble in his own voice. "You all right?"

7, blond head bowed, arms shaking, just nodded in response. Avarice moved to his side, gripping his arm as she studied his face. She bowed her head, then tilted up to catch his eye. Omen saw something powerful pass between them, and he retreated quickly, feeling like he was intruding.

All around, befuddled people milled about trying to make sense of their prolonged blackouts. Those affected by and released from the Widow Maker's song wondered how they came to be on the beach or on the cliffs. Panic fluttered as they discovered their friends and neighbors slumbering on the ground, ensorcelled by magical sleep. But soon delighted murmurs rose, and they took in the sight of the myriad of Sundragons. Trusting fully that the mere presence of so many Sundragons meant that all was once again well, the Melians left, bewildered but unhurt.

"Help the others inside," Avarice called to the servants, releasing those her spell had put to sleep. The Daenoth servants rushed to obey. The two gardeners that Omen had punched groaned in pain as they limped away.

Omen felt guilty and didn't look in their direction as they left.

Turning his attention to his father, Omen asked again, "Dad, are you hurt?" Beside him, Kyr had calmed down and leaned heavily against him. Omen kept one arm around the boy, reassuring him.

"No. Just tired," 7 replied, shaking himself as if trying to wake up.

89

"We're about to have company," Lilyth pointed skyward.

Two dragons circled overhead. Omen recognized them by their secondary colors: Lord Amar and Lady Frey. They hovered briefly, back claws extended downward as if they intended to land directly on the balcony. Their great reptilian bodies blocked the sky entirely, the wingspan of both dragons shadowing everything around Omen. But before their claws touched the stone pavers of the patio, both forms shimmered with light, and from one instant to the next the dragons vanished from sight utterly. Instead, two tall, golden-haired people — a man and a woman — stood beside them.

Omen recognized Lady Frey immediately — breathtakingly beautiful, draped in a white gown, golden hair swept back from her brow and revealing the still, inhuman dark sapphire tones of her eyes. The man beside her was clad in a blue tunic that reminded Omen of the uniform the Untouchables wore. He could have been Lady Frey's brother, so similar in appearance were they. Tall, golden-haired, with bright golden scales edging the side of his brow and gleaming in the fading evening light. Omen had never seen Sundragon Amar's human form before, but would have known him immediately by the sky blue jeweled tones of his eyes.

"Thank you for your assistance, Prince S'van," Sundragon Amar said without preamble, inclining his head to 7. "Did you kill the creature?"

"No." 7 sounded regretful. "I'm fairly certain I only frightened it."

"The thunder rang and a thousand voices slipped their chains, and sailed off to the distant shore." Kyr, still speaking in Kahdess, startled them all. Both dragons looked shaken.

You don't see that very often, Omen thought, an icy chill running down his spine.

7 clapped the boy on the shoulder. "Poetic, Kyr," he smiled faintly. "But that's a fairly accurate assessment of what happened. The instant I attacked, the Widow Maker threw a thousand imprisoned souls into my path while it made its escape. The full force of my attack hit those minds, not the creature itself. It's frightened and angry, but uninjured."

Dad freed a thousand souls?

"Angry enough to attack again?" Lady Frey asked, her attention on the immediate threat.

"I have no way of knowing," 7 admitted. "Perhaps. It's thousands of years old — possibly millions of years old. There's no guessing what it will do. It's a survivor — it may not risk attacking again, or it may come for revenge for all the souls it lost."

"Something has gone terribly wrong for a creature like the Widow Maker to swim the ocean freely," Amar replied.

Omen shot a worrying look toward his mother.

Avarice shook her head minutely.

This has something to do with the Autumn Lands! But how much can I say about Indee's quest without triggering the hex mark on Kyr?

Avarice gripped his shoulder. "Omen, take Kyr and the cats and go and search the neighborhood. See if any of our neighbors need help. People may be hurt."

He wanted to protest, but the sharp, pointed look his mother gave him kept him silent. He'd have to trust her and his father to deal with the dragons, find out what they could and perhaps convince them to aid in getting Indee to lift her hex. He hesitated, warring with his own curiosity. *They'll tell me afterward,* he assured himself.

"Come on," he steered his brother away from the group, and reached out to grab hold of a fistful of Tormy's fur. "Let's go see if anyone needs help."

"I is betting people is needing dinner!" Tormy purred eagerly. "We is checking on them so they is eating dinner."

"I is betting people is needing to *give us* dinner!" Tyrin added as he squirmed out of Kyr's hands and climbed onto the boy's shoulder again. "I is not liking that song we is hearing. The dragon song is being better."

"Omy's music is betterestest," Tormy agreed thoughtfully as he capered after Omen back inside and then once more into the city.

❖

It was nearly noon the next day before Omen had a chance to talk to either of his parents. Both were gone when he'd returned the night before with Templar in tow. Neither Templar, Liethan nor Bryenth had been affected by the Widow Maker's music — all of them able to shield their minds despite being fairly unskilled with psionics. Omen's friends had spent the bulk of the attack desperately trying to stop people from heading down toward the beach.

Still can't wrap my mind around how quickly everything happened.

Afterward, Bryenth had returned to his Hold to aid his father and the other Hold Lords. Liethan had raced down to the docks to see what troubles had unraveled there. But Templar had remained in the park to help a boy who had fallen from a tree when the music had caught hold of him. The crack to the child's skull had required a healer, and Templar had stayed until help arrived.

We got lucky. Omen recalled the look on his father's face. *Maybe luck isn't the right word.*

Templar had been excited by the prospect of a quest to Kharakhan and a trip into the Autumn Lands, and he'd returned home through the Cypher Rune Portal in the Daenoth Manor to seek permission to travel with Omen from his father. *Wonder if Antares will allow it.* Omen felt hopeful.

After filling their bellies, Kyr and the cats had seemingly forgotten the events of the day and had curled up to sleep soundly — exhausted and mindless of the worry that gnawed away at Omen.

He could understand Templar's excitement — the prospect of a quest was thrilling. But the thought of taking his little brother into such danger shook him to the core.

What am I going to do? If the Widow Maker is already watching, how are we supposed to cross the entire Luminal Sea? His sole consolation was that his father seemed capable of chasing the creature off. *But at what cost?*

As the morning wore on, Omen grew more and more nervous. An inexplicable feeling of doom swished around in his stomach. He couldn't settle down and ended up pacing around the manor aimlessly. His parents searched him out at noon. His mother led Kyr and Tyrin away to try on a new coat she'd been making, and Omen was left to speak freely with his father.

"Your mother and some of the dragons spoke with Indee," 7 began without preamble. He motioned Omen to follow him down the main staircase to the foyer. "According to Indee, only when Khylar is free can the hex be removed from Kyr's hand."

"Do you believe her?" Omen asked. Tormy blithely

93

skipped ahead several steps, bounding down the stairs like a fluffy, bouncing ball.

"Doesn't matter." 7 smiled, clearly amused by the question. "You're stuck. You and Kyr have to go to Kharakhan, and you have to find out what happened to Khylar."

Knowing he couldn't say anything that might indicate refusal for fear of activating the hex, Omen carefully worded his next question. "And what about the dragons? Didn't they have some issue with this?" He couldn't imagine the dragons would be pleased by Indee's hexing — not that any of them would stand against her. She was the wife of one of the most revered dragons in Melia, and the Sundragons followed a strict hierarchy.

"No one is going to criticize her, Omen," 7 replied. "And the dragons are more concerned about protecting the country. They are glad of your aid in helping to investigate what has gone wrong with the Autumn Lands. The Widow Maker should not be here, and no one can explain why that is."

"So we're going to Kharakhan?" Omen hadn't really expected anything else, but the mere possibility sent a shiver of anticipation down his spine, despite his unease. Tormy hopped across the foyer with a bounding leap and greeted the doorman, who reached up to scratch the huge cat behind the ears.

"You and Kyr are going to Kharakhan," 7 amended. "We all spoke last night — the dragons are afraid the Widow Maker will attack the city again. They've asked me to stay here to fight it."

Omen's heart skipped a beat as he realized what his father was saying. "But if Kyr is the one attracting it, won't it follow us instead of coming back here?"

"We don't really know if Kyr is what attracted it," 7 said

after a few beats. "And after what happened, there is a good chance it will return here for revenge. It is a collector of souls, and to save itself, it had to give up thousands of those souls to block my attack. For a brief moment I felt its unspeakable rage. It knows who I am, and it knows what I did. It is just as likely to return here to try again."

"Can you stop it?" Omen asked, concerned.

7 gave a thoughtful shake of his head. "Don't really know. That's not really the sort of thing you can truly know until it happens. But I do know that I'm the only one in the city who has any chance of even attempting it. You saw what happened yesterday. If I hadn't driven it away when I did, a lot of people would have died."

"I get it." Omen understood the deep sense of responsibility that kept his father from going with him, but that didn't mean he wasn't frightened by the realization that he would be on his own. *He has to choose between all the people in the city or his son.* "I can handle this on my own." The doorman had pulled open the front doors, letting Tormy outside. The large cat was spinning in circles in the front courtyard, chasing his tail.

"Yes, you can," 7 agreed. He paused a moment to watch Tormy spin happily around in circles — a breeze had picked up, unseasonably cool despite the summer sun. "You're strong enough. You just have to stay focused. I talked to Kadana last night — she's agreed to take you to Kharakhan."

"I'm surprised anyone would volunteer their ship under the circumstances," Omen said.

"Kadana is just as worried as everyone else, but like the dragons, she knows that something has to be done. Someone has to find out what happened, and the only way we

95

can do that is by going to Kharakhan. Her family is there. She won't let a sea serpent stop her from getting home. And her ship is fast and has a number of magical protections on it. She's got the best chance of getting across the sea safely. And she has sense enough to sail hard and fast and escape anything hunting you."

Omen swallowed nervously. "Maybe having Kyr with me will make it easier — he'll be our early warning. We'll know to change course ahead of time."

"Maybe." 7 let out a short breath. "I assume Templar and Liethan will go with you."

"I don't think I could stop them," Omen agreed. "Bryenth will want to come, but I suppose he'll be expected to stay here and protect the city as well. And Tormy and Tyrin will come too of course."

"Of course," 7 shot an amused look at the large cat who was now gripping his tail fiercely between his paws and cleaning the end of it with frantic licks. "Still, you'll need someone smart as well."

"Templar's smart," Omen said defensively.

7 blew out a laugh. "Someone smart who also has good sense."

Omen paused momentarily. *Good sense?*

The hesitation made his father laugh even harder.

"Go talk to Shalonie." 7 nodded as if approving of his own idea. "She's the only person besides me who can build a Cypher Rune Portal in Kharakhan. Once there is a portal there, you can return home as soon as you find Khylar. And you're going to need someone like Shalonie to find your way into the Autumn Lands in the first place."

"I thought all I had to do is go into the Mountain of Shadow to get into the Autumn Lands?" Omen asked.

Night's tongue! It's already getting complicated.

"The Mountain of Shadow has openings to a thousand different realms and dimensions, and it's filled with traps and riddles," 7 explained. "Shalonie has studied what little we know about the Mountain — she'll be your best bet for getting through it. You and Tormy head over there now. I'll send word ahead."

"What if I trigger the hex again?" he asked.

"Your mother says the hex is activated by either imply-ing or actively refusing to rescue Khylar," 7 began, only to be stopped by Omen's protest.

Wasn't that mentioning a refusal? "Dad!" He tensed, waiting to hear any sign from inside the house that Kyr had been injured.

7 glanced at him. "The hex was meant to bind you and Kyr — you're the only ones who can't refuse. And you shouldn't really talk about it either. You'll figure it out. Now go on with you. You can't delay."

Omen gave a curt nod. *Fine, I can do this! Get Shalonie, cross the ocean, don't get eaten by the Widow Maker, save Khylar, get the hex removed, come home. Good sense not required.*

"Come on, Tormy." Omen reached up and put a hand flat on the big cat's shoulder. "Let's go see Shalonie."

He wondered how he would explain the hex without triggering the mark. A smile spread on his face. *Shalonie's smart. She has good sense. She'll figure it out.*

"Is you thinking Shalonie's mommy is still being mad about the bunnies?" Tormy mused, gazing thoughtfully up into the summer sky.

Omen faltered a step, glancing uncertainly at his father. 7 tensed as if bracing himself for what was coming.

"What bunnies?" Omen asked warily. Shalonie's mother, Hold Lord Tatharion, wasn't the friendliest of people. She didn't care for all the foreigners in Melia — and despite his having lived in the city most of his life, she still considered Omen an outsider.

"The ones I is chasing into her sitting room," Tormy explained guilelessly. "They is running, I is chasing. When bunnies is running, I is having to chase them, Omy. I is sorry about the broken stuff, but I is not sorry about the chasings."

"That would probably explain the bill I received from their Hold last week," 7 quipped. "And the angry letter."

"Oh yes!" Tormy agreed happily. "She is saying lots of letters — and words too! I is not knowing most of them, but Tyrin is learning them. Come on Omy! We is got to get started on our quest."

"Right." Omen sighed heavily as he followed after his now purring cat. *I'm supposed to have trouble getting past Shalonie's guardian Hold Dragon, not her mother!*

Tormy trotted across the courtyard in the direction of the Tatharion Hold, his long plume of a tail high in the air; Omen trailed behind.

Chapter 7: Shalonie

SHALONIE

S halonie sighed with relief as she finished signing her last piece of correspondence for the day. All morning, she'd been writing letters to the families of various business partners while dealing with routine Hold business and trying to research anything she could find on the creature that had threatened their shores the day before. *Widow Maker. Not much written about you.* She shut a thick tome on Melian creature lore, the pages crumbling and warped. *What do you want from us?*

Knots tightened in her stomach. *They all tried to jump in the ocean. To drown themselves.* The Sundragons' song still swirled through her head. *Thank Melia.* She muttered a quick prayer to the first of the Sundragons, the mother of them all. *Thank you for keeping our people safe.* "And thank you for the Daenoths." She still didn't know the entire story, but she had a strong suspicion that 7 and his family had done more than their fair share in keeping the city and its citizens protected during the attack.

Shalonie prodded a stack of missives freshly arrived from the province of Miran. *It never ends.* "But it's enough for today."

Her efforts, however diligent, seemed constantly hampered by her mother's interference, and Shalonie was looking forward to having some time to herself. Her mother, one of the twelve Hold Lords of Melia, had found yet another excuse to shirk her responsibilities, leaving the Hold business to her daughter as she had since Shalonie was old enough to forge her mother's signature.

"I have completed the books, my lady," the Hold accountant said as he shuffled into the room, holding the heavy, leather-bound accounting ledger containing the city's finances. This year, the Tatharion Hold was responsible for all the collective finances of the country, a task that came around every twelve years. *Could be worse — I could be on trade agreements like last year. What a nightmare!*

With the opening of the borders, trade had become far more complex as new currencies constantly flowed into the land. At least the shared governance of the twelve Holds insured that no one Hold Lord was ever burdened with any one complex task for too long.

"Thank you, Stenic," Shalonie told the accountant while reaching for the heavy book. Stenic, though nearly a decade her senior, was still considered quite young by Melian standards. He shifted nervously as she opened the books and glanced through the most recent records. *What lovely penmanship. Pity he can't add.*

"The numbers are off again, Stenic." Shalonie added the columns in her head. "This first page is short twenty-seven silver; it won't balance on the next."

Stenic frowned. "I rounded," he said. "Your mother told me to."

Stenic, like most Melians, was not prone to lying. It was entirely possible that her mother had told him to round the numbers. *Mother doesn't understand accounting either.* But even if he had rounded all the numbers, he still would not have reached the totals on the page.

"You cannot round the financial records, Stenic," she told him, deciding to give him the benefit of the doubt.

He pulled at his collar uncomfortably, his eyes on the book she still held in her hand. Shalonie's thoughts flashed again to the events of the day before — the haunting music that had invaded all of the city, the sudden death march of nearly the entire population toward the ocean, the sudden transformation and flight of their Hold Dragon to defend the city. *Stop!* she told herself. *Stop it.*

Stenic, regardless of his weakness as an accountant, possessed a rudimentary psionic shield and had been the only person besides her who had been unaffected by the Widow Maker's music. Stenic and Shalonie had frantically worked to bar the rest of the household from marching to their doom. Under the circumstances, she was inclined to forgive his shortcomings. "Never mind that. I want to thank you again for yesterday."

He cleared his throat as if he wanted to say something. Seconds passed, but he remained silent.

Can't find the words. She gave him a tight smile. "I'll correct the numbers. Go pay Teleon and his crew for repairing the docks last week and tell them we have more work for them. The school needs a new roof before winter."

Seeming relieved that he did not have to deal with the books any longer, Stenic inclined his head in a respectful bow. "At once, my lady," he agreed, and then hurried out the large double doors of Shalonie's office.

"And Stenic . . ."

"Yes, my lady?"

"Good work yesterday," Shalonie said sincerely. "I couldn't have—"

"Thank you, my lady," Stenic said quickly, embarrassment tightening his voice. He bowed and left.

He is a good man, Shalonie thought. *I should find him a*

different position. Maybe promote him to . . . I don't know. I'll make something up. She glanced around her office, wondering what her father would do in her position.

The room was actually her father's office, but as Shalandor Tatharion Lir Drathos had not set foot in Melia in over a year, Shalonie had commandeered it for herself. Even when her father was in residence, he rarely took time to sit at his desk and deal with the work of the Hold. When he did, he conjured solutions for complicated problems with ease and breathtaking speed. Shalonie admired his ability as a problem solver, but she knew that only consistent leadership would allow the Hold and Melia to flourish. *And consistent leadership means me. And if I'm going to do the majority of the work, I might as well have a nice desk to sit at.* To her delight, her father's office was lined with bookshelves that held some of the most prized manuscripts and scrolls in the city. Access to these references allowed her personal research to move forward.

"Shalonie!" her mother's voice echoed through the white marble halls of their Hold.

A moment later Shalonie heard distinctive, slipper-clad steps as her mother swept through the office doors.

Lady Alisina Tatharion Lir Drathos, Hold Lord of the Melian Provence of Miran, more than lived up to her commanding title. She was tall and beautiful, regal by all accounts, her golden hair worn in braided circlets around her head like a crown. And certainly she was dressed as befitted any queen, in a gown of white and gold splendor, cut according to the latest Melian fashion. The blue gems she wore around her pale neck likely cost a king's ransom, as did the matching bracelet around her left wrist. In comparison Shalonie, clad in simple leathers, her own golden hair pulled back in a messy braid, looked like a commoner.

Taking in Shalonie's messy appearance and the worn leather tunic and pants she preferred, Alisina feigned over-exaggerated shock. Shalonie remembered her boots had mud on them from her foray into the woods in the early dawn hours in search of a rare plant she needed for an experiment. She decided to stay behind the desk.

"Why aren't you dressed?" Alisina demanded indignantly.

Shalonie frowned down at herself. Considering she was planning on spending the rest of the day crawling through the catacombs of the city library, she was dressed appropriately. *Some of those old rooms are caked in dust — and unless I missed my guess, there is a walled-off room in the northern basement that's been sealed for centuries. It's not like I can use a pickaxe and a shovel in a dress.* "What are you talking about? I'm—"

Her mother cut her off with a curt wave of her hand. "Never mind, I'll send the maids to dress you and fix your hair. You're hardly presentable like this!"

"Presentable?" Shalonie asked with unease. "Presentable for what?"

"Our afternoon luncheon at the Garden!" Alisina exclaimed as if Shalonie were exceptionally slow-witted.

The Garden, a private courtyard near the Melian park, was expressly reserved for the ladies of the twelve Holds. Surrounded by stone walls, the sanctuary had been designed in concentric circles that featured seasonal Melian blooms, charming statues, and a many-tiered center fountain. Some of the finest chefs in the city clamored for the honor of preparing scrumptious meals at the Garden. And many of the ladies of the Holds took genuine pleasure in hosting Garden events, working tirelessly to impress and delight their peers.

"We brunched in the Garden yesterday," Shalonie reminded her mother. "For three hours, if I remember correctly!" *We talked about fashion — for three extremely long hours! And then all hell broke loose.* "Mother, I am exhausted after—"

"We will be discussing the . . . event!" her mother informed her sharply. "It is your duty to reassure the ladies that the danger has passed."

"I spent hours meeting with the other Hold Lords last night discussing the *event*!" Shalonie reminded her mother. "While you took a nap."

"I was affected by the music, Shalonie!" her mother huffed to her. "You were not. It was terribly distressing. And if I am distressed, so are all of my friends. You have to explain how the dragons saved all of us."

Shalonie bit her lip, holding back her remark. "I'm sorry, mother," she breathed heavily. "I do understand — but as I said, I've already spoken with all the Hold Lords. They'll all be very busy today — there were people who were actually wounded. And ten people on the docks nearly drowned. They're still being treated by the healers. No one will have time for another luncheon."

"There are a dozen ladies coming to my gathering," her mother insisted. "You have responsibilities, Shalonie! You cannot spend your days fiddling about with frivolous pursuits when you have responsibilities to this Hold!"

"Frivolous pursuits!" Shalonie exclaimed, disheartened. She lifted the heavy leather accounting book from the desk. "I have been working on Hold business all morning. And now I have to spend another hour fixing all the mistakes that your accountant made before I give the books to Lord Geryon!"

"Stenic is a very nice young man." Her mother frowned. "A few addition and subtraction errors are not the end of the world, Shalonie!"

"They will be when we hand the books off to Hold Lord Sive next year!" she said simply.

That at least caught Alisina's attention. Her mother had the good sense to flush uncomfortably. If there was one person Alisina did not want to anger, it was Hold Lord Sive.

"I promise you, he will find every single one of the mistakes we make," Shalonie said. *The man is like a ferret.* "And you know him, he will not keep silent about it." *A really loud ferret.*

"Then you can fix those pesky things tonight," her mother insisted. "And while we're on the subject of Hold business, why did you cancel the carriage I commissioned?"

Exasperated, Shalonie tugged at her braid. "Because we already have three carriages. We don't need another."

"We have summer, fall and winter carriages," Alisina told her indignantly. "We don't have a spring carriage."

"We don't need a spring carriage," Shalonie said. "That sort of excess is obscene, Mother. People will talk!"

"People will talk if I don't have a spring carriage." Her mother stomped one of her slipper-clad feet.

"We don't have any place to keep it!" Shalonie tried to sound reasonable. "Our carriage house only has room for three carriages."

"Which is why I have also commissioned a new carriage house," her mother replied simply, seeming quite pleased with herself.

105

Shalonie frowned — the Hold's lands were extensive, but theirs was a very old Hold, already quite built out. There was no room for a new carriage house. "Built where?"

"The grove, in the south yard," her mother replied dismissively.

"The White Grove!" Shalonie clarified. "Mother, there are wood sprites living in those trees. You can't cut them down."

"I don't recall giving wood sprites permission to move into my trees," Alisina replied. "They're certainly not paying rent. And beyond taking care of trees that are now in the way of my new carriage house, they have no practical use."

"Wood sprites belong to the realm of faerie, Mother," Shalonie reminded her. "I think both Deldano Holds will have something to say about their abuse. The Deldanos are of faerie. They have a vested interest in the wood sprites' wellbeing."

Alisina's eyes flashed with anger. "*I* have no *interest* in what the foreign Hold Lords have to say regarding my managing of my own land."

"Hold Lord Bryon was born and raised in Melia. He is as Melian as the rest of us. And Hold Lord Beren's children are Nythira's children. They could have no older bloodline!" While Lady Nythira had been several years older than Shalonie, she had always been a dear friend, and her death had struck Shalonie extremely hard. She did not like hearing her mother so readily dismiss Nythira's young children.

Alisina glared at her daughter. "Hold Lord Bryon's heritage is questionable at best as his mother was unmarried when she had him. And do not forget he spent several years living in Haze, that vile cesspool. Sometimes the vocabulary that comes out of that man's mouth is positively shocking. And Hold Lord Beren isn't Melian at all. Kharakhian and faerie. It turns my stomach to see him rule a Hold. Until his children are of age, that seat should remain empty!"

"That is not the dragons' will, Mother," Shalonie stated, starting to shake. In such matters the Sundragons always had the final say, and even her mother would not speak out against them. "And I do not think they will take kindly to you cutting down the White Grove."

"Then it is a good thing they will not learn of it," Alisina told her. "As I forbid you from telling any of the Deldanos my plans. Do not forget, Shalonie, I am the Hold Lord, not you. You will do as I say. And do not interfere again in my private purchases. It is not your place. Now, do you prefer to dress here, or shall I send the maids to your rooms?"

"I don't have time to go to another function," Shalonie protested. "I told you, I have work to do! I need to finish the books, and I need to get to the library."

"The library! You were there last week!" her mother howled. "You don't need to go again."

"Mother, my work requires . . ."

"Yes, yes, your little translations!" her mother huffed, waving her hand at the pile of papers on Shalonie's desk. "That is not work; that is a hobby! And as a Hold daughter you should have more appropriate hobbies. No one cares about dead languages! If there were anything important in any of your scrolls, the Hold Dragons would translate them for us. They do not need you."

"The things I'm working on are tens of thousands of years old, maybe hundreds of thousands," Shalonie protested, trying to keep her voice down. "The only dragons that could possibly translate these would be the Ancients themselves."

Her mother looked positively horrified at that. "Shalonie Tatharion! Please tell me you have not tried to seek an audience with the Ancients over such a ridiculous thing!"

Outraged that her mother would even make that suggestion, Shalonie sputtered, "What! Of course not! I would never bother the Ancients!"

"See that you don't!" Alisina declared and then turned on her heel and swept through the doors of the office. "I'll send the maids!" she announced. "And from now on, your access to the city library is rescinded!" She then reached out and pulled closed the office doors.

Shalonie stared at the closed doors, amazed when she heard the distinctive sound of a key being turned in the lock. *She locked me in!*

Stunned, Shalonie leaned back into the soft leather of her desk chair. It wasn't as if being locked inside bothered her — opening the doors wouldn't be difficult. But the idea that her mother could rescind her access to the library was unspeakably horrible. She might be the heir to the Hold, but her mother was still the current Hold Lord. If she ordered Shalonie banned from the library, the librarians would have no choice but to obey. As it was, she had to sneak into half the places she typically visited, simply because her mother had forbidden her. Every excursion she'd ever taken outside of Melia had been done secretly because she'd been forbidden from leaving the city. If Shalonie hadn't had access to the various transfer portals in Melia, she never would have gotten anywhere with any of her research.

A gentle knock at the door startled Shalonie. She looked

up, guessing it was probably the maids her mother had threatened to send. But the voice coming from the other side of the heavy wooden doors was most definitely not a maid's.

"Lady Shalonie, may I enter?" The sonorous voice belonged to their Hold Dragon, Lord Geryon Lir Drathos.

Shalonie leaped to her feet, grabbing a piece of chalk from her desk blotter. "One moment, Lord Geryon!" she cried out and raced toward the doors. With swift, sure motions of the chalk, she drew a sigil upon the doorframe, and instantly the lock clicked. She yanked open the doors immediately, inclining her head to the Sundragon.

Lord Geryon had been the Tatharion Hold Dragon for centuries. He was one of the Hold Dragons who spent the majority of his time in human form. Tall and fair, with the golden hair all the Sundragons possessed, he had eyes of the purest amethyst. The jeweled eyes of the dragons were one of the first things that marked them as inhuman, as did the faint markings of golden scales along their hairline and the sides of their faces. Though beautiful and elegant, their features were unusually angular — not unlike those of the elves. But it was their movement more than anything that marked them most as dragons. They were prone to unnatural stillness, and when they did move, the movements were sharp and precise in a way that seemed almost mechanical — as if despite the human forms they occasionally wore, they were still the enormous scaled beasts that ruled the sky.

"I heard raised voices," Geryon told her, his tone deep and sympathetic. "Are you all right?" If Geryon had been anywhere in the Hold during her conversation with her mother, he'd heard more than simply raised voices. The dragons' senses were acute in the extreme.

"The same old arguments," she said, feeling more hurt than she had allowed herself to realize in the heat of the argument. For the majority of Shalonie's life, Geryon had acted more as a father to her than her own father, Shalandor. How her mother and Shalandor had ever come to be married, she couldn't imagine. Her father had spent the majority of his life wandering from one adventure to another. It was his stories, usually told in long letters written to her in ancient languages she had to work to translate, that told of exploring old ruins and organizing archaeological digs in haunted lands, that had sparked Shalonie's desire to travel. But while Shalandor thought nothing of abandoning his duty to Melia, Shalonie could not. It had been their Hold Dragon Geryon who had taught her about her duty to the land and Hold, and it was because of him that she performed the duties her mother regularly abandoned.

"I came for the books." Geryon's gaze flicked briefly toward her desk where the finance records lay. "I saw your . . . accountant leave."

She winced apologetically, a pained expression creeping across her face unbidden. "Please allow me to correct the numbers first," she told him. *It's not fair to Geryon to make him fix all the mistakes.* She knew other Holds were not run with such thoughtful draconic consideration — there were even a few Hold Dragons who never took human form; certainly, they didn't check and correct accounting ledgers. Yesterday all of them had been pointedly reminded of the dragons' true purpose to their land — guardians, and Melia's main defense against invasion.

Geryon smiled, familiar with the prickly relationship between Shalonie and her mother. "Stenic is still not adding the numbers correctly, is he?"

"He was very brave yesterday, but honestly!" Shalonie let her exasperation fly. "The man trained to be a baker. Why mother insisted he take over his father's job as Hold accountant I will never know. He is ill-suited to the position. I actually think there is something in his brain that makes him transpose numbers. He's a good man. But numbers are not what he excels at."

"Your mother is a firm believer in tradition — to her detriment." The translucent membrane of Geryon's inner lids stretched across his amethyst eyes in a slow reptilian blink. "It was fortunate that Stenic was here to aid you."

"I told him how grateful I am for his help." Shalonie considered. "He is a valuable member of the Hold . . ."

Shalonie appreciated that Melian society was founded on ancient traditions, their devotion to their guardian dragons the most sacred tradition of all. But she found blind adherence to any law unbearable. "If anything, yesterday earned him the right to do what will make him most happy. I'm all for tradition when it makes sense, but a tradition that forces a child to follow in a parent's footsteps when so ill-suited to it, makes no sense."

"Not all would agree with you," Geryon replied mildly.

Shalonie looked up, searching his face to determine if she was being chastised. His jeweled eyes seemed more amused than reprimanding.

"But you agree with me?" she responded, fairly confident in her belief. "I've wondered about something for a long time now. You've never been vocal about it . . . but you like the Deldanos."

He inclined his head fractionally. "Most of us do," he agreed. "They have been a refreshing change to the leadership of Melia. The Deldano children are likely to usher us into a new age. Beren's two eldest, Chant and Tess, have already had several standoffs with Lord Sive, and have come out the victors — that they can do that before reaching their majority, is impressive indeed."

Shalonie chuckled, knowing that Beren's twin Melian children, though only ten years old, were forces to be reckoned with. The days Beren let the two of them take his seat at the Hold Council were some of the most enjoyable meetings she'd ever been to. *Unpredictable to be certain.*

"I know lowering the magical barrier that protected Melia from the rest of the world was controversial," Shalonie said, mentally lining up the course to her real question. "But the dragons were right. Melia needed new blood. And it isn't only the Deldanos. They brought the Daenoths, the Corsairs and Machellis with them. The foreigners may bring a whole host of new dangers to our land, but they are powerful allies. 7's actions are a perfect example."

Geryon's eyes flicked to the open window. "We could not have stopped the Widow Maker without him."

True shock ran through Shalonie, making her body tingle from her scalp to her fingertips. *Is he admitting the fallibility of the Sundragons?*

"Sooner or later those dangers would have come to our shores regardless, considering the other issues with the barrier." The moment the words left her mouth, she saw that she had said too much.

Lord Geryon froze, the unnatural stillness coming over him.

Shalonie counted her thundering heartbeats. *One, manticore. Two, manticore. Three, manticore.*

Geryon's head turned slowly, his movement more draconic than human. A flickering light burned deep in his jeweled eyes, reminiscent of the fire the dragons were known to breathe. "Other issues?" he asked, measured.

She paled and placed her right hand over her heart in apology. "I'm sorry." She inclined her head to him. "I'm not supposed to know about that. I shouldn't have said anything. I have not shared it with anyone else."

He held her gaze. "Shared what?" he pressed.

There was no lying to a dragon. Not only would it be the height of disrespect — something Melians instinctively avoided — but the dragons' senses were so perceptive, they could see and hear and smell a lie. Deception was pointless, and Shalonie made no attempt to prevaricate. "I know the barrier was failing," she said and cleared her throat gently. *That's also why you have made no mention of putting it back up even considering the threat of the Widow Maker.*

Something shifted in Geryon's gaze. He did not seem angry or upset. He looked mostly puzzled and perhaps a little intrigued. "How?"

"The Cypher Runes," she informed him. "It's what I've been studying."

He drew his golden eyebrows together in a frown. "The portal runes?" he clarified.

"Yes, but they're not merely portal runes," she said.

Melia was home to ancient transfer portals that could transport a person safely from one location to another instantaneously. To date she and 7 Daenoth, working together, were the only people to successfully build a new portal since the originals were crafted centuries ago. Despite her youth, Shalonie was considered one of the foremost experts on portals, and her accomplishment of creating the new

113

portal in the Daenoth home was counted a marvel among Melians and dragons alike.

"The Cypher Runes can be used for other things — perhaps everything," she explained, pointing toward the sigil she'd drawn on the doorframe.

Geryon turned to study the chalk mark, reaching out to touch the firmly drawn lines. "Did she lock you in?" he inquired curiously.

Shalonie laughed at that. "Yes, I believe I'm being held captive for the sake of another luncheon in the Garden."

He cocked his head to one side. "And you unlocked it with this sigil, not an opening spell?"

"Yes, it's a Cypher Rune," she replied. "Just like the portal runes, just like the marks on the barrier stones."

That drew his attention back toward her, his eyes filled with curiosity despite his body's unnatural stillness. "You believe it is the marks upon the stones that created the barriers and not dragon song?" He did not sound upset by the idea, just baffled.

"Yes . . . I mean no!" She shook her head. "It is the dragon song and the magic you pour into it that activates the stones, but the sigils direct the power. That's how I knew they were failing. The sigils are wrong."

"The barrier stones have stood for thousands of years, unchanged," Geryon informed her. His tone was not a denial of her words, but it was obvious he wanted more of an explanation.

"They weren't wrong — not thousands of years ago. But they are now," Shalonie replied. "Magic isn't static, it changes, it evolves. And the sigils would have had to change and evolve with it, in order to keep the outside world at bay. It would be my guess that the original sigils likely weren't even carved into stone. Trees would have been more practical as they would have changed and grown over the years and required the runes be constantly adjusted."

Geryon's eyes widened fractionally. "The original barrier foci were carved into trees," he admitted. "But that was thousands of years ago. You could not have known this. They were eventually carved into stone to make it more permanent."

She had suspected as much. "Which means the original understanding of the marks had already been lost. They were not meant to be immutable. Not unless you were attempting to seal off a dead world — which was never the intention of the barrier. Magic was meant to flow freely back and forth — otherwise Melia and everyone inside the land would have died."

He inclined his head. "It was one of the reasons we took down the barrier. We felt things had become too static, too unchanging. Melia needed new life, needed change. And the barrier had been failing for decades, perhaps even centuries. We were not certain how much longer we could maintain it. It seemed every year we were pouring more and more magic into it — had it not been for Lord Sylvan, the barrier would have fallen long ago. His spells alone sustained it — and to do so he had to constantly craft new spells, each more powerful than the last. But the one thing we could never discern was why they were failing. We assumed the fault lay in us, in our magic, or in the stones themselves. Do you mean to say it is in the marks upon the stones?"

"Yes," Shalonie replied, amazed that the dragons had been dealing with this issue for perhaps centuries without any guidance, or any hope of success beyond their own stubborn nature and exceptional gifts of magic.

"It's a language, an ancient language, and very complex," she told him, moving toward her desk and pulling out a notebook from her secret stash. She opened it and showed him the many pages she'd filled with sigils and runes of all types. "When I was studying the transfer portals I started to recognize patterns, and I started to realize I had seen similar marks in other places: my father's journals, books, scrolls, old ruins — from all over the world, and from other realms. But they're not simply a language — the runes form mathematical equations, complex equations that control how magic interacts with them. I've only started understanding how they all go together, how these equations are written and balanced. Which is when I realized that the runes on the barrier stones are out of balance with the rest of the world."

He stared at her with wonder.

Shalonie shifted self-consciously.

"And you can fix them? Balance them?"

"No." She shook her head, alarmed that perhaps she'd inadvertently claimed some knowledge she did not possess. "I don't know nearly enough yet," she said feverishly, speaking faster and faster. "I've only just started piecing this together. I was able to build the new transfer portal because I had numerous working portals to compare it to. But the understanding of the runes themselves has been lost for eons. I think this language is likely hundreds of thousands of years old, maybe even millions of years old. I don't even have a complete understanding of the basic alphabet of the runes, let alone a working vocabulary."

"But you are pursuing proof of this theory?" he asked,

holding up her thick notebook.

She nodded. "Trying to anyway," she admitted. "It hasn't been easy."

"What do you need?"

She considered the seriousness of his simple question. "I need to find more runes. I need a complete alphabet." She interrupted herself as ideas exploded in her head. "I suspect there may be hundreds if not thousands of characters in the language. I need to understand how the equations are formed. I need to see other examples of runes working. I understand how the Melian portals work fairly well, but I need to see other portals in other lands, portals that have nothing to do with Melia, portals that use different magic systems so that I can compare them to see what makes ours different. Plain and simple, I need more information."

Geryon handed back her notebook. "Perhaps I have something that can aid in your search. Wait here a moment." He left the room, moving swiftly down the hallway toward the office kept for his own private use. Neither she nor anyone else in the Hold ever entered his rooms, for no Melian would ever dare intrude upon a dragon's private domain. But she had always been curious about what things she might find inside — ancient scrolls and books only the dragons had gazed upon.

He returned a few moments later, carrying a slender sword in a golden scabbard. He held it out to her.

Shalonie stared at it, her mouth gaping. She took in the craftsmanship and markings upon the hilt and the scabbard. Sunlight coming in through the large windows that lined the marbled hallway caught upon the golden metal of the weapon and sheath and highlighted the amethyst gems that adorned the hilt. She knew this blade was not made from any common gold. She recognized the deep amethyst color. She'd known it her entire life. This blade was made from Geryon's own dragonscales.

"I had this crafted for you the day I saw your father teaching you the sword," he told her, holding out the weapon. Gifts made from dragonscales were rare beyond belief, and more precious than any treasure. "I was told not to give it to you until you had completed a certain task."

"Told? By whom, and what task?" she blurted out, hesitant to even reach out for the blade.

"By the Ancients." He smiled warmly, and Shalonie felt her heart skip a beat at the possibility that the Ancient Melian Dragons, veritable gods of the land, might know who she was.

"The task was simple," he continued. "I was to give you this blade on the day you thoroughly surprised me. You have discovered an answer to a riddle that we have been struggling with for centuries. You have exceeded all of my expectations." He lifted the blade in both hands, holding it out to her and urging her to take it. "There is not a single door in all Melia that this will not open, regardless of the decrees of the Hold Lords."

He seemed to enjoy the look of wonder she gave him as she lifted the blade from his hands — taking care not to actually touch his skin — one did not touch the Sundragons of Melia for any reason.

She fully understood what he meant by doors being opened: carrying this blade, the highest mark of the Sundragons' favor, she could go anywhere in Melia, even the library her mother had forbidden her access to.

As she took the blade in her hands, she could feel Geryon's own magic in the golden metal. The warmth of the song that made up his soul resonated in the fibers of her heart. She, like all Melians, was tied through blood and magic to the Sundragons, possessing a piece of the Ancient Dragon Melia's own soul within her heart. There was no more fundamental connection to a Melian's heritage than a Sundragon's scale. It was that connection the dragons had used to awaken the Melians from the Widow Maker's grasp the night before.

"The city library!" she exclaimed like a delighted child. "The libraries of the Twelve Holds!" Her eyes widened as she thought of one of the other places she'd never set foot in. "The archives of the Untouchables in the Temple itself!" Possession of this sword would open the doors to all these places. There wasn't a Melian in existence who would deny access to one who possessed a dragon blade.

"Or the archives of the Ancients in the Dragon Lands if you so desire," Geryon told her with a smile.

A hard shockwave washed over her. *Access to the Dragon Lands! I am losing my mind!* To be allowed into the very realm of the gods themselves was nearly unheard of. *Few Melians in history have seen the Dragon Lands!* She might be the heir to a Hold, but she had not done anything of worth. *To be granted such an honor.* She trembled with excitement and fear. "Lo . . . rd . . . Ger . . . yon . . ." she began, barely able to form words.

He held up his graceful hand, silencing her protest. "Learn whatever you can, Shalonie. Go wherever you must, in Melia and beyond. I only ask that you take care, and do not wander the world alone as your father does. We cannot lose you, too. You will be cautious, yes?"

"Of course, my lord. I promise." She silently swore to herself that she would follow his directive, would surround herself with whomever she had to in order to explore all the dark places of the world in relative safety.

"Good," he agreed with sudden humor. "Now, if you'll excuse me, I believe I have a White Grove and group of wood sprites to save. Perhaps I shall suggest to your mother that she donate one of her carriages to charity. She has so many of them, after all." He strode away, moving down the hallway silently as mist, and vanished into the depths of the Hold.

Shalonie sank down into a chair near the hearth, her hands gripping the sword tightly, her eyes still on the golden sheen of the weapon. Her mind whirled as she tried to formulate a plan. Her entire life she'd had to scramble to gather material to further her research. Now she had so many libraries open to her, she wasn't certain where to start.

"Shalonie?"

The new voice startled her, and Shalonie looked up with a flinch. She stared blankly at the young copper-haired man standing in her doorway. Though he had not been announced by any servant, Omen Daenoth had entered the Hold and was standing in the doorway to her office. His odd eyes — one silver, one Deldano green — shone with a mix of hope and anticipation.

Shalonie suspected any announcement of his arrival had gone to her mother who had promptly ignored it — her mother did not care for the foreigners who lived in their city, however elevated their bloodlines.

So then, how did he get in?

She glanced past Omen but could see no servants in the hall.

Omen took a tentative step into the office.

He's sure gotten tall.

120

"Omen?" she asked, wondering what had brought him to her home. *If he's here, where is the giant cat?* A moment later she heard the sound of something crashing and shattering on the floor near the kitchens. *There's the giant cat. So quiet, so stealthy, so graceful.*

Omen cringed at the sound. "I'll pay for that." His voice was as melodious as any Melians, but she suspected as he aged it would deepen to an exceptional baritone. "Tormy has a hard time keeping track of his tail," Omen said sheepishly. "Do you have a minute?" He moved into the center of the room. "I need your help with something."

Shalonie stood, taking the sword and fixing the scabbard around her waist. She didn't normally wear a blade, but this was one sword she would not be leaving lying about. She saw Omen raise one eyebrow.

"Dragonscale? Impressive!"

Though Omen himself was not Melian, he had lived most of his life in the city. Shalonie knew he understood the sword's significance. For a moment, she allowed herself to bask in the awed look he gave her.

Not often one gets a look like that from Omen Daenoth.

"What can I do for you?" she asked. She felt as if a heavy weight had been lifted from her heart.

"Well." He shifted from one foot to the next as if nervous or not entirely certain what to say. "I suppose you know all about the Widow Maker." He gave a self-deprecating smile at his own obvious statement. "Of course you do . . . For complicated reasons, I've been charged with figuring out why the Widow Maker is in our waters and how it escaped the Autumn Lands." He stopped and shook himself as if changing his mind mid-thought. "Actually, my quest has nothing to do with the Widow Maker, but if I solve one problem, it will also hopefully solve the problem with the Widow Maker. But to do any of it, I actually need to go into the Autumn Lands."

"Really? That's going to be difficult," she told him, very curious where this was going. "Your best bet would be to go to the Mountain of Shadow in Kharakhan and hope you can find a portal."

"I know," he said. "My ship leaves tomorrow."

Sun and scales! She forced herself to remain calm and keep the alarm from her face. "You're going into the Luminal Sea with the Widow Maker just off our shore?"

"Yes," he replied. She could see the worry in his eyes, though he kept his features neutral. "I don't have a choice. And after what happened here, I have to do my part, whatever the risk. And I know it's a lot to ask, considering the danger. But . . . you . . . actually know things. . . I need your help."

"You want me to come with you." It was a statement, not a question. She breathed slowly to calm the pounding of her heart. *He's asking me to come with him.* The idea of heading out to sea with that monster just off the shore was terrifying. But going into the Mountain of Shadow, of seeing the raw magic of that mystical convergence, of entering the fabled Autumn Lands and perhaps seeing some glimpse of the ancient magic of the faerie realm — that was a dream come true.

And this is exactly what Lord Geryon just tasked me with! Find out more about the Cypher Runes, find a way to protect Melia.

"I'm in!" she exclaimed, fear and excitement rolling through her. "I'll do it."

Chapter 8: Shilvagi

OMEN

Conley was back on duty when Omen, pleased with himself, returned from Shalonie's Hold. Conley bowed and held the door as Tormy, also pleased with himself, gamboled into the entry hall.

Omen gave Conley a tight smile because he didn't know what to say to the man. *Sorry the squid monster scrambled your brain. But hey, isn't it neat how my dad chased it off? And as a bonus it released the souls of thousands of drowned people. That could have been you. Have a nice day.* As Omen hurried after Tormy, he couldn't shake the uncomfortable feeling that, despite their big win the day before, the threat wasn't over.

Wonder how Kyr's doing. I didn't say anything to trigger the hex at Shalonie's — I think. Concern continued to tug at him. *Hopefully, Tyrin kept him distracted. They're probably eating.* Omen followed Tormy toward the kitchens. *Hope Kyr didn't climb into a cupboard and fall asleep. That boy can sleep anywhere. Just like the cats.*

Lilyth caught him in the hallway before he passed the drawing room. His ten-year-old sister was a miniature version of their mother and had somehow even managed to master Avarice's wicked smirk. She used it now, willful as if pleased by whatever news she was about to impart. "Mother wants to see you in her office immediately," she told him, hands on her slender hips, silver eyes gleaming.

"What for?"

Lilyth's gleeful smirk disconcerted him, and he felt tempted to lift the information from her mind. But his father's constant praise of Lilyth's psionic skills made him hesitate. *Not sure I want to get my butt kicked by my little sister. Her shield never faltered yesterday.*

Lilyth twisted from side to side with a persnicketiness not uncommon to girls her age. "Mother had words with Indee, loud words, and she's decided you're not going on your trip after all."

"What?" Omen couldn't hide his astonishment. *Wyvern dung!* "Kyr's still hexed! Mother can't decide that! I have to go! What did Indee say to her?"

"Lots of words that Tyrin would love to learn," Lilyth replied, and then she turned on her heel and sauntered off, her inky-dark curls bouncing with each step. "Better not keep Mother waiting," she called over her shoulder. "You know how she gets when she's riled up. Maybe she'll ground you too."

Lilyth's monumental grounding was a point of bitter contention for the girl. Five months ago she had used the newly installed Daenoth transfer portal to travel to Terizkand all alone in search of a Tormy or Tyrin of her own. As punishment for an act that had nearly gotten her killed, she was forbidden from receiving anything new for an entire year, no clothes, no books, no jewelry, no gifts, no prizes — and certainly no talking cat. And as there was nothing in the world the girl wanted more than her own talking cat, she burned with indignation at her punishment.

Omen wondered if Lilyth might have helped Avarice's mood deteriorate. Still, considering how insistent Avarice had been about the seriousness of Kyr's hex, it didn't make sense that she would now forbid him from going. *Unless*

Indee angered her. But if I even hint that I'm not going, the hex will activate and Kyr will be injured. Worried and irritated, he turned away from the kitchens and stormed toward the west wing and his mother's private office. *It's not like I'm not already worried enough!*

He didn't bother to knock when he got to the large ornate door. Instead, he pushed it open and strode inside, determined to present a strong front. *Sometimes aggression is the only way to get her attention.*

Stepping into the room, he glanced briefly through the enormous wall of windows at the sun gleaming on the vast ocean below. Turning his eyes toward his mother's desk, he realized that she was not there. Instead of his mother, a young man was sprawled in a plush velvet chair set in front of Avarice's desk.

Momentarily taken aback, Omen swallowed the words of his prepared tirade and blinked at the stranger with confusion.

The man was quite young, barely older than Omen. His clothing, deep blue velvets finished with fine brocade piping and soft suede city boots, marked him as a noble instead of a servant. At first glance, he appeared foppish — rings on all of his fingers and several small hoops adorning his ears. His eyes were lined with dark kohl, and a faint shimmer of gold traced his cheeks in the manner of the drug-addled Venedrine elves that ruled over the Sul Havens. He was also unarmed, which Omen marked as unusual.

The stranger was silver-eyed like every member of the Shilvagi Machelli clan. His shoulder-length black hair shimmered with red highlights. Golden-skinned and sharp-featured, he had a sensual mouth that twisted with a smirk reminiscent of the one Lilyth had just flashed. But more than that, save for his gender, the man was the exact likeness of his mother, as if he were some long lost twin brother. *And I know she doesn't have a twin brother.* He had met all of his uncles, Avarice's brothers — tall, feral, muscular brutes who were more ruthless than refined. This young man seemed nothing like them. *Must be a Machelli though, same eyes, same face, same attitude, but I've never seen one unarmed. He looks more like Mother than even Lilyth does.*

The man did not rise or react to Omen's presence beyond giving him that infernal smirk and drumming his jewel-adorned fingers on the arm of the chair. Typically the members of the Machelli clan gave him at least a perfunctory sign of respect — born out of a long, wary association with his mother.

Doesn't he know who I am?

"I'm looking for my mother," Omen announced.

The young man glanced around the room. "This is her office," he remarked. "Probably a good place to start your search."

"You're not another long lost brother, are you?" Omen asked flatly.

The stranger laughed at that. "Find a lot of those, do you?"

"With remarkable frequency," Omen admitted. "But I was actually referring to my mother this time. Are you my uncle or my cousin?"

"No idea." An elegant shrug underscored his supposed ignorance. "Possibly both."

Omen was surprised by the man's indifference. All Machellis he knew could and would recite their lineage ten generations back. Close family ties were vital to the Scaalian clans. "You don't know how you're related to my mother?" he prodded. *He's obviously related. The similarity between him and Mother is startling.* Omen grew uncomfortable. *I hope this isn't one of those bad stories.*

"Not a weasel's fart of a clue who my parents are," the man said dismissively. "I was told not to discuss such things in polite company. Unfortunately, Avarice has failed to inform me who is considered polite, so I confess I'm at a loss. Have I offended you, or should I go into more detail? I tell a very good salacious story. True or not."

Omen wasn't about to let the man's flippant jabber distract him. "But you are Machelli?"

"I've been told I'm definitely Shilvagi, and apparently that makes me a Machelli." He yawned, slowly bringing his delicate, ring-clad fingers to his lips. "Devastation."

"Excuse me?" Omen was confused by the non sequitur.

The young man laughed again, as if at a joke. "My name," he explained. "It's Devastation."

Devastation Machelli. Doesn't get more Machelli than that. Omen drummed his fingertips to his thumbs. *Never yet met a Machelli without a hex name.* He was starting to appreciate the value of "hex" names, as his mother called them. *Might have done Kyr some good to have extra protection. Even if it is only superstition.*

His father's mother, the Queen of Lydon, had thrown a fit over the Machelli naming tradition when Lilyth was born. "Drivel and irrational nonsense! A little princess needs a proper name to set her up right in life," Omen's grandmother had insisted. "You can't call her 'Sepulcher' Daenoth! That is insane!" She had gone on to tell 7 once again that he had married a lunatic.

Omen, who had been privy to the ugly conversation, had received the bribe of a bowl of honey custard and a new pony in exchange for never repeating his grandmother's words to his mother. He'd kept his promise. And 7 had brokered a truce between his mother and his wife.

Lilyth had been eight months old before Queen Wraiteea had realized Avarice's compromising deception: Lilyth meant "assassin" in her native Scaalian tongue.

"Devastation Machelli," Omen said slowly, a new thought occurring to him. "Can you turn into a wolf?"

Devastation raised one eyebrow. "Not that I've ever noticed."

"Rat's feet!" Omen sighed. "They say we Shilvagi used to be able to transform into wolves. But I've yet to meet a single one that can actually do it." *Turning into a wolf would be fun!*

Before Devastation could conjure a reply, Avarice burst into the room and strode past Omen. Grabbing onto the back of her desk chair, she regarded both of them with a stern expression. To Omen's surprise, Avarice did not comment on the young man's failure to rise out of his sprawled pose, though he noticed her knuckles turn white with her tightening grip.

Not displaying the least bit of fear, Devastation gave Avarice a warm, overfamiliar smile.

That, more than anything, set Omen's nerves on edge. As an afterthought, he remembered that he had intended to meet his mother's ruling with aggression. He opened his mouth to protest. "Mo—"

"Good, you're both here," Avarice cut him off.

"Father said I had to go!" he pressed on loudly as if already in the middle of the argument. "You implied it was the only way to help Kyr. And now Lilyth said you've had words with Indee and are going to forbid—"

"Stop!" Avarice waved her hand before he could say any more.

He winced, realizing that his careless words could have triggered the hex.

Avarice glanced at the ceiling, then plopped down on the chair behind her desk with an exasperated sigh. "Honestly, Omen, why do you continually rise to Lilyth's bait?" she asked, agitated. "I told Lilyth to tell you I wished to speak with you — she made up all the rest for your benefit. And you fell for it like a three-year-old nogwirt . . . Indee is eight months pregnant. Do you really think she came here just so I could have words with her?"

The wind taken from his sails for a second time since coming to the office, Omen looked down. His shoulders sagged. *I am so stupid!* "I see your point," he stammered out, feeling sheepish. "Sorry. What did you want then?"

Avarice inclined her head, satisfied. "Another of Lilyth's little tricks," she scoffed. She turned her attention to Devastation who appeared increasingly delighted. Avarice twisted her wolf head guild master ring. "As it turns out, my son has been tasked by Indee'athra Set-Manasan to go into the Autumn Lands to rescue her kidnapped son King Khylar." She had slipped into her cold, business-like cadence.

"How curious," Devastation remarked, raising one dark, upswept eyebrow. His lips twitched as if he found the idea amusing, but wasn't sure Avarice would tolerate a smirk.

"Lucky for you," Avarice stated plainly, "you will be joining him. Are you agreeable?"

Startled by his mother's declaration, Omen frowned. *What good is he going to be?*

"Am I meant to be agreeable?" Devastation inquired.

"Yes, you are," Avarice informed him.

Devastation smiled broadly and placed one of his bejeweled hands over his heart, inclining his head. "I am honored to serve you, my lady," he replied, no trace of mockery or bitterness in his tone at all and yet said with perfect insincerity.

Why would she put up with that?

"Good choice." She opened a desk drawer and pulled out a flat, rectangular wooden box. "Have you introduced yourself to my son?" she asked Devastation while tapping the carved lid in a deliberate sequence.

"Yes, and we've exchanged details of our lineage." His eyes twinkled mischievously. The sunlight glinted off the multicolored jewels in his ears.

"Wait a minute!" Omen cut in, feeling he'd lost the thread of the conversation somewhere. "Why is he coming with me?" *He's a foppish city boy!*

"Honestly, Omen." Avarice opened the box but did not remove its contents. "I'm sending a Machelli operative with you on your trip. Why else would I send him if not to spy on you? If you are too slow-witted to figure that out for yourself, I don't want to hear about it."

Despite the fact that she was always unfailingly blunt with her children, Omen was taken aback by the harshness of her tone. He stared at her for several moments, neither of them saying a word. He broke first and glanced back at Devastation. *He looks like an unarmed, overly pampered noble.* "Why are you sending a spy?" Omen whined, hating every moment of this conversation.

Avarice leaned back in her chair. "If you, my dearest catastrophe, had been kidnapped by mysterious Autumn

Lords and taken forcibly into an alien land, do you imagine I would go and rescue you myself, or would I say, no, I can't be bothered, I think I'll force my friend's fifteen-year-old boy to do it for me?"

Omen blinked, the thoughts connecting like a lock snapping shut. "Crows' toes! When you put it like that, it does seem a bit . . . strange . . . " his voice trailed off.

"Telling you what?" Avarice prompted, looking impatient.

He sighed. "That something else is going on here," he admitted. "Something that she didn't tell us."

"Exactly," Avarice replied. "Which is why I'm sending Devastation." She turned to the young Machelli. "Dev, Omen is in charge of this little venture. You will do whatever he tells you. And you will report everything back to me in excruciating detail. And when things inevitably go horrifically wrong, you will do whatever you must to fix it. Understand?" She pried a small leather-bound book from the flat box and handed it across her desk to Dev.

"Perfectly." Dev nodded, seeming unconcerned with the underlying threat. He took the book from Avarice, leafing through the pages. "Ah, I'm journaling. How fun."

"Hey," Omen protested. "What makes you think it will all go horrifically wrong?"

"You're fleeing across the Luminal Sea with an ancient leviathan hunting you," Avarice told him. "Assuming you survive that, you have to go into the Kharakhian wilderness. If things don't go horrifically wrong, then you've probably landed in the wrong country. Now get out of here, both of you. I have important matters to attend to." She shooed them both toward the door with a wave of her hand. "Oh, and Dev," she called after them. "Lose the make-up and the jewelry. I don't want some Kharakhian warlord mistaking you for a pretty girl and carrying you off. You're sailing to Kharakhan not Revival. Try not to make a spectacle of yourself."

"But I'm so good at making spectacles." Dev looked genuinely disappointed.

"Omen has a big, giant orange cat, a potty-mouthed kitten and a little brother who talks to the dead. They can create spectacles all by themselves," she insisted.

Dev sighed dramatically and inclined his head in acquiescence. Then he followed Omen out the door.

"So, is it true you have five parents?" Dev asked brightly, his eyes gleaming with mischief. "How exactly does that work?" The innuendo in his voice was unmistakable.

Horrified, Omen looked back through the office door at his mother who glared at both of them. Omen quickly grabbed the door handle and pulled it shut.

"Not the way you're thinking!" he protested, mortified that Dev had implied something unsavory in front of his mother. *Why do people keep harping on that?*

"Oh, what a pity." Dev sighed, looking disappointed yet again. "Here I was hoping to hear all the juicy details."

Grumbling, Omen glared at him. "So why did she pick you exactly?" he changed the subject.

Dev shrugged blithely. "I'm extremely disobedient," he explained. "I imagine she thought you'd like that in a traveling companion."

"Disobedient?" Omen asked, perking up at that. Disobedience was something he could work with. "So then you don't mean to spy on me?"

Dev laughed. "Of course I intend to spy on you. She's paying me. I said disobedient, not foolish."

"And the part about the ancient leviathan doesn't frighten you?" Omen challenged. *He doesn't exactly look like the brave sort.*

Dev looked perplexed. "What's the worst that can happen? It eats us alive? I can think of worse ways of dying. I'm sure it will be loads of fun."

Annoyed, Omen turned away from the Machelli. Feeling at odds with himself, he briefly wondered if it would be worthwhile to pay Lilyth back for her little trick. *Maybe I'll steal her diary and read it on the trip.* He laughed under his breath at the thought and headed in search of his brother and cats.

Chapter 9: The Golden Voyage

DEV

Devastation Machelli leaned against one of the wooden posts lining the path that led down to the Melian docks. All around him, scores of dockworkers and wharfies hurried along, going about their morning business.

The first rays of early sunlight fell on scores of tall ships moored in the port of Melia. Their bone-colored sails fluttered and snapped in balletic unison as a mild summer wind played across the water. The ancient pier sparkled like a kaleidoscope as laborers unloaded cargo from all over the world and filled cavernous holds with valuable Melian treasures. Merchants bustled from ship to ship like bees flitting over lavender fields. But despite the constant movement around the port, no ships set sail, all firmly anchored in the bay.

They are still a little worried about the Widow Maker. Not as naive as I thought.

Most of the Melian fishing fleet had remained in port as well. A few brave souls had ventured out for a predawn run, but none had gone beyond the protective ring of the bay. Their haul, small in comparison to most days, was all the more precious, and the lively bray of workers resounded through the upper and lower fish markets.

Several workers tipped their caps in greeting as they passed. Dev nodded back, bemused by the overt friendliness. *Melians! They'd invite the thief who robbed them to stay for tea.*

The short time he'd spent in Melia had convinced Dev that the Sundragons had to be out of their minds for opening the border to outsiders. *Sweet, innocent Melian souls.*

It was obvious to Dev that unscrupulous sailors from far away places like Kharakhan and Terizkand would easily take advantage of the overly trusting Melians — were it not for the enormous, terrifying dragons stationed in strategic places throughout the city.

At least the Sundragons keep vigilant watch over their people.

One such dragon waited upon the cliffs near the port to greet arrivals. Blinding sunlight glittered off the creature's golden scales, making the behemoth impossible to miss; nor could anyone discount his sword-like talons as he gripped the rocky perch.

"Keep away from the dragons," Avarice had warned Dev when he'd first arrived in Melia. "They'll smell the Shilvagi in you immediately and know you for a Machelli. And lies won't fool them."

Considering most words Dev uttered were lies, he imagined any number of interesting conversations he could potentially have with the dragons. *Interesting conversations I don't need.* He had no desire to speak to a dragon, interesting or otherwise. Where he'd come from, dragons were mindless, terrifying grotesques who devoured people; he wasn't quite ready to believe that somehow the Melian Sundragons were different.

Civilized. Educated. Kind. Whatever faerie tales they've spread, I am not buying it. Dragons are predators, pure and simple.

He'd been somewhat surprised when Avarice had sum-

135

moned him from Terizkand the day before, sending a servant to lead him through the transfer portal in the Terizkandian royal palace. While Dev frequently found himself infiltrating the various parties and decadent gatherings of the Terizkandian upper class, he'd avoided the castle and the nobility. *And now I'll be traveling with the Terizkandian crown prince. Lucky me.*

Avarice had always seemed fond of him, mostly he suspected because she'd recognized a kindred spirit — someone who had to fight and claw and cheat to survive. Unlike Avarice, Dev had attained no rank or pedigree, nor had he the parentage to place him among people of power. To the rest of the world, he was a nobody. And he preferred it that way.

While Avarice had sketched out strict parameters for his involvement in this trip and the duties he was to perform, Dev didn't understand why she thought he would make a suitable companion for her son, Prince Omen Armand Locheden Daenoth, Prince of Lydon, Scion of the House Machelli, the House Deldano, and blood-child of the Elder God Cerioth, The Dark Heart.

There is more to this than she's let on.

Dev knew Avarice realized he was not the boy he appeared to be. His youthful countenance was the product of a curse and not age. Omen and his friends, however, would accept him as a peer — a fact Avarice was depending on.

Just one of the boys with the whole wonderful world before us. He chuckled bitterly, wondering if Avarice's decision was a wild miscalculation or pure arrogant madness.

Possibly both, he mused, nodding to yet another group of Melians who smiled happily at him as they went about their work. *Considering they were attacked by ghastly monsters just the other day, they're remarkably cheerful.*

He glanced briefly down at the leather satchels resting by his feet. The bags contained supplies he felt would be needed in the weeks ahead. Inexplicably, not once had a single person eyed the bags with the intent to steal anything. *Melians! My bow isn't even tied down. Some lightfinger could sell it for a tidy sum at any weapons shop.* The bow itself was a Terizkandian recurve that he'd won in a dice game from a Venedrine elf — and like most things owned by the elves it was of the finest make.

A sudden commotion further down the street caught Dev's attention, and he spotted his quarry approaching from the direction of Daenoth Manor.

Omen Daenoth was impossible to miss in a crowd, and not just because his constant companion was the giant orange cat trotting blithely beside him. It also wasn't just the windblown locks of his copper red hair, or his bizarre multicolored eyes — one Machelli silver, the other Deldano green — that set Omen apart. Though only fifteen, Omen towered over the men around him, his bloodline instantly clear to anyone who cared to look. Despite teasing Omen the day before, Dev knew more than he'd let on about the true nature of Omen's lineage and how the bloodlines of a dark god, some powerful elemental savage, and a Deldano healer had been bestowed upon the boy at his birth.

He'll be remarkable one day. If he doesn't get himself brutally slaughtered first.

Armed today, Omen wore two thin daggers strapped to either leg and carried a large two-handed blade strapped to his back. Dev suspected lesser men would have difficulty wielding such a weapon. *Kharakhian steel. Used to hunt trolls. Probably the only weapon he couldn't easily break.*

137

No doubt Omen had been trained his entire life in any number of deadly fighting styles. *Neither Avarice nor 7 would have left his martial education to chance. If they've let their fifteen-year-old son wander freely in the world, he knows how to defend himself.* At least Dev hoped he did. *If he doesn't, this job is going to be much harder than I'd like to imagine.*

Half a dozen Daenoth servants rushed past Dev, all carrying parcels and packages to be loaded onto the ship ahead of the arriving passengers. Dev raised an eyebrow as they passed. *Supplies for the cat?* he wondered. *I suppose the beastie does eat a great deal. Probably costs a fortune to keep a creature like that.* Neither Omen nor the elvin boy with him was carrying traveling bags. Dev guessed the servants bore whatever belongings they might require. *Hope the brats aren't too spoiled.*

Dev frowned as he took in the sight of the boy walking next to Omen: Kyr Daenoth, though Dev knew his true name to be Kyr De'Kyrel, last of the Venedrine Royal House, and blood-child of Cerioth as well, Omen's half brother, and from the stories he'd heard, a mystic. Dev's own history with the darker side of things left him leery of anyone who spoke with the dead — according to Avarice, Kahdess, the Language of the Dead, was in fact Kyr's native tongue.

What powers the boy might possess, Dev did not know, and Avarice had made a point of informing him that Kyr was to be protected from any harm. How a child of the Elder God Cerioth had come to be cherished by Avarice Machelli was something Dev did not know; but looking at Kyr, Dev understood her concern. Kyr possessed none of his brother's strength or fortitude, his frail body delicate even by elvin standards. Though he had the grace and fine features of his Venedrine kin, with sun-gold hair and large violet eyes, there was a leanness to his frame, a gauntness in his face that suggested long periods of starvation. The boy appeared to be no more than ten years of age, though his bloodline made it impossible to judge. Dev wondered at the wisdom of allowing Kyr to join them on this trip.

Of course if he's the one who was hexed, I suppose there is no choice. Indee has to be a right harpy to curse such a child. I wonder if the crew of our ship knows he's a mystic and will likely draw the Widow Maker's interest?

An erratic movement on the boy's shoulder caught Dev's attention, and he smiled faintly when he spotted the small orange shape half-hidden by Kyr's golden hair. *Must be Tyrin.* Dev had heard of both cats of course — but had yet to speak to either of them. He had to admit to a certain curiosity as he wondered how smart the creatures were.

Omen paused suddenly and waved toward an approaching woman. The pretty blonde smiled and enthusiastically waved back. Curiously, while the Melians around them were nodding politely to Omen, most of them stopped and bowed respectfully toward the woman, despite her presenting a far plainer appearance than the foreign prince. *Shalonie Tatharion, then. Hold Lord's daughter.* He supposed the golden sword strapped to her leather belt was enough to mark her rank.

That's quite a sword. Hope she can hang on to it.

Shalonie's bearing was a combination of stuffy scholar and tomboy, her clothing — beige linen and sturdy cloth under a soft leather hooded cloak — was far more practical than the colorful fashions of a Melian noblewoman. Her blond hair was bound into a thick braid woven tightly

139

around her skull and secured with a soft piece of leather — but Dev suspected that unbound her locks would tumble past her waist in a fall of gold. When the girl spotted Omen and returned his greeting, her bright smile gave her an air of radiant beauty that more than made up for her unfashionable appearance. *Avarice claims she's renowned for her intelligence. And from what I understand that dragon blade is the highest mark of favor known in this land. I wonder why she's joining us? And why the dragons are letting her?*

Shalonie fell into step beside Omen, greeting both cats and Kyr as they walked.

Dev straightened as Omen spotted him, noting with some amusement that he seemed at first not to recognize him. Without the excessive jewelry, glittering face paint and colorful clothing expected in the Terizkandian Garden Courts, Dev supposed he looked more like one of the wild-born Machellis of Scaalia. *More like one of Omen's younger cousins.* Dev scooped up his own traveling bags, slinging the various straps over his shoulders, and waited — bow in hand — as Omen and Shalonie approached.

Omen nodded to him, and then turned solicitously toward Shalonie, his Melian-bred manners apparent in his instinctive move to introduce the lady in his company. "Shalonie, may I present Devastation Machelli. He'll be . . . traveling with us."

Dev caught the hesitation in Omen's words and couldn't help but smirk. "My lady." He bowed his head in greeting. "And by traveling he, of course, means spying. Please call me Dev."

Omen glared at him, looking outraged by his words while Shalonie looked on amused.

"I'm sorry," Dev apologized immediately, rather enjoying Omen's taciturn mood. "Was I supposed to lie about that? Avarice didn't mention it."

"Generally when you're hired to spy on people you're expected to keep it a secret," Omen informed him, seeming annoyed.

"Ah," Dev nodded. "I didn't see the point. Avarice told you what I was to do, and I've been led to believe that Lady Shalonie is quite clever. I have no doubt she'd figure me out immediately. It seemed rude to lie."

"Is you going to spy on me?" Tyrin asked from his perch on Kyr's shoulder. The little cat's tail lashed back and forth.

"No." Dev shook his head emphatically. "In fact, I was told most pointedly by Avarice that I was not to inform her of anything either you or Tormy did."

Tyrin's whiskers flared at that, and his amber eyes narrowed. "Not fair!" The little cat punctuated his unhappiness with a strident *meow!*

Dev tried not to laugh.

Tormy stalked toward the group, sat down beside them with purpose and folded his tail around his paws.

Dev noticed with some alarm that even seated Tormy was taller than he was.

"Yes. Not fair." Tormy gave Dev half a dozen short sniffs. "On account of the fact that we is very interestingly-ness."

"Most interestinglyness!" Tyrin agreed.

"My apologies." Dev inclined his head to both of the cats. Inwardly, he laughed at the looks on both Omen's and Shalonie's faces as they realized what he was doing. "Would the two of you like me to spy on you as a personal favor?"

"Yes!" the cats both agreed in unison, and Omen sighed

heavily.

Dev flashed them a grin. "Consider it done."

"Are you green?" Kyr asked, and Dev blinked, caught momentarily off guard. He looked toward Omen for an explanation, but small Tyrin seemed to take matters swiftly in paw.

"He is Dev, Kyr," Tyrin informed him. "And he is really real which is sort of green on account of the fact that you is liking green. And he is writing letters for us to Avarice so we is telling her all the new words we is learning."

"I like studying my letters," Kyr announced, and then reached out and very slowly and deliberately poked Dev in the shoulder, his face set in an expression of wariness as if unsure what to expect. Judging by Omen's glower, Dev guessed he was not supposed to react. He graciously allowed Kyr to complete his peculiar and uninvited prodding.

Kyr smiled when his finger came in contact with the leather of Dev's coat, and he nodded toward his brother — satisfied. "He's not imaginary, Omen," the boy said solemnly.

"Glad to hear it, Kyr." Omen smiled back dolefully. "Come on, let's keep going."

Guessing he wasn't going to get an explanation for the boy's odd behavior, Dev fell into step beside them. *Avarice did warn me that Kyr was a handful. Maybe Cerioth's blood breeds madness?*

The fish merchants along the pier all noted the presence of the two cats and swiftly began setting out their meager catch in an effort to garner the felines' attention. The enterprising tactics worked splendidly. Tormy's tail twitched widely as they set foot on the merchants' boardwalk. No doubt, living in Melia, Omen had spent hours exploring the shops, stalls and taverns, seeking exotic items from foreign lands. He likely spent more than his fair share at the markets purchasing tuna and swordfish, clams and crabs for his hungry cat.

"Omy . . ." Tormy purred searchingly, his nose twitching with interest.

"I guess a shrimp or two can't hurt," Omen said and flicked a coin to a nearby runner. "Bag of wiggles for the cats."

The Melian boy snatched up the coin in mid-stride. "My lord." He tipped his cap.

The young runner returned shortly with a large paper-wrapped bundle brimming with near-transparent raw crustaceans. Omen tossed another coin to the boy. "Walk with us, so the cat can keep moving while he eats. And fling a small one to the tiny fluffball."

Not fazed by the request, the boy peeled open the paper wrapped around the collection of large Melian shrimp. He snagged a bite-sized critter with extra long antennae and flicked it to Tyrin who was still seated upon Kyr's shoulder. The orange kitten snatched the treat from the air with itty-bitty razor claws and bit down heartily. Dev had to laugh at the sight. *Shrimp is almost the size of the cat.*

"Pity we can't simply portal to Kharakhan. We could be there and back again before dinner," Omen said as they walked along the boardwalk toward the pier where their vessel was waiting.

Dev had to agree it would have been far preferable. He didn't much care for ocean travel. And despite his flippant remarks to Omen the day before, he didn't relish the possibility of meeting the Widow Maker far out at sea.

"There are no established portals between Melia and

Kharakhan," Shalonie said earnestly. "I can work on setting one up once we're there, but don't forget it took your father and me three months to set up the first portal to Lydon."

"But only one month to set up the one to Terizkand," Omen said encouragingly.

And much appreciated. The transfer portal in the Daenoth Manor had allowed Dev to travel instantaneously from Terizkand to Melia. He looked at Shalonie with new respect.

The young woman conceded with a nod. "We learned a lot the first time. But Kharakhan has other issues — random magical energies that like to corrupt teleport spells. A corrupted teleport spell could rip you apart and scatter you across the world. You wouldn't want to take the chance. Setting up a stable portal will be challenging." She shaded her eyes against the bright glare of the sun and studied his face. "We'll be fine. I suspect your father injured the Widow Maker more than he let on."

"Probably," Omen agreed, too quickly.

Dev didn't feel particularly confident.

Omen stopped abruptly, a wide smile crossing his face. "There she is — the Golden Voyage, my grandmother's flagship."

They'd rounded a corner of stalls and now had a clear view of all the ships docked in the deep-water bay along the wharf. Dev's eyes widened when he realized which ship Omen was referring to.

"Kadana's ship is fantastic!" Shalonie exclaimed, admiring the gleaming green and gold vessel.

They surveyed the galleon. The Golden Voyage would be their home for several weeks, if the crossing to Kharakhan went smoothly. Sporting three tall masts, the

Golden Voyage wasn't much bigger than the other anchored ships, but judging by the enormous crates that were disappearing into its depths through the great opening on the main deck, Dev guessed this ship was crafted with elaborate enchantments that contained hidden holds and magical rooms, which could expand beyond its given physical dimensions. *If Kadana is the only captain brave enough to set sail at the moment, I'm guessing the ship will be packed to the brim with goods.*

"That's Ven'tarian made," Dev said, calculating the market value of the vessel. *Worth a king's ransom. Ironic.* He noticed the dark shape of a little monkey swinging from one of the mast ropes and couldn't help wonder how the little creature would get along with the two cats.

"Grandmother bragged that her ship is the height of comfort and there would be plenty of room for Tormy," Omen told them.

"Do you know how rare a Ven'tarian galleon is?" Shalonie spoke in a hushed, almost reverent voice. "The spells are woven so tight, legend says the ship repels water like a duck. It's priceless. How did Kadana come by it?"

"She told my dad she won it in a card game," Omen said, his tone suggesting he was unsure if it had been the truth or a joke. "Come to think of it, there are a lot of things she claims to have won in card games."

"Look at all the water!" Kyr exclaimed in delight, ignoring the brilliant galleon before him and looking past the twisting ropes, the furled sails, and high decks where hardworking sailors prepared for departure at a devilish pace. Kyr had eyes only for the great swells of waves crashing beyond the port's breakwater. "I bet there's fish out there."

"Fish!" Tormy mumbled, still chewing. "I is loving fish!

Fish is being good — is we getting fish? I is wanting fish, Omy. Is you cooking us fish now, Omy? It must be being lunchtime!"

Dev found himself impressed with the cat's appetite despite being forewarned. He'd seen the elaborate spread in the Daenoth dining room that morning. He had no doubt Omen and the cats had just come from breakfast. *And now the cat is hungry again. Feeding that bottomless stomach may become a problem.*

"You are eating shrimp right now!" Omen reminded the cat.

"They is empty," Tormy complained. He looked at the crumpled paper wrapper with sad eyes, transparent swimmerets still stuck between his teeth.

The Melian runner looked at Omen, hopeful.

"Fine. Another helping." Omen handed a small coin pouch to the boy. "Have them wrap up a couple of their largest tunas too. He'll be hungry when he gets on board."

The boy dashed away.

"The never-ending gullet," Shalonie teased blithely. "Good thing they're so cute."

Tormy and Tyrin preened in unison.

"Now settle down, Tormy." Omen patted the cat's hind leg. "We're going to Kharakhan. We're getting on Kadana's ship, remember?"

"I 'member 'member. I is liking Grandma Kadana!" Tormy chirped happily. Just then, they spied Kadana emerging from the main cabin onto the deck. "Hello, Grandma Kadana!" the cat called out.

Dev took in the appearance of Kadana Deldano, the ship's owner and captain. While he knew cursory stories about the Deldanos, he had never met any of them, and

Kadana's appearance was not quite what he was expecting. From what he understood, the matriarch of the Deldano clan was entirely human despite the mixed heritage of some of her descendants, and she'd fought in several of the Kharakhian wars. She should have been well into her seventies, and while magic could go a long way toward prolonging youth, it usually required at least a trace of non-human blood to work. The woman who had stepped out onto the deck of the Golden Voyage was young and strong. Dressed in leathers dyed in the green and gold of the Deldano crest, Kadana stood taller than most men, her muscular form lean and hard from long years of battle. Her honey-gold curls pulled back with a leather tie revealed a tanned, smiling face.

"Omen, did you say Kadana is your grandmother?" Dev interrupted. "She looks like she's in her thirties. Is she a Melian?" He knew that though technically human, the Melians aged much slower than people of other nations, blessed with long life by their draconic guardians.

"Don't be a dolt," Omen said gruffly. "She's from Kharakhan. Born and raised."

Kadana shouted out rapid-fire orders in a robust voice that carried well past the deck of the Ven'tarian galleon. The sailors responded without hesitation, obeying swiftly with the effort of workers aiming to please a valued leader.

They clearly respect her.

"So, whose mother is she?" Dev continued his inquiry, though he already knew the answer. He could see Omen beginning to prickle at the blunt questions about his heritage and wondered how long it would take him to realize Dev only asked because Omen's reaction was so amusing. "She's not 7's or Avarice's?"

"Neither. She's Beren's mother. Deldano obviously."

"Right, how exactly are you related to Beren again?" Dev needled. "You never really explained that part."

Omen sighed. "Beren is a bardic healer. When I was born . . . You know what, I don't want to talk about it. It's none of your business."

"Do you call her grandma?" Dev pressed.

"Shut up!" Omen waved a gauntleted hand. "Kadana, over here."

Kadana waved back, motioning them aboard and directing them toward the gangplank. Omen nodded and steered Kyr forward.

"Are we going swimming?" the boy asked, utterly bewildered.

"No Kyr, we're getting on the ship," Omen said.

"Wait, wait, wait, wait, wait!" Tormy fluffed his ruff and dug his claws into the wooden planks of the wharf. His voice rose with each iteration of *wait*. "We is doing what? Wait, wait, wait, wait, wait! No one is saying anything about a ship! A ship that's in the water. Water is wet, wet is bad. I is not bad, I is good. I is not getting wet!"

Now I understand why Avarice and 7 didn't want to accompany Omen to the docks! Dev bit back the laugh engendered by the sudden realization on Omen's face. The young man looked at his cat with baffled trepidation.

"Is there a ship?" Kyr asked in confusion. "Is it real? I see water. I don't think I know how to swim. Do you want me to try to swim, Omen?"

Omen's look of alarm grew. "No, we're going on a ship . . . see . . . it's right there—"

"Is sailors knowing how to curse?" Tyrin asked abruptly, curiosity underscoring his purr. "I is thinking it might be fun to be a sailor. I is thinking of climbing that big tree in the middle."

"What tree?" Kyr looked around for the tree in question.

"The three big trees on the boat!" Tyrin replied. "The ones with the sheets!"

"Am I carving trees?" Kyr asked Omen, his eyes gleaming eagerly.

"No, you're not carving the trees." Omen was starting to look overwhelmed, and Dev almost felt sorry for him.

He can't even get his brother and cats on the ship. That doesn't bode well for the rest of the trip.

He saw the frazzled look Omen threw Shalonie. The girl patted his shoulder. She turned toward Kyr and took his arm, her smile dazzling. "Would you be so kind as to help me up the gangplank, dear sir?"

Kyr looked startled but smiled back shyly. "Of course, Shalonie. The numbers tell the story. You can hear the ticking of time on the wind. I checked the clock before we left, so it's time to leave." It was Shalonie's turn to look bewildered. They started for the ship.

"Problems?" an amused voice came from behind them, and Dev stiffened. He hadn't heard anyone approaching. While Omen turned toward the sound with a look of relief, Dev felt a cold shiver claw down his spine, apprehension nicking each vertebra.

Standing behind them was Templar Trelkadiz, Crown Prince of Terizkand, son of the Nightblooded warlord Antares. Dressed from head to toe in embossed black leather armor, two slender swords of white bone strapped to the sword belt at his left hip, Templar was as tall as Omen. And though only a couple of years older than the Daenoth cub, Templar had a trace of his father's intimidating air

about him. The jostling Melians around them seemed to instinctively give Templar a wide berth. Dressed for travel,
Templar carried a bulky pack slung over one shoulder. He
leaned insolently against a post as if he'd been watching —
and judging — for some time.

How did I miss his arrival? Dev berated himself. There
was nothing in this world he mistrusted more than the
Night Lands — and anyone associated with them. Templar
was the crown prince of Terizkand, and there wasn't a single person in the kingdom who wasn't aware that the royal
Trelkadiz family was Nightblooded. Even if Templar's family had tried, it would have been impossible to hide the
curse. At the first sign of anger, the eyes of the Nightblood
glowed yellow with fire. It was said that as a child Templar
had once grown so angry that his blue eyes had permanent-
ly turned yellow, forever revealing his true nature.

Not that the Terizkandians care. While most people
shunned even the whispering of anything Nightblooded, the
denizens of the kingdom of Terizkand were different in that
regard. In conquering Terizkand, King Antares had at the
same time freed the population from the giants who had en-
slaved them. The Terizkandians reveled in the power of
their royal house.

But Dev's history with the Night Lands was mixed and
sordid, and he knew better than to trust any of their kind, no
matter how pleasing their appearance or helpful their manner.

*Avarice can't possibly trust Templar. And yet she said
nothing against him.*

"Cats! Water!" Omen explained in exasperation. "Tormy
is refusing to get on the boat."

"Ah, pity." Templar shrugged nonchalantly. "Guess he's

going to miss out on all the fish and the mice."

Tormy's ears perked forward. "What? What fish? What mouses? I is liking fish and mouses. Where is being my fishies and mouses?"

"On the ship," Templar explained. "The ship is full of mice and the ocean is full of fish. We'll have an entire voyage of every type of fish dish imaginable. Fish breakfast, lunch and dinner."

"And mouses?"

"All the mice you can catch, maybe some rats too," Templar replied. "But of course if you're not going . . ."

"Wait for me, Grandma Kadana!" Tormy took a mighty leap from the dock, catching hold of the upper edge of the main deck railing, claws digging into the polished wood. He pulled himself upward, back claws scrambling against the hull and scoring the fine green paint.

A group of sailors nearest the railing shrieked as the enormous cat crawled like a fluffy predator onto the deck, and then flounced happily toward their captain.

Shalonie and Kyr took a few quick steps to catch their balance, laughing as they steadied each other in turn. "Wheeeee!" Tyrin giggled.

Kadana let out a hearty belly laugh and patted the giant cat's orange flank. "How're you doing, my boy?" she greeted, seeming undisturbed by the cat's antics or the damage done to the ship's paint.

"I is being here for the mouses!" Tormy explained, making Kadana laugh even harder.

"Aren't we all," she said as she led Tormy away from the railing.

"Tell me again why we can't portal to Kharakhan?" Omen asked out loud.

"Don't worry. Ocean voyages are fun, especially with the added threat of ancient leviathans," Templar assured him. "Is this your spy?"

"Devastation Machelli, a pleasure," Dev inclined his head. *No sense in angering the Night Dweller.*

Templar chuckled. "Now there's a proper Machelli name if I ever heard one."

The runner returned carrying two great sacks filled with wrapped packages.

"I'll get those." Omen offered. "Nice work."

"Afraid Kadana won't feed us?" Templar started. "And where is your gear?"

"Loaded everything earlier, and Liethan stowed all the extra supplies on the ship last night. He already spent the night on board. Getting a full crew wasn't easy — considering." Omen took a final look around. "Guess that'll do it." He held the fish bags securely, avoiding spillage. "This should get Tormy through to lunch."

"We'll be fishing the entire way to Kharakhan just to keep your cat fed." Templar looked around. "Bryenth isn't coming?"

"His duty is to stay and help protect Melia. The dragons are worried that . . ." Omen trailed off with a meaningful look around the docks, not wanting to say aloud what Dev knew he was thinking.

They don't want the Melians to know that the Widow Maker could attack again at any moment. According to what Avarice had told Dev earlier, there was a good chance the creature would want revenge on 7. *Also a good chance it will follow our ship and attack us.*

"What about you?" Omen asked. "Your father didn't mind you shirking your duties to travel with me?"

Templar feigned affront. "Shirking my duties! My father sent me out into the world to be an ambassador for Terizkand and to make valuable allies. That's what I'm doing."

Omen looked pleased. "Your father considers me a valuable ally?"

"Of course," Templar reassured him and then immediately shook his head. "Well, no, he considers your parents valuable allies. And he likes the idea of Indee being grateful to us for helping her out. But he did say you weren't the most annoying friend I've made in the past few years. And for him that's practically a compliment."

"Swell." Omen sighed. "Did your father really tell you to be an ambassador?"

"Absolutely," Templar replied. "I believe his exact words were, 'Get out of here you annoying brat and go do something useful.' The title of ambassador was of course implied — you just have to know how to read him."

"Right." Omen motioned toward the ship. "Let's get aboard." He headed up the gangplank.

Dev followed Templar, shaking his head at the folly of joining this group. *Two sons of Cerioth, two talking cats, and a Night Dweller. I must be addlebrained to join them. At least Shalonie seems normal enough.*

Kadana met them on the main deck. Without fuss, she motioned them to follow her to the upper navigation deck where a golden-haired, blue-eyed young man waited by the ship's wheel. Judging by the tanned skin, bare feet, simple breeches, and thin cotton shirt, Dev guessed the young man was Liethan Corsair. Though he remembered the Corsair had a title of some sort, he also knew that the Corsairs tended to forgo formalities.

"I've spoken with your father," Kadana began without

153

preamble, turning toward Omen. She kept her voice down so that it would not carry to the sailors. Most of their attention was taken up with preparing to cast off the lines while avoiding the enormous orange cat that was inspecting the ship. Kyr and Shalonie stood by the mainmast, and little Tyrin had already dug his claws into the wooden beam and had started climbing upward toward the ship's monkey.

"If we have good winds, we have about three weeks of water ahead of us," Kadana continued. "It's my hope that if we stick to the summer route we'll avoid the main hunting grounds of the leviathan. But I also understand that there is some concern about Kyr attracting the creature?"

Omen glanced briefly toward his brother. The boy was watching his little cat climb, staring worriedly up at him. "The dragons seem to think that the Widow Maker is attracted to mystics," he admitted. "He could hear the song before everyone else did. Don't know if that means anything."

Kadana shot a quick look around the ship's many decks. "We had a hard time getting a full crew for this voyage. Everyone is on edge, and it's our job to keep things running smoothly. Sailors are a superstitious lot — so watch your words. And if you can, keep Kyr from speaking in the tongue of the dead. That won't go over well."

"Understood," Omen agreed, though to Dev he sounded uncertain.

"Let's cast off then," Kadana announced and started shouting orders to the sailors below. Dev leaned against the rail guard, keeping out of the way while Omen and the others headed back down to the main deck.

"Bye Melia!" Tormy shouted from the forecastle. "Be a good Melia. We is being right back. Don't go nowheres."

"I is a &$!*^!! pirate," Tyrin squealed and danced on the rigging like a thing possessed. "I is the orange scourge of the many seas!" The tiny cat let out a wicked chitter.

"Well, at least I'll have plenty to write to Avarice about," Dev remarked to himself, and looked forward across the endless expanse of white-capped water.

Chapter 10: Navigation

SHALONIE

S halonie stood next to Haptis, the ship's navigator, and listened with great interest as he explained the workings of the helm.

When she'd first come on board the Golden Voyage, she'd been delighted to learn that Kadana expected everyone in the group to take on a job. *Understandable. They're light on crew for this journey.* She pressed her lips together to keep from smiling. *I should be scared, but this is so exciting!* While she had plenty of her own research to keep her occupied, she'd always felt actively learning from an expert in the field — any field — was eminently more valuable than simple book learning. Seeing the sheer amount of magic present on the vessel made her positively giddy.

The magical artifacts crafted by the fabled Ven'tarian Sorcerium are legendary! The ship was priceless, especially considering the Ven'tarians no longer existed. Known for their extraordinary ability to bind elemental spirits inside artifacts, the Ven'tarians, it was rumored, sought more and more powerful beings to bind. They had destroyed themselves and their entire people when one ambitious Ven'tarian sorcerer had attempted to bind a Night Lord.

Ven'tarian magic wasn't a form of magic Shalonie practiced — the binding of any living creature seemed inherently wrong to her. But she knew that Ven'tarian artifacts were valued beyond compare and had never imagined she'd be sailing on one of their vessels.

"And this, my lady, is the helm control," Haptis pointed out the ship's wheel which possessed a myriad of extraordinary buttons and levers, each embedded with glittering charms. He explained some of their functionality, though he frequently bowed his head and said sheepishly that he didn't understand how most of it worked and hadn't yet figured out half the devices.

"Been sailing for nigh on forty years with the Corsairs," he told her after pointing out yet another lever he didn't understand. "But I never did see the likes of this vessel. And you should see the maps."

He motioned toward a large platform table covered with pieces of vellum. *Secured with golden clips. Must be ensorcelled or they'd blow away.* Just above the platform on a raised upper deck, Tormy stretched out in the sun, his amber eyes gazing curiously down at the one piece of vellum that lay rolled open on the platform. A small corner fluttered in the breeze, but the vellum itself did not move.

Beside him, leaning against a rope-bound crate sat the dark-haired Machelli spy, Devastation. While the supposed youth professed to know nothing about ships or sailing, he had adapted surprisingly well. He looked relaxed and content in the job he'd been given: mending a spare sail torn on the last voyage. He was barefoot, like the majority of the Corsair sailors, and while he claimed to have never sewn anything in his life, his hands moved with swift deftness, neatly stitching up white canvas as well as any master tailor. *He's either an amazingly quick study or a pathological liar.* She couldn't decide which.

He is a Machelli, she reminded herself. *Deceit, deception, and manipulation are tools of their trade. Come to think of it, there are probably Machellis named Deceit, Deception, and Manipulation.*

Dev winked when he noticed the assessing look she was giving his stitching work. His silver eyes twinkled with amusement as if aware she'd caught out his lie.

Shalonie averted her eyes, then cursed herself for doing so. *He's going to make something of that.* She forced herself to look at him again.

Dev possessed sharp, chiseled features that made him more pretty than handsome, but he also had a strangely wicked and equally boyish charm.

Shalonie blushed despite herself.

"Never sewn anything before?" she asked him lightly.

"Not a stitch," he agreed. "Never thought it a skill I'd have any use for. Never saw the point in learning."

"And it shows," she told him, eyeing the perfect row of stitches he'd already completed. "You're terrible at it." She doubted even the first mate would find anything to complain about with his work.

"I know," he sighed apologetically, seeming anything but remorseful judging by the gleam of mirth in his eyes. "Probably have to rip it out and do it all over again."

Stifling a smirk, Shalonie turned her attention back to the navigator. *Dev is Omen's problem,* she reminded herself, relieved. *Not that I think Omen knows anything about him. Avarice must trust Dev, or she wouldn't have sent him along . . . Would she?*

While Shalonie had many mixed thoughts about Avarice, she knew the woman would never endanger her family — would in fact go to horrific means to safeguard them if it came right down to it. *There are stories . . .*

Dev looks no older than Omen himself, but I would bet

gold that he's far older than he looks. As a Melian, Shalonie knew not to judge a person's age by their looks. Melians all possessed an extraordinarily long lifespan. Though not as long-lived as the elvin races, they outlived humans significantly. But the possibility that a Machelli had managed to trick death a time or two would not surprise her.

"This is the route we are taking, my lady," Haptis interrupted her thoughts. He pointed to the map stretched out on the large platform. Thin black lines and numbers, as well as silver sigils and symbols written in several languages, trailed over the heavy vellum.

"This is saying 'map' I think," Tormy explained. He reached out one of his enormous paws and covered the large black letters at the top of the vellum, claws carefully retracted as if he understood the value of the page. The words he covered in fact said "Luminal Sea Navigation." The cat's attempt to read made her smile. Curiously, he nodded his head in a rhythmic pattern as he studied the words. *Is he sounding out the letters?*

"There is being lots of silent letters in the word 'map' isn't there?" Tormy announced. She realized that he had counted the marks and somehow determined there were too many letters to spell the word *map.* That indicated he did at least understand that "map" was a very short word. *How smart are these cats?*

"Lots," she agreed sagely. *Tyrin must be with Kyr and Omen in the galley. Bet he'd have something to say about the map as well.* The little cat's penchant for learning new curse words always made her laugh, even at the most inappropriate times.

Tormy nodded. "It is being written in Kharakhian, and

that is having lots of silent letters," he explained. He looked up suddenly, ears perked forward. "I is reading Kharakhian," he sounded astonished. "I is brilliantnessness!" Both Dev and Haptis chuckled at that, but neither man corrected the cat.

Tormy reached out then and pawed curiously at the long golden chain attached to the top of the map by a jeweled stud. The chain was long enough to span the map from corner to corner. It ended in a clasp.

Shalonie guessed a small object should be clipped to it. But the object was missing.

"Is this being our longitudinousnessness?" Tormy asked, batting at the chain playfully.

"Ah, no, Master Tormy," Haptis explained. "Longitude is marked here." He traced the long lines running vertically down the map. "We're here." He pointed to a spot marked with wavy lines indicating currents and wind patterns. "I don't actually know what the chain is for," he admitted. "The others say I should remove the chains and melt the gold down — worth quite a bit. But the Ven'tarians don't do things without reasons — and all the maps have these chains. I imagine they have a use — just haven't managed to work it out yet."

"They're Proximals," Shalonie told him, having seen similar devices in the course of her studies. "There should be a small glass or crystal ship figurine attached to the ends of the chain, but it's likely the ship's last navigator took it."

"Proximals?" Haptis frowned. "Never heard of such things."

"I'll show you," Shalonie said, searching the deck for something to use. She spied the small wooden pipe attached to Haptis' belt and motioned toward him. "Let me have

160

your pipe. And Dev, give me a spare piece of that sail, small bit should do."

Both Haptis and Dev looked equally curious but did as she asked. Haptis emptied the bit of burnt leaf from the pipe first, rubbing it clean on his trousers before handing it over to her. Dev slipped a knife from a hidden sheath under the sleeve of his linen shirt and cut off a small corner of the white canvas sail he was mending.

Tormy's tail twitched wildly as he watched.

Shalonie took the pipe and the canvas. She stuffed the white material inside the pipe's leaf bowl and then motioned to Dev. "Let me see the needle," she told him. He snapped the line of thread connecting his sewing needle to the sail and handed the thin piece of metal across to her. She carefully scratched small, thin symbols into the side of the pipe. "This won't work as well as the actual Proximals, but it should be enough to demonstrate the magic," she told them. "The pipe will represent the ship."

"What's the piece of sail for?" Haptis asked.

"It connects the real ship to the pipe — the magic in a Proximal is entangled with the object it represents." Shalonie finished carving the necessary marks. She took the end of the golden chain attached to the map and wound it around the shaft of the pipe. She held both tightly in her hand for a moment, channeling a surge of magical power into the pipe. It wouldn't by any means be the magical artifact the Ven'tarians would have created, but she hoped her Cypher Runes would approximate the device. *The marks should be enough to direct the magic.*

She felt the chain warm in her hand and could barely suppress a titter, knowing that her guess as to the purpose of the chain had been correct. It was likely that the missing crystal ship would have had an earth elemental locked inside it. Her spell would replicate its magic without imprisoning a living entity. *Cypher Runes are truly superior to other magics.*

"There!" she said, collecting herself quietly. She released the chain and pipe, and they watched as the pipe began sliding across the map. It appeared to come to a rest in the very location Haptis had marked as their position.

"It's still moving," Shalonie said. "Just too slowly to really see — it will match the position of the actual ship in the ocean with the pipe's position on the map. Ven'tarian ships never get lost."

"That's marvelous!" Haptis leaned over the platform to get a closer look at the map and the pipe. "How accurate is it?"

"The original Proximal would have been extremely accurate," Shalonie told him. "This one's a mock-up. The magic won't hold long because a pipe doesn't really represent the ship — maybe a day at most. Get Kyr to carve you a figurine of the ship — the more accurate the representation, the more accurate the spell, and the longer it will last. A good figurine could last you at least a year before the magic would need to be renewed. The original one probably had an earth elemental inside it — they never wore out." She handed the needle back to Dev, who quickly threaded it and continued sewing.

"Kyr?" Haptis asked. "The strange elvin lad with Prince Armand?"

"I think he prefers to be called Omen, but yes, I meant the boy," Shalonie told him. She glanced over at Dev before adding, "The Machellis have these odd superstitions about names."

"Says the girl who just turned a pipe and piece of sail into a magical artifact." Dev laughed, seeming to take no offense. "Names, words, symbols — they all have power. With the right words a Night Dweller can steal your soul. Wouldn't recommend that."

"Fair enough," Shalonie conceded. *Seems to know more about magic than I suspected. Aside from Avarice, the Machellis are known for their blade work, not spell casting.*

"Boy seems a bit touched in the head," Haptis continued, still focusing on the idea of getting Kyr to do something for him.

Shalonie felt a lump form in her throat.

"Kyr is being very touching," Tormy agreed sweetly. "He is scratching my ears all the times. And I is purring on account of the fact that I is liking having my ears scratched. He is being good at the carvings too."

"You won't find a better sculptor," Shalonie told the navigator. "And if you explain what it's for, he's likely to put his own brand of magic into the carving — it will make it all the more powerful."

Haptis nodded with difficulty, but his mistrust was obvious.

Shalonie found her admiration for Omen growing. The constant prejudice against Kyr had to be a strain. Their elevated status prevented people from saying hurtful things outright, but the side glances and the barely concealed signs to ward off evil whenever Kyr lapsed into Kahdess had to be wearing.

It's a wonder Omen doesn't get into more fights.

She knew the cats with their often-loud commentary, or good-natured brand of destructive clumsiness, couldn't be easy to manage either. Yet Omen handled all with good humor and grace. *And a sizable bank account,* she amended. The sheer amount of food that Tormy consumed would bankrupt a less prosperous family.

Haptis peered at the map, then glanced out at the ocean swells rising and falling around the great vessel. Off their starboard bow, Shalonie spotted two fishing skiffs skimming along the top of the water, floating inches above the waves, dragging a net between them.

Air elementals kept the small boats aloft, both controlled rather superbly by Templar who'd managed to master their power the moment he'd climbed aboard. The Terizkandian prince had no trouble manipulating the magic needed to keep both vessels under control — something the ship's fishing master had taken full advantage of, assigning Templar the duty for the duration of the trip.

"Well, at least my calculations were not off," Haptis said, looking back down at the map and then back up again at the waves. "I wondered. It's nice to know for certain."

Shalonie paused at that, glancing over at Dev who looked up abruptly.

"You were worried about something, Haptis?" the Machelli asked sharply, his silver eyes narrowing. Apparently he too had heard the note of concern in the navigator's voice.

Haptis tugged uncomfortably at one of his earlobes. "We're taking the summer route," he began haltingly. "Different seasons, you take different routes, ride different currents." He pointed to various lines along the map. "This route is calm in the summer— peaceful. Little in the way of rough weather. But with the appearance of the Widow Maker, we have to steer wider south than usual to avoid the

Mourner's Straits where the leviathan appears on Haunter's Eve. Adds some time to the trip, but it's easy sailing. But I've never seen the water this choppy so early in summer."

Shalonie cut her gaze toward the water where the skiffs rose and fell, the air elementals keeping them aloft over the ocean surface. The water didn't seem particularly choppy to her — though she could see whitecaps all around them. But she wasn't a sailor and had spent very little time on board a ship. Haptis had lived his entire life at sea. "Do you think we're off course?" she asked bluntly.

The man shook his head. "No, my lady," he replied. "Sailed these waters for years. Never seen the sea like this in summer. Smells more like an autumn wind. It's just with all the talk of the Widow Maker, we're all afeared — jumping as if we had the Night Fleet itself at our stern." Haptis shuddered and gripped a silver medallion hanging around his neck. Shalonie recognized the symbol of Lethune, the sea god revered on the Corsair Isles, carved into the medallion's surface.

He doesn't look confident, Shalonie noted as a cold shiver moved down her spine.

"Oh, looky! He is having a concertina!" Tormy exclaimed excitedly. He scrambled to all four paws. "I is loving concertinas! I is dancing!"

As the large cat went galumphing down the stairs to the lower deck, fluffy orange tail barely missing Dev's face as he ducked to avoid the furry menace, Shalonie frowned down at the maps. The small wooden pipe had moved a bit farther along the surface of the vellum, holding steadily to the course the navigator had mapped out.

The summer path is peaceful, she reminded herself, whitecaps notwithstanding.

165

Chapter 11: Galley

OMEN

"Everyone has to have a job on the ship, Kyr," Omen responded to Kyr's quiet grumbles.

"That's Kadana's rule. Even nobles," the ship's chef Mégeira explained. "And we're short crew this trip."

Omen flicked the wooden spoon he held in his hand, agreeing with her. "Grandma Kadana said we have to earn our keep while we're on board. Liethan is a deckhand for the length of the trip." Omen turned from stirring the giant pot of fragrant Melian fish stew. "And she wants you and me in the galley."

The gimbaled stove rolled a tiny distance to the side as the force of the waves increased, allowing several heated pots and pans to ride out the movement.

"Better than mending sails like Dev." Omen adjusted the cast iron cauldron, careful not to touch the small sun stone burning its heat in one of the stovetop's round openings.

Of course, Shalonie gets to work with the navigator.

The long row of carved wooden storage cabinets rattled as kitchen requisites bounced along in concert with the waves below. Carved sigils covered every inch of the cabinets, the binding magic keeping the insides cool with the help of tiny ice elementals. Omen wondered if the creatures would try to escape their confines if the rough, bouncing sea provided an opportunity.

Never know with children of the elements . . . Kadana has no dearth of magic onboard, that's for sure.

166

Kyr sneezed and looked up at him from a hunched-over crouch; the boy picked at a brown potato with a long knife. "But the cabinets are talking. And these eyes are looking at me. Makes my nose tickle."

"Peeling potatoes is like writing poetry. After your first million spuds, you get it down." Mégeira laughed. "It'll teach you to not joke about hardtack and fish fat."

Omen eyed the older woman. Mégeira was queen of the kitchen, and the galley was her realm. The Golden Voyage's cook didn't strike Omen as a poet, however. He noted her dark, silver-streaked braids and her large dark eyes, surrounded by hairline cracks that were beginning to mar her smooth olive skin.

She's from the Corsair Isles. He revised his initial impression. *They eat, drink and breathe poetry. Of course she knows poetry!*

"Spuds notwithstanding, I didn't joke about the food," Omen reminded the woman. "Templar did."

"And your friend Templar has been impressed into fishing duty." Mégeira stuck a spoon in the broth and tasted with her eyes closed. "Delicious. Perfect amount of saffron. The leeks are bold, but I like what they do." She carefully considered. "The captain was right. Omen Daenoth, you are a master of Melian cuisine. Well done, boy."

"Look at all these potatoes!" Kyr exclaimed as if seeing the mountain of yet-to-be-peeled potatoes for the first time. His eyes grew wide as saucers as if a thought had just occurred to him. "Can I eat them, Omen?"

"All of them?" Omen teased.

Kyr nodded solemnly. "Sometimes I get hungry and there's nothing but rocks to eat. I don't like rocks. Potatoes are better."

Sadness tugged down the corners of Omen's smile. *My poor brother.*

Kyr paused in mid-thought, a frown crossing his brow. "How will they fish? The boat goes far too fast to cast a line. And this ship isn't a fishing vessel. Are there even nets? How will they fish?" Panic caught in Kyr's throat. "Tyrin could fall in and drown. Deep in the dark of the sea. There is no mercy. Only cold, cold, cold and dark, dark, dark."

As Kyr's tone rose in intensity, Mégeira turned and stared at him, her teeth grinding together as the muscles of her jaw worked. Omen saw the furtive movement as she pinched a small bit of salt and threw it over her shoulder.

Warding off evil.

"The captain makes her own luck." Mégeira sounded rattled by Kyr's outburst. "The cold cabinets keep food fresh, but supplies last only about a week with a full crew. We used to live on hardtack, salted beef and brown ale for the rest of our journeys. But the captain makes her own luck. You should go see." She seemed suddenly eager to dismiss the brothers from her kitchen. "I imagine that's where your friend and your cats are right now. Young master Liethan won't be far." She cleared her throat. "You should go."

Changed her tune. All of a sudden she can't wait to get rid of us.

"Are you sure you don't want us helping with the rest of the meal prep?" Omen asked, slightly dispirited. *Kyr's words really bothered her.*

"What about the rest of the potatoes?" Kyr asked, unaware.

"I have an idea," Omen said before Mégeira could answer. "Let me try something." He didn't want to leave the job unfinished.

He focused his thoughts on the potatoes, picturing the whiteness that lay beneath the thick skins. He imagined removing the skins like one would remove a coat. A familiar musical tune filled his mind, instantly bringing forth the psionic pattern that triggered his mental power. A tiny thump hammered against the back of his skull, just behind his ears. He ignored it.

On his prompting, one potato rolled from the stack, freshly peeled and gleaming with moisture, its skin in a crumpled heap.

Many, Omen thought and repeated the procedure, the music swelling in his thoughts.

Thump. Thump. Thump. He ignored it.

The mountain of potatoes shifted slightly and wobbled into perfect stacks, peeled and ready to be cooked.

An audible gasp came from Mégeira. "Salt and sea protect us."

"Omen," Kyr sang out with delight. "You used your psionics to peel the potatoes. That's genius! 7 would love that!"

Omen was sure his father wouldn't approve of using psionics as a kitchen shortcut, especially since he felt ragged with exhaustion as soon as he unchained his mind from peeling the spuds.

A cantrip probably would have been easier.

"Maybe we'll keep this to ourselves," Omen suggested. "Though it gives me another idea . . ."

"Off with the two of you," Mégeira shooed them out, her voice ringing of false bravado. She cast a sideways look at Omen and Kyr in turn. "Send the cabin boy to serve, and tell the captain that dinner will be on in half an hour, an hour for the crew."

"Come on Kyr," Omen said with a cheerfulness he didn't feel. "Let's see what Tormy and Tyrin are up to." *At least she's as bothered by me as she is by Kyr now.*

The boy returned the long kitchen knife to a wooden butcher block nailed to the counter. He smiled at Mégeira. "I'm sorry about the whispering. The elements don't like to be imprisoned."

Omen ushered his brother out of the galley before he could speak again.

Even from below deck, Omen could hear Kadana's lively laughter up above, accompanied by a rousing round of applause and . . .

Is that a concertina?

Omen and Kyr emerged on deck to a most curious sight. Tormy floated five inches above the wooden planks. He hopped midair from side to side in an impressively rhythmical jig fueled by the comical concertina stylings of a stocking-capped sailor. The man's silver curls bounced merrily, and his aged fingers scrunched and elongated the odd little instrument.

Tormy's paws never touched the deck.

Omen could feel the warm tingle of magic emanating from his cat. He'd never sensed Tormy actively manipulating the energies around him before.

I had no idea he could do that. Since when can my cat use magic?

"Tormy!" Omen yelled out, his surprise bubbling up in an uncharacteristically high-pitched squeak. Excitement swelled through him at the realization. *My cat can do magic! My cat can fly!*

"Omy! Omy! Omy!" The giant cat yipped. "Kadana is saying I is stomping like a dragon. I is saying I is floating like a feather. Then I is floating!"

"Your cat . . ." Kadana spat out between gales of laughter. "Arp was playing. Your cat started dancing . . . Almost put holes in the planks. I told Tormy to get his twinkle toes off my ship. And he did." Kadana failed to gather her mirth. She'd turned red in the face and sputtered incoherently.

"This is being funnessnessness," Tormy hollered and sprang over three startled sailors' heads to softly land at Omen's feet. "I is flying like the little skiffs."

"Skiffs?" Omen asked, more confused than ever.

"The fishing skiffs." Tormy nosed toward the open sea. "Templar is catching fishies for dinners."

At a considerable distance, two small wooden skiffs hung over the water as if suspended by ropes. Strung between them, like a hammock, a bulky net swayed in the breeze, its wiggling bounty providing counter to ever-increasing gusts.

"Feeeeeeeeesh!" Tormy exclaimed in ecstasy.

Omen strained against the intense reflection of sunlight on the water. He could barely make out Templar's mop of long black hair whipping against his billowing white shirt.

Adroitly Templar helped the other sailor in his skiff tighten the ends of the net and scoop up the sides so there'd be no escape for their catch. The other skiff mirrored the action. Both skiffs turned toward the Golden Voyage in harmonious unison and started a rapid approach.

Omen stood dumbfounded. "Your little skiffs fly?" he asked. "How?"

"You're honestly asking how Kadana acquired yet another piece of jaw-dropping magic?" Shalonie joined them at

171

the rail.

"Seemed practical," Kadana said and wiped the last tears of laughter from her eyes. "The fishing's good out here. The skiffs are easy to control if you have a little magic talent, which your friend has in spades. Templar can ride them like a goblin rides a moor pony."

Not that I've ever seen a goblin, or a moor pony for that matter.

"The skiffs talk like the cupboards," Kyr mused. "Even over a distance."

More elementals?

"Where's Tyrin?" Shalonie said out of nowhere. "I thought he was with you in the galley."

"Tyrin!" Kyr gasped and slammed against the railing so hard Omen thought the boy's thin body would topple overboard.

As the skiffs raced toward the ship, Omen spotted a small orange dot against Templar's white shirt. He realized the kitten had been balancing on Templar's shoulder, but at that very moment the little creature began a clawed descent down Templar's sleeve.

"He's going for the fish!" Omen shouted. "Templar! Templar!"

* *Templar! Grab Tyrin!* * But even the psionically sent warning came too late. They all watched in paralyzed horror as Tyrin swiped at the ropes, missed and tumbled, snout first, toward the waves below.

Omen blasted a psionic shield under the tiny cat but the waves crushed his erratic energy, sending a blast of agony back at Omen. He collapsed to his knees in time to see his giant orange Tormy hurtle the rail and jump into the waters below.

"No!" Omen's mouth tried but failed to form the word. His head felt like it would burst as the pain of the returned psionic blast ricocheted around his skull. Far away, he heard Kyr wailing a long string of Kahdess words. His voice sounded raw.

"Kadana! Do something!" Shalonie shrieked.

Kadana's strong hands lifted Omen. "Breathe, boy. Breathe! And open your eyes."

She held him up against her strong body, trapping him against the railing.

He watched, helpless, as Tormy bounced over the sea foam crests of the wild ocean waters. The cat's paws never touched the surface.

"Tormy's nearly there," Kadana murmured, her words barely gilding over the concern in her tone.

Like an enormous hawk, Tormy swooped down on the tiny orange speck making its way toward the top of a violent wave. The water reached up and pulled the small cat under. Tormy scooped his paw down, the pads squeezing together to form a leathery ladle. He completed the arc of the swipe, depositing what appeared like a tiny sopping ball of dark orange yarn back into the skiff.

"He's got him!" Omen blurted out and fell back against his grandmother. The agony of the returned psionic blast had folded in on itself, leaving only a dull ache. He felt as if his body and mind were wrapped in itchy, wet wool. His eyelids ceased to obey and fluttered closed.

It's all the potatoes fault!

He was only vaguely aware of a large furry form settling down beside him.

"Omen!" Kadana said his name sharply. "Omen! Wake up!" Two quick slaps sparked across his cheeks. He opened his eyes to see Kadana smiling at him.

"There you are, my boy!" She helped him to his feet. "Can't say I've had many of my grandsons faint on me. Granddaughters maybe." She chuckled lightly. "You'll be fine."

Omen squeezed her hand. "Thanks . . . Did Tormy really fly?"

"Yup, saved the little one," Kadana said, sounding impressed.

Tormy lay in a side crescent a few feet away, licking at his wet front paws with great care. Omen crouched down beside him and wound his fingers through Tormy's damp ruff. The big cat purred softly. "You saved your brother. You're a hero."

"I is being a great adventuring cat," Tormy agreed. "I is flying, but I is not being a bird. I is not having wings. Maybe I is being a wizard. I probably is needing a hat."

Omen nodded. "You can have all the hats you want." The cat's innocent pondering warmed his heart.

"You frightened me!" Kyr shrilled from a few feet away, still sounding horrified. "Kyr will be alone if all the green is gone; there is only dust and shadows that scream and claw."

Omen frowned as he pushed through the circle gathered around Kyr. The boy was holding a sopping wet orange kitten in his hands.

It's bad when he starts referring to himself by name.

"It's fine, Kyr," he told his brother gently and placed a hand on the boy's frail shoulder, trying to calm him. Residual fear made Omen's heart pound with the beat of a military march.

Don't know how calming I can possibly be. I'm still

sweating like a hog in summer. He snatched back his hand. "Everything's fine." He tried to sound confident.

"Yes, Omen's right," Shalonie echoed the sentiment and clapped Omen on the back soundly.

Omen could see in Shalonie's eyes that she too was merely playacting for Kyr's benefit as Omen repeated, "Everything is fine."

"Fine!" Templar snarled as he climbed aboard the ship. "My stars!" He staggered to the deck and sank down against the railing. Weakly, he watched as the sailors started to pull the tangle of filled nets on board. "Sure, everything is fine," he spat and glared up at Omen. "If you don't count the fact that my brain is bleeding. Bit loud there, Oh Psionic Master! I thought Lilyth was bluffing when she said you Daenoths could rip through a psionic shield. Do you have to be so bloody loud about it?"

Oops, Omen thought. *My father did warn me not to try that with someone else. I should know better!* He and his family frequently communicated telepathically. 7, Lilyth and Omen could do so with ease, having trained together for years. He and Templar had never practiced the skill. *I'm lucky he didn't lash out at me. We both could have ended up hurt.*

"I was trying to get you to help Tyrin," Omen said apologetically. "I didn't think you saw him going in."

"I didn't," Templar admitted. "But I couldn't do anything to help him after you shouted like a mad beast. You stunned me. Blasted right through all my defenses. Why on earth does anyone need psionics that powerful?"

"Potatoes," Kyr answered earnestly, still clutching Tyrin to his chest, even though the little cat was wiggling in an effort to shake the water from his fur.

175

"Right — sorry Templar," Omen cut in before Kyr could elaborate.

Let's not spread the potato story around.

Omen stepped around Tormy to help his friend back to his feet. Despite Templar's claim that his brain was bleeding, he appeared to be recovering swiftly.

"I should hope you're sorry! There's something very wrong with you, Omen Daenoth," Templar huffed, though Omen could see that he was not really angry.

"There I am," Templar lamented for Omen's benefit, "out on the water, trying to catch fish for your cats—"

"I is catching them too!" Tyrin piped up, still squirming in Kyr's tight hold. "I almost had that little &*^#%@!"

Templar laughed at that. "It was a swordfish, Tyrin. It would have pulled you under."

"Fish have swords?" Kyr exclaimed, eyes widening.

"Not those kind of swords," Omen assured him. "Tyrin, you almost drowned!"

"I is catching dinner!" the little cat protested. He looked suddenly horrified and turned his amber gaze toward Kyr. "We is still liking dinner, right?"

Kyr nodded. "And lunch too," he assured the cat. "But I like the green better. I will eat rocks if the green stays."

Wondering if his brother would ever get out of the habit of calling the people in his life "the green," Omen smiled assuredly. "No one is going anywhere, Kyr. Tyrin's fine. Tormy's fine. I'm fine. Everyone's fine."

Kyr nodded, but his face was pinched with worry. "Is everyone real?"

While his question sparked looks of confusion from everyone around them, Omen understood what he was asking. "Yes, Kyr. Everyone is real."

"Even the people in the water?" the boy asked, gazing back out at the ocean waves. "They're very loud and they didn't help when I called to them."

Kadana frowned. She looked to the sea, then to the two skiffs tightly secured to the deck. "Everyone made it back in," she stated, self-assured, though Omen could see her doing a swift head count of the sailors on deck.

"Not real then," Kyr turned away from the waves. "Just shadows. Fish with swords and angry faces."

"Why don't we all go see about dinner," Kadana suggested. "This is probably the most excitement you'll get all trip. Summer crossings to Kharakhan are very peaceful."

"Not summer," Kyr muttered. Omen patted the boy on the back and steered him below deck.

177

Chapter 12: Dinner

OMEN

O men gaped through the open door into the great
cabin. "It's . . . different . . . bigger!" he exclaimed, intrigued.

Kadana beamed and waved the six hungry youngsters
into her private quarters. The cats, one large, one small,
padded behind the group, giggling and whispering to each
other. All Omen could make out were the words "flying"
and "fish."

The captain's plain cabin had been lavishly transformed
into a spacious dining room, fully prepared with an extravagant feast. A long mahogany table, twelve formal, heavily
embroidered chairs and a long dark wood buffet took up the
space Kadana's bunk and desk had formerly occupied.

*Where did all that fancy furniture come from? How does
it fit?* Omen bit his lower lip. The curiosity sparked by the
depth and breadth of magic so casually on display gnawed
at him.

*Kadana isn't a spellcaster, but she surrounds herself
with the most extraordinary magic.*

Large, enchanted golden orbs placed strategically
around the room emitted a golden glow and lent a warm
and inviting atmosphere to the already comfortable space.

Kyr glared at the humming orbs as he entered. "Shh!" he
snapped at the lighting. "You're being rude."

More elementals!

The cabin's smell of cedar planks and sea salt had min-

178

gled with the delicious fragrances of a sumptuous meal and drew Omen's full attention.

Sweet. Exotic. Spice. Can't wait to dig in!

All flat surfaces were laden with an abundance of bowls steaming with crisp vegetables and scented grains. Plates of every conceivable shape had been piled high with samplings of delicacies from the sea. Omen eyed a porcelain oval brimming with squid ink pasta.

That looks so good. His mouth watered involuntarily. *How did Mégeira fix all of this? I was in the kitchen all morning, and I only saw half this stuff.* He noted a deep serving bowl with his Melian fish stew. *Center stage.* He smiled to himself.

Kadana stood at the head of the table, filling seven goblets with a bubbly pink liquid.

"A toast!" she called out as a cabin boy in stark white passed drinks to Shalonie and Liethan.

As the companions took their seats, Omen surveyed the offerings on the sideboard buffet. He noted several empty vessels.

More coming. Yum!

"To a successful journey!" Kadana raised her glass. "Enjoy! We can't eat like this every night."

Omen rushed to accept a goblet and drained it on cue. *Hope Tormy didn't catch that last part.*

"Melian sparkling wine?" he asked his grandmother.

"I suppose." She studied the bottle still in her hand. "Beren had a few cases of Litranian wines sent up. They're all very good. Even if this one is pink."

Litrania. Never visited that region. Omen made a mental note.

Two cabin boys pushed several of the chairs to the far

179

wall, making room for Tormy at the table.

Omen took a fried shrimp from a delicate silver bowl and dipped the morsel in the accompanying red sauce. The sharp bite of horseradish brought water to his eyes.

"Tasty," Omen said, waving his hand in front of Tormy's face. "Not for cats. Too spicy. You'll cry."

The myriad of muscles in Tormy's fluffy orange face did a dance of perplexed outrage. "I is not crying!"

"Just have the shrimp without the sauce."

Defiantly, Tormy dipped his tongue into the vessel and licked up most of the spicy sauce.

"Nightfire!" Omen dove to the sideboard and reached for the carafe of cream next to the strawberries.

"Omy! Omy! Omy!" Tormy wailed. "Hot. Hot. Burn. Burn!" Tears dripped down the cat's face.

Stunned, nobody moved as Omen dumped the entire carafe of cream into an empty soup tureen. The company also heroically refrained from laughing as Tormy shoved his large pink tongue into the thick cream in an effort to soothe his burning mouth.

The cat let out a sigh of relief and proceeded to clean the tureen of every remnant of the soothing liquid.

"Attaboy, Tormy. That'll put hair on your chest!" Dev passed the carafe to a petrified cabin boy. "I think we need more cream."

"What's not &#*@^$! hot?" Tyrin hopped next to the shrimp bowl and sniffed an oval platter with a spread of a dozen steamed lobsters. "Can I have a whole lobster?" He brazenly pawed at a crustacean roughly his own size.

"Why don't you take that one?" A wide smirk crossed Kadana's lips, and she filled a different goblet with amber liquid from a cut crystal bottle. She did not offer the drink to the boys or Shalonie. "Eat. Eat! The cats already started."

"Your cabin . . . changed?" Omen ventured as he sat next to Kadana. He picked up a shrimp heavy with fried batter and coconut shavings.

Mmm. No need for sauce.

"The Golden Voyage has rooms that are larger than they should be, a galley kitchen that allows for both cooking and cold storage, a saltwater converter, and captain's quarters that I can change as I see fit. The only thing it can't do is fly." Kadana had a jolly sparkle in her eyes as she switched from the amber liquid to dark red wine. She nodded to the cabin boy to fill her guests' glasses as well.

"But you have flying skiffs," Liethan threw in, sipping from his glass with care. "I've never seen flying fishing skiffs before. My Grandpa Seth would love those."

"I acquire things," Kadana said simply.

"How?" Shalonie asked outright.

"A combination of brute force and cunning," Kadana answered, the look on her face oddly both carefree and serious. "That's what I hear say."

Omen found his wild grandmother more and more interesting by the minute.

"Of course," Shalonie agreed. "We've all heard the songs."

"Mostly lies," Kadana countered jovially. "Especially those written by Beren."

Omen sputtered his drink. "The Ballad of the Bloody Beast?"

"Lies."

"The Rhyme of the Rescued Realm?"

"Lies."

"The Death of the Mother of Swords?" Liethan picked

up his wine. "Well, I suppose that one isn't true. You're obviously alive."

"Actually, that one is true." Kadana looked smug.

Liethan put down his goblet.

"But how did you acquire this ship?" Shalonie pressed. "There must be thousands of people who wanted it."

"And I am the one who won it." Kadana chugged her wine and poured herself another before the serving boy could reach her. "And I'm the one who can keep it. I make my own luck. Always have."

"Lady Kadana, you've said you won the ship in a card game," Dev fished for more.

"On the Golden Voyage, I'm captain not lady," Kadana corrected lightly. "It was a card game like no other, the conclusion of an adventure that changed the course of all of our lives."

Omen perked up. His own mother rarely spoke of her youth, the time she had spent traveling the world with Indee, Kadana, Beren, Kylee, Arra and Simetra Corsair, and Diemos, the scariest of them all. He looked forward to the story.

"It was winter. Many winters ago. We had fought our way through to the top of the Mountain of Shadow."

Both Omen and Shalonie simultaneously gave small starts. They looked at each other.

"We'd been searching for some artifact or another." Kadana settled into an obviously abbreviated version of the tale. "Beren spotted it first, on a wall. He grabbed for it. At that point, Kylee was barely alive and wouldn't have made it if Arra hadn't called up her powers to bind the last spark of life in Kylee's body."

"My middle name is Kyel — named for Lady Kylee,"

182

Liethan added between bites of butter-drenched crab.

Omen tried to picture the scene. Lady Kylee lived in Melia, on Dragonberry Lane. His mother called her a thief, but Lady Kylee had always been generous and kind to him. He had a hard time picturing the delicate, dark-haired Daoinee woman as part of his mother's legendary — or infamous — group of adventurers.

Kylee sure never brags about it.

"Something about Arra throwing that spell right as Beren touched the artifact opened up a random portal," Kadana continued casually as if she were telling them about the weather outside. "Threw each of us for a spin. We all ended up in different, wildly strange places."

Shalonie stayed silent, but Omen could tell she was drinking in every bit of information.

"Don't know much about the others, but found myself at a card game with heavily armed, very powerful looking people — Not people exactly . . . things really. Didn't know who they were. Didn't know the rules," Kadana said with laughter in her voice. "But I played like my life depended on it."

"Which it did?" Dev asked, sounding sure of the answer.

Kadana nodded, as expected.

"Bluffed my way through the round." She poured herself another goblet of the red wine. "Put everything I had in the pot. I knew once the game was over, I would have to fight. I was just trying to gain time, to prepare."

"And you won?" Shalonie asked, a mix of disbelief and awe on her face.

"Everyone had dropped out." Kadana scooted her chair closer in. "Except this giant tattooed wizard. He must have been seven feet tall, covered in green and blue sigils all over his body."

"A Ven'tarian sorcerer," Shalonie gasped.

"That's right," Kadana said, impressed. "But I didn't know that at the time."

Her fingers reached for a gooey lobster roll. "He threw a little carving of a galleon into the pot. Said that was the key to the most fabulous ship in the world. Trouble was, I had nothing else to throw in."

"What did you do?" Liethan asked, completely absorbed in the telling.

"What could I do?" She popped the entire lobster roll into her mouth and chewed heartily.

Omen looked around. Everyone's eyes were glued on Kadana, including the cats'.

That's some good, fast story weaving.

"I put Beren in the pot and won the hand," Kadana finished, deadpan.

Shalonie gasped again, her eyes wide. "You put your son up as collateral in a card game?" She sounded genuinely upset.

Kadana shrugged it off. "I won. And I got the key to this boat."

"But Beren?" Shalonie dug in. "How old was he?"

"Beren could take care of himself," Kadana said, unfazed. "Ask him sometime where he ended up. Funny, he never wrote a song about that." She laughed heartily. "Between getting the key and getting the ship, I had my hands full. Didn't make it back to Kharakhan for years, and by then everyone had scattered to the four winds."

Omen couldn't tell if there was an edge of sadness in Kadana; it seemed unlikely.

"It all worked out." Kadana reached across the table to

heap her bowl full of Omen's Melian stew. "It always does."

Omen checked on the cats, who gobbled and slurped with abandon. Seeing his brother had only piled potatoes on his plate, much to the horror of both Tormy and Tyrin, Omen sighed. "You can't eat just potatoes, Kyr," he told him.

Kyr shook his head. "I'm angry at the fish," he insisted.

"All the more reason to take your revenge and eat them," Dev suggested, holding out a plate of seared Luminal sea bass to the boy.

Omen laughed at that, more so when he saw the startled look on Kyr's face. To his surprise, Kyr took the platter and began piling fish on his plate.

"If that is true, I will be vengeful," the boy agreed pragmatically.

Tormy, who had moved on from the cream to swordfish steaks, purred happily. "We is being very vengefullnessness, on account of the fact that feeesh is good."

"Kharakhan. You boys will love it." Kadana poured a thick, blue substance into a tiny glass and threw it back. "You too, Shalonie. Spent the best of the worst of my misspent youth in Kharakhan." She laughed, a harsh sound. "Ended up settling down there too."

"You're sure she's your *grandmother*?" Templar whispered smugly, which made Kadana laugh with a raucous edge. She poured another glass of the blue alcohol.

Mother did say she drinks a lot.

"I'll tell you all you need to know about dealing with Kharakhians." Kadana grabbed a whole lobster off the center platter and cracked it open with her bare hands. "Hit 'em hard." She chewed like a hungry dog and threw back another gulp. "Amandirian ice wine. Not for the inexperienced drinker." She stoppered the bottle and directed the cabin boy to carry it away. Oddly enough she did not appear even slightly drunk, her gaze still clear, her movements unhampered by inebriation.

"And . . ." Omen prompted, wondering what he would need to know about dealing with Kharakhians.

"That's it." Kadana shrugged. "Just hit 'em hard. If they get back up, hit 'em harder. Pretty straightforward."

The dessert course ended further discussion.

"This should be an outstanding crossing." Kadana tapped her spoon against the caramelized sugar top of her custard. "You'll see. Easy. This time of year the weather is fantastic, and the ocean is smooth as butter. Nothing to worry about."

Chapter 13: Dessert

SHALONIE

For Shalonie, dinner had proven to be a curious affair. As she carefully cracked the burnt sugar top of her vanilla custard, she reflected on the goings-on. While Tormy's antics with the overly spicy food and Kyr's amusing declaration that he was mad at the fish were certainly entertaining, she found Kadana's stories as disturbing as they were enlightening.

"The Ballad of the Bloody Beast," "The Rhyme of the Rescued Realm," were not, as Kadana had insisted, all lies. Shalonie had researched the songs quite thoroughly when she'd first heard them. Having grown up in a land of music and song, she was well-versed in the embellishments bards tended to add to their stories. But far from embellishing these tales, Beren Deldano had in fact left out several of the more extraordinary parts of the stories — concerned perhaps that the actual events would have been too unsavory for a Melian audience.

Like "The Ballad of the Bloody Beast." It hadn't been only the beast who'd been bloodied. The song failed to mention the entire city that had been massacred and eaten prior to the battle that had ended the monster's vicious rampage. *Wholesale slaughter generally doesn't pair well with a catchy tune,* she thought. *Or maybe it does.*

The other stories were even worse in some regard, and Shalonie found it intriguing that Kadana shrugged all the tales off as lies. *Perhaps that would make sense in a room*

187

full of children. Shalonie frowned as she looked around. Neither Templar nor she were children, and certainly Devastation Machelli had seen his fair share of darkness.

Omen is only fifteen, she reminded herself, though it was hard to reconcile the young man's actual age with his physique. Tall and powerfully built, there were no men on board the ship who would be a physical match for him — save Templar. *Blood of a god.* She shook her head. *I can't begin to predict what Omen might be capable of one day.*

Still, I suppose it's possible that Kadana sees us all as children. Liethan was Omen's age, and while the Corsair boy himself possessed the faerie blood of his grandmother, his golden looks were still boyish and carefree. *Grew up around Corsair sailors. Probably knows more curse words than Tyrin ever will.*

Certainly Kadana looked at Kyr and saw a child, skinny, harmless and innocent. Though from what Shalonie knew of his past, Kyr was older than all of them, and far from innocent, having endured the most horrific conditions known to any immortal. He possessed the same divine blood Omen did, but in his case that had been all that had kept him alive where a mortal would have perished.

In spite of all that, the boy appeared to be the soul of innocence, hardly different from the two cats. *Perhaps that's how Kadana sees all of us,* Shalonie reasoned.

"Now, you never did tell me what this trip is all about," Kadana proclaimed after finishing another of her many stories.

Shalonie glanced over at Omen, curious. Truthfully, beyond knowing he needed to go to the Mountain of Shadow, she didn't know the details either. *He's been surprisingly mum on the subject.*

"Um . . ." Omen glanced uncertainly over at Kyr, who seemed entranced by the contents of the footed bowl in front of him — ever so cautiously tapping his spoon on the caramelized sugar to get to the velvety cream beneath. "That's actually a bit complicated."

Neither Kyr nor the cats were paying much attention to the conversation, focused instead on their desserts. Templar and Liethan exchanged knowing looks. *They know what's going on.*

"Complicated?" Templar demanded. "What's complicated about it?"

Omen sighed heavily. "It got complicated," he explained. "More complicated. It's a bit hard to explain . . . or speak about . . . or . . . if I even hint that I'm not . . . actually I can't say that either . . ."

He trailed off, and Kadana slammed a heavy bottle down on the table in front of them. "I hate complicated," she said. Then grinned. "Grain-cast on the other hand — never complicated. Especially if it's made from Kharakhian barley. " She pulled the cork from the bottle labeled just "Grast," a common name for the hard grain-made drink. She began filling their goblets with the amber liquid. "Drink up."

Shalonie smiled, though she made no move to obey — she wasn't a drinker beyond the occasional glass of Melian wine. *No, thank you.* The boys, however, were quick to comply with the order, all attempting to mimic Kadana as she threw back her head and drank the fiery liquid in one gulp. Dev alone managed, seeming as unaffected by the drink as Kadana herself. Kadana had swallowed an obscene amount of alcohol that evening and still showed no signs of drunkenness.

While Omen, Templar, and Liethan all grimaced at the burn of the drink, Kyr shrieked in outrage and grabbed Tyrin's bowl of cream and gulped it down.

Kadana burst out laughing. "Never did meet an elf who liked grast," she admitted. "Probably should have said something."

"Kyr, stick to the water," Omen urged, patting his brother on the back.

The boy spoke through pressed together teeth. "I don't know how to swim. And the fish with swords is mean. It can see with its hands."

Laughter filled the room at that pronouncement.

"Fish don't have hands, Kyr," Omen reminded the boy indulgently.

"If they have swords, they have hands," Kyr insisted, seemingly unaffected by the laughter, or perhaps simply not understanding the reason for it. "Lots of hands, and arms. Too many arms."

"Is he drunk?" Kadana asked in fascination.

"No," Templar replied, his yellow eyes twinkling. "This is what passes for normal in Omen's world."

Kyr smiled ethereally at Kadana, his face lighting up with happiness. "I like Omen's world. It's green." His smile faded then. "My world wasn't green. We won't go back there. Omen promised."

"No, we won't go back there," Omen agreed, a wistful sadness in his eyes.

Shalonie only knew the vague outline of Kyr's past, but it was enough for her to understand the impact of the boy's words. Judging by the looks of those around the table, they too understood enough to let the topic drop.

"Tyrin's sleepy." Kyr held up the small ball of fur in his

hands, presenting it to the room. Tyrin was curled into a tight ball, sound asleep. While Tormy's eyes were still open, the cat had placed his enormous head down on the edge of the table and was half asleep himself. "Is it bed-time?" Kyr asked. "I wish the boat would stop going up and down. It's hard to sleep."

"Up and down?" Kadana laughed, and indeed to Shalonie the motion was hardly noticeable, the magic of the Ven'tarian ship keeping their progress smooth and steady. "Have to take you sailing in a storm one of these days, my boy, then you'll get some serious up and down. Summer crossings are peaceful. But sleeping is a good idea. Sunup comes early."

Taking that as their cue to retire, they all began to rise. Shalonie paused to thank Kadana for the fine meal and the stories. She was looking forward to doing more research on the Ven'tarian ship come morning and wondered about the spells that kept the boat so steady in the water. She had spied the web of silver embedded into the outer hull of the ship when they'd boarded, and suspected there were spells laid in the metal that controlled the ship's movement and accounted for its steadiness as well as propulsion. She couldn't help but wonder if she could use a Cypher Rune to mimic the spells — something that could calm the waters or steady a rocking ship in a storm.

"It's too late for that one," Kyr told her as she exited the cabin. "You'll need the one for the lightning."

"I'll keep that in mind, Kyr," Shalonie told the boy. She smiled quizzically at Omen who spread his hands in apology.

Shalonie had been given a cabin of her own when she'd come on board, though she knew all the others were sharing various rooms. While the ship's magic expanded the interior, it wasn't infinitely large. Still, her cabin was spacious enough, with a soft bed that was suspended from the ceiling on chains so that it would sway with the natural motion of the vessel. There were more magical globes to light the room, and the fire elementals within them flared brighter as she stepped inside.

She kicked off her boots, and unlaced her jerkin, stripping down to a thin undershirt before climbing onto the bed and pulling out the small notebook she'd placed beneath her pillow. The notebook, bound in soft leather, was small enough to carry around. It was filled with good quality paper, bleached the purest white, so that even a soft mark showed up well against the surface. She'd brought this one along to record her latest findings, and now found herself scribbling down all the things she'd observed about the ship and the countless spells woven throughout it.

Chapter 14: Ghosts

OMEN

"In a night and a day, they were gone . . ." An urgent murmur woke Omen. Still half-asleep, he turned his head toward Kyr's hammock and tried to make out the continuous swell of distressed words coming from the boy.

They had been at sea for a week, and so far all had been peaceful.

"Light!" Omen commanded. The fire elemental orbs placed throughout the cabin blazed to life. "Soft," he amended, and they dimmed to a warm glow. He blinked sleep from his eyes.

"Swallowed through and can't return. But yet return . . . now . . ."

Kyr's quiet litany had been going on for some time — hours perhaps — Omen realized.

"Has Kyr been sleep-talking for long?" he asked Tormy, who lay curled in most of a ball next to him. The cat's bushy tail and fuzzy shank draped off the swing bed, the strain of his weight stressing the chains suspending the frame from the ceiling. Omen was glad he'd thought to reinforce the hooks with a minor carpentry cantrip he'd learned from Liethan's uncle, Catlar.

Tormy sniffed the air. "Kyr is being fast asleep."

"You can tell that by scenting?"

"Peoples is smelling differentnessness when they is being asleep." Tormy ran a paw over his cheek, straightening out a whisker that had gone astray. "The awakenessness smell is fadenessness when they is sleeping long."

"Kyr is saying the same words over and over for a longestness time." A perplexed Tyrin crouched on a beam just above the boy. "I is saying, 'Get up.' And he is not get-upping." The tiny cat sounded anxious.

Omen tried to push himself to his elbows, but the sway of the ocean made moving unexpectedly awkward. His eyes focused on the wound-up hammock where Kyr moaned and babbled, caught in his swinging bed like the very noisy filling of a canvas-cased sausage.

"They ride on the currents beneath the waves. Faces in the water." Kyr lashed about wildly, the confines keeping his wide swings restricted to worm-like wiggles. "Their arrival brings blood and screams."

That's it!

On wobbly legs, Omen braced himself against Tormy's back and stood up. "Kyr!" He called out as he scrambled on his breeches and boots. "Kyr!"

"The crown swims now there is no other way to go," was all Kyr replied.

"Shake him!" Tyrin wailed. "You is better waking-upping Kyr now."

Omen unwound the canvas hammock and shook Kyr's shoulder.

Kyr's eyes opened wide, but he was far from awake. Even in the dim light, the inky black of his wide pupils eclipsed the sunset violet of his irises.

Omen started to reach out to Kyr psionically, but instantly a multifaceted wave of colors flashed in front of his mind's eye like a warning beacon. *Blast! Forgot about the shielding bracelet Dad gave him! Only way past it is to*

194

take it off, and I don't dare do that!

He retreated as fast as he could. But the mere blink brought back the remembrance of the maelstrom of madness he'd seen rage in Kyr's brain, the thousands upon thousands of voices incessantly screaming at the boy in Kahdess. When he'd connected to Kyr on the day of The Dark Heart's attack months ago, Omen had understood the true scope of his brother's strange gift for the first time. *Curse more like. And he bears it without complaint. My poor brother.*

"Kyr, wake up!" Omen's voice cracked with panic. *What if he never wakes up?* The flare of colors had faded from his sight, and he thought he saw both cats glaring at him with accusation and expectation. Tormy had leaped from the bed and was standing beside him.

"I'll get help!" Omen said. "Tyrin, stay with him and . . . purr."

Tyrin yowled and hopped down onto Kyr's chest.

"Don't let them set foot on the deck," the boy whispered, unraveling Omen's nerves further.

He stumbled through his cabin door and into the corridor, keeping a firm grip on Tormy's fur.

"The singing. The singing," Kyr called from behind them and started in on a song made of words so strange that an icy chill swept through Omen, as if the words themselves spoke of something forbidden and destructive, the very sounds holding infection and ruin.

I know that from somewhere. He couldn't place it.

The cabin door to his left swung open, and Dev Machelli emerged from his room. "Omen!" he hissed urgently. "Silence him before the sailors throw him overboard!"

Startled, Omen turned. "He won't wake up."

195

"I've got something for that." Dev crossed the corridor and entered Omen's room. Worried, Omen followed.

"What are you doing?" he demanded, not trusting the man with his brother.

Dev pulled a small vial from some hidden pocket, yanked out the stopper, and held the vial under the boy's nose. Tyrin reared back in distress and hissed hard and low at Dev. But Kyr immediately woke, flinching in shock and proclaiming, "Bad smell!"

"Hurrah! You is being awakenessness!" Tyrin announced as Kyr awkwardly swayed in his hammock.

"Kyr!" Omen crossed to his side. "Are you all right? You were talking in your sleep and you wouldn't wake up."

"You have to keep them off the deck, Omen," Kyr pleaded.

"That's what you said in your sleep." Omen grimaced. "Keep who off the deck?"

"Grandma Kadana is being on the deck with Templar and Liethan," Tormy announced, still waiting in the corridor. "I is hearing whisperings from the sailors as they is being affearednessness of the lights in the water."

"Lights?" Omen stared at his cat. "There are lights in the water? We're days out to sea. There can't be any lights — unless we've met up with another ship." He gripped Kyr's arm. "You all right now?"

The boy nodded glumly. "Bad smells and bad voices."

"Stay here with Tyrin." Omen was already on the move. "I'll go check the deck and see what's going on."

Omen emerged from below deck to discover the ship shrouded in a heavy fog. Small wisps of white drifted past him, hugging the wooden planks of the deck. The elemental lamps burned brightly, trying to hold back both fog and darkness.

Tormy padded softly up beside him, his whiskers flaring as he raised his nose to sniff the salt air. Omen could see Kadana at the wheel with Arbrios, her first mate. The sound of sloshing waves against the side of the ship was different in the muffled fog.

We're hardly moving.

Near the mainmast Liethan worked with the small group of sailors that made up the night crew. They were tugging on ropes, trying to position the sails to catch the cold breeze. Kadana called out orders periodically.

As Omen headed up to the higher deck to speak to his grandmother, he saw Templar standing nearby, peering out into the shrouded darkness.

"Is the fog normal for this time of year?" Omen asked Kadana as he neared.

"No," she stated darkly. "Normally you'd only see this in midautumn. Never in summer."

"These are ill portents," Arbrios groused, leaving Omen hesitant to mention Kyr.

"There!" one of the sailors on the lower deck hollered. "Another one."

Omen turned to look where the man was pointing. A strange bobbing light, pale blue in color, danced in the mist just off the starboard side of the ship.

Templar immediately rushed ahead to get a better look.

Omen joined him. "Any idea what that is?" he asked, keeping his voice low so that it didn't carry farther than Templar and Tormy.

"If I had to guess, I'd say it's a haunting of some sort. Ghost light. It has the feel of necromancy to me," Templar whispered back.

"Kyr was rambling again," Omen told him. "Said we should get everyone off the deck."

"Hard to sail a ship that way." Templar gave a quick look around. "Only a handful of crew right now."

One of the sailors bellowed suddenly, and Omen turned toward the sound. Positioned near the forward mast, the man slowly backed away from a human-sized figure pulsing with light.

Rat's teeth!

The unnatural form was of a man, but it glowed with a pale bluish light. Dark liquid dripped from its body with every step it advanced.

Paralyzed with dread, Omen could only watch as a crab crawled from the ghost's mouth, ran up its face, and disappeared into a hole where the left ear should have been.

Templar drew one of the white bone blades he wore strapped to his belt and rushed toward the ghost. Tormy followed, the large cat hissing ferociously. Omen snapped out of his stupor and charged ahead.

Though the incorporeal figure had no weapons, it reached both knobby, barnacle-encrusted hands out toward Templar. The prince swiped his blade without hesitation, cutting through the glowing shape as if it were only smoke. The form scattered into billowing mist and blew away into the darkness.

"It has substance," Templar called out to the crew. "I felt some resistance when I cut through it."

"There's another one!" a nearby sailor blared.

Omen spun. A tall, dripping ghost stood only inches away. Cold air surged over his skin, raising the hairs on his arms.

For a second he found himself staring, slack-jawed, into

dead, glowing eyes. The stench of rotting fish and seaweed struck his nostrils just as a bony, ice-cold hand closed over his left wrist. His skin burned at the touch, the grip tightening steadily like a vise.

Instinctively Omen staggered back, pulling his hand away. But it was only when Templar sliced through the glowing ghost's spindly forearm that Omen's wrist was freed.

Omen stared at the blisters forming around his wrist. "Don't let them touch you," he warned the others, not certain if the burn had been caused by heat or extreme cold. Both possibilities were disturbing. *These disembodied whatevers can hurt us!*

He needn't have bothered with his warning. Kadana's crew had already abandoned their posts and fled from the few glowing shapes that had appeared around them.

"They're in the water!" someone yelped.

More forms rose from the mist and stood upon the waves, bits of seaweed clinging to them and blowing slowly in the churning fog.

The Golden Voyage was surrounded. Unearthly shapes pressing slowly forward — men, women, children — all glowing, all in various states of decay. Foul water dripped from them as they reached upward as if imploring the sailors on board to help them climb.

Lost souls.

Two more figures materialized on the deck. Templar raced forward to cut through them. "No need to panic!" he called out to a crew already well into the throes of panic. "I'll get rid of them. They're just harmless shapes — keep clear, and I'll cut them down."

"Go on then!" Backed against the wheel, shielding her

first mate, Kadana swiped at two nearly transparent specters with her broad, triangular dagger.

Liethan, holding on to two separate ropes as he'd been abandoned by the men helping him, called out to Omen, "Grab these and tie them down. The sail will swing free if we don't."

Omen didn't question him. *Don't know ships or sails.* He leaped forward and wrested the ends of the ropes through metal fastenings set in the deck. His fingers started to twist a knot he'd forgotten he'd learned. *Thank you, Lily's dopey five strand braid.* The ropes pulled away from him, cutting into his skin, but he curled his fingers around them and worked on completing the knot despite the slick moisture of blood mixed with sweat.

"If we can—" Omen strained to formulate a plan while fighting to complete his task, but his words were cut off. Far out to sea familiar music sounded over the waves and wind.

The Widow Maker had begun to sing as it had in Melia, weaving its terrible tune and ensnaring the minds of all who heard it.

Urgolath's song! Omen's stomach dropped. *I can hear it . . . Kyr was warning me.*

Mournful and melodic, the song of the Widow Maker reached across the water with vicious intent. Omen felt the beating pulse of the percussion throb through the ship's deck and tremble through the waves surrounding them. The notes, haunting and echoing, nearly disrupted the low background sounds of his own psionic shield. Urgolath sang of loss and sorrow, calling the living to join the dead.

"Shield your minds!" Omen called out as he fortified his own shield. He knew the moment the warning had left his

lips that it would do no good. Liethan, Templar, and
Kadana all had enough minor psionic ability to shield
themselves from the song's harrowing effect — but he
doubted the crew could protect themselves.

"Omy! Omy!" Tormy wailed, confirming his fear. The
large cat held down two sailors who were trying to leap
from the ship. He'd stuck his claws through the sailors' belts
and pinned them in place. But a third sailor, a tall woman
with brown hair, was moving past him, her blank gaze on
the water rising and falling with each wave.

In a surprising move, Tormy hopped forward and kicked
the woman in the chest with one of his back feet, knocking
her down. Tormy wiggled and squirmed, still keeping hold
of the two men, and then promptly sat down on the fallen
sailor.

The shock of Tormy's impact and of having a horse-
sized cat sit on her snapped the woman from her stupor.
"It's going to eat me! The cat is going to eat me!" she
screamed and flailed about.

"I is not eatings you! I is savings you!" Tormy protested,
discombobulated.

"Grab the others!" Kadana shouted out as she caught
hold of the back of Arbrios' belt, holding him in place when
he too headed toward the ship's railing.

Liethan caught two sailors nearest him, and wound the
long rope he was holding around both their bodies. The
rope, still attached to the mainsail, held them firmly fixed
in place though they still tried to shuffle toward the rail.
Across the deck, more apparitions manifested — two ghost
women draped in long white gowns, shells, and seaweed
tangled in their dripping wet hair. The left arm of one had
been eaten away, but both forms walked forward toward Li-

201

ethan, hands extended imploringly.

Templar raced ahead and cut through them, once again scattering them into the mist.

"Omen!" Shalonie's voice rang through the night air as she, Kyr, and Dev emerged. Dev slammed the door leading below deck shut behind them, pressing his shoulder against it forcibly. A loud thump sounded, and it tried to swing open, bodily moving Dev who pressed harder to keep it closed. Kyr pushed against the door with his feeble strength.

"All below are ensnared." Shalonie threw her back against the wood, pressing her feet against the deck. "They'll jump overboard."

"Need something to bar the way!" Dev shouted as another hard thump nearly threw him back.

Omen looked around for some sort of bar or barrier even as he shoved his hands up against the wooden frame. His strength far outmatched Dev, Kyr, and Shalonie's might combined, and the door held firmly. "Barrels maybe?" Omen suggested, spying a number of large wooden barrels tied off to one side.

"We have to get this lot locked up first!" Kadana called down. She had tied off the spokes of the wheel to a steadying rope and was dragging her first mate toward the lower deck. The sailor beneath Tormy was still wailing in protest, sounding as if she were being murdered. Tormy, upset and agitated, thrashed his tail from side to side, striking the screaming woman in the face with each flick.

An animalistic shriek rained down upon them, and Kyr danced away from the door as he pointed. "Omen! The crow's nest!"

Omen looked upward to see the young, ginger-haired

lookout who had been up in the crow's nest, climb over the edge of the wooden frame. With him was the ship's monkey. Tail firmly wrapped around the rail, back feet clinging fiercely, the little creature tried to pull the sailor back from the edge. The monkey chittered and cried in distress, its frantic gestures showing Omen that even though it could not talk, it still understood the danger.

The song of the Widow Maker rang onward relentlessly, beckoning. Only the steady purring thrum of Omen's shield kept his mind clear of its influence.

Without warning, the lookout jumped, his body hurtling downward toward the deck. The monkey screamed. Immediately, the small creature raced down the mast pole after the man.

Omen shifted the song in his mind, adding a new tune to the base of his shield as he reached outward with his psionics toward the plunging sailor. The pattern he needed formed instantly, and he grabbed the tumbling body, the impact of weight and force driving him to one knee as he focused all his attention on saving the sailor before the man's head could strike the deck. He was vaguely aware of Dev, Shalonie, and Kyr trying to hold the door he'd just abandoned, but his mind was centered on the cushion of force around the young man.

He slowed. Stopped. Inches above the planks.

Carefully, Omen lowered the sailor to the deck even as the little monkey leaped from the shrouds and landed on the sailor's chest. The creature cried and whimpered as it slapped tiny hands against the young man's cheeks as if trying to coax some sign of life from him. The pitiful whimpers pulled at Omen's heart.

"He's all right," he tried to tell the monkey, forgetting

203

momentarily that the fuzzy animal wouldn't understand his words. Omen tried to stand back up. Pain flared through him, and he had to gasp in a few deep breaths to steady his flailing shield. *I can do this.* He reset the calming purr of his shielding song, his eyes moving instinctively toward Tormy as if to remind himself of the sound of the cat's purr.

Tormy still struggled with the three sailors he was holding in place. The woman caught under him was still hollering in terror. *At least her fear is keeping her mind free of the song.*

Kadana passed by Tormy as she dragged Arbrios downward. She grabbed hold of the woman's arm and hauled her from beneath the large cat's orange rump. "On your feet! A big, fluffy, orange cat sat on you!" she snapped. "Get over it!" The woman fell silent as she stumbled after Kadana, the voice of her captain breaking through her panic.

"We need to get them below." Kadana moved toward the door that Dev and Shalonie were just barely holding shut.

"It's just a matter of time before they break through," Dev warned. "And sooner or later someone will think to go through a porthole. We have to stop this blasted song!"

"Omen, can you do what your dad did back in Melia?" Templar's question was underscored with doubt.

Omen quaked, remembering the terrible sound that had echoed through his mind when 7 had blasted the Widow Maker. He also remembered the dire warnings his father had given him. *If I attack it, I'll likely end up brain-dead.*

"No," he admitted freely. "I can't begin to understand what my father did. My powers are not trained to that extent."

"Can you shield the ship from the song?" his grandmother asked quickly.

Omen squirmed at having to say *no* again. "I can probably shield four or five other people, but not for long. Certainly no longer than an hour."

"It doesn't know who is on board," Kyr announced suddenly. "It wonders, it fears, and it hears my voice when I
speak of the dead. But it doesn't know."

"Is that importantnessness, Kyr?" Tyrin asked urgently.
The kitten poked his head out from the boy's coat pocket.
Omen knew that Kyr's mind was protected from the song
by the bracelet around his wrist, and he was glad that his
father's guess that the cats were not affected had been correct.

The door behind them thumped hard again, shoving Dev
forward. Templar reached out to help brace it, holding it in
place.

"We are surrounded by fish," Kyr whispered to the little
cat, and Omen smiled sadly at the boy. His moments of
strangeness took him down paths that Omen couldn't comprehend.

"I don't know what. . ." Omen began only to trail off as
Kyr's words replayed in his head. "It doesn't know . . . there
may be something I can do after all." He looked up brightly. "I don't know if it will work, but I can at least try."

"If you can think of something, do it!" Kadana urged.
She waved one hand through the air as if to encompass her
ship. "No wind, no momentum and this blasted song —
we're dead in the water."

Omen, heart pounding in his chest, moved forward toward the railing. He chose a spot next to Tormy who was
still holding fast to the two sailors he'd pinned. The great
cat was less agitated now that he was no longer sitting on
anyone, and no longer being accused of eating anyone.

Tormy rubbed his fuzzy head against Omen's side as he approached and immediately the soft purr began rumbling through the cat's body, reinforcing the shield Omen kept around him. He smiled faintly. *This may destroy my mind. What will happen to the cats and Kyr if I'm gone?*

He shuddered, trying to force the dark thought out of his head. *I have to try. We're dead in the water if I don't.*

He felt Kyr move up to the railing, taking a place by his side. The boy stared impassively out at the shapes of long dead men and women standing up on the waves. *He must see things like this all the time.*

"All right," he whispered to himself. "Focus, Otharian pattern to reach out, and then the Loiritic pattern. Why didn't I learn the last two! Blast." He steadied his breath.

He was familiar with the Otharian patterns, which he used to push or blast his powers outward. Of all the patterns, those came easiest to him, and the songs of the various forms were clear and waiting in the back of his mind. He only needed the weakest of them for this — just a simple battle tune, percussion, and melody springing eagerly to the forefront of his mind. He held on tightly to the energy that formed as the pattern emerged.

Now for the Loiritic pattern for the suggestion. Of the five, he'd only learned the first three — he'd used the third, the strongest he knew, but that song was harder to pull forward. *Like singing in a round. Hold both songs together.* He entwined the two tunes, Otharian and Loiritic, creating a new melody that throbbed in his head. He felt pain creep in just behind his eyes. *Hold it! Hold it!* he scolded himself.

Now the suggestion. Just a hint, just a thought. This has to work. He formed the image of his father in his mind, pictured him as clearly as possible, standing there beside him

206

at the railing. He thought of his father's eccentric thought patterns — sharp angles and vectors spinning off into chaos in a way he could never fully comprehend. The illusion had to be convincing enough to trick the Widow Maker.

Power built within him. His skin grew hot, the throbbing of his pulse carrying the baseline of the song beating through him. The image formed, clear and bright. He could almost see 7 standing there beside him, golden hair damp with mist. *Now!* Omen pushed outward, briefly lowering his shield to push the thought forward.

It wasn't precisely an attack on the mind of the Widow Maker — it was just a touch followed swiftly by a desperate retreat back behind the waiting shield. He pushed the suggestion outward, and for one brief moment he touched the mind of something old and monstrous, an entity beyond his understanding, vast and fragmented as if made up of thousands of different minds. A thousand eyes turned toward him, focusing on the intrusion, focusing on Omen.

He backed swiftly away. *Shield! Behind your shield!* Omen cursed at himself as he tried to reach safety once more before the eyes spotted him. They locked on. *Not going to make it!*

"He'll take them!" he heard a clear voice beside him shout out in Kahdess. Kyr, gripping the railing, screamed into the waves and fog. "This time he'll take them all! All your souls will be gone and you'll be alone forever!"

The boy's words did the trick. That along with the image of 7 standing there at the railing poised to attack was enough.

Omen heard a terrible, rage-filled scream in his head as Urgolath withdrew its haunting attack. The lights vanished; the shapes faded from the water; the song at last ended. The ship drifted slowly forward, only a simple fog barring their way as the sound of water against the bulkhead washed over Omen.

He crumpled, Tormy bracing him on one side, Kyr on the other. But there — just at the very back of his mind — Omen caught the image of something huge and dark, hundreds of long tentacles, eyes on long waving stalks, a vast mouth filled with gnashing teeth. He saw it rip its way out of a cave and rush forward into the open sea, bent on vengeance.

The others raced toward him, freed now of the burden of holding back the sailors wanting to jump overboard.

I want to go swimming. Omen sighed heavily, his head pounding with pain. He felt his grandmother's hand close around his.

"You did it, Omen!" she praised. "You defeated it."

"No," he shook his head, trying to clear it. *The water looks so nice. So cool.* He felt overheated. "I just scared it," he explained. "I made it think 7 was on board about to attack it. It has to lower its mental shield to sing. It won't dare sing again if it thinks 7 is going to steal more souls from it." *I want to swim.*

He heard Kadana chuckle; he felt too weak to raise his head to see. "Clever! Now if we had some blasted wind we could outrun it for good and make port."

"I might be able to get the ship's air elementals to rustle up some wind if I experiment a bit," Templar suggested.

"Can't outrun it," Kyr spoke softly, but they all heard his words. He was sitting beside Omen on the deck, staring up at the sky. "It's in front of us."

"Are you sure of that lad?" Kadana asked gently.

Kyr smiled. "I hear it thrashing and wailing as it swims

the open seas. Always hungry, now vengeful."

I want to swim. Omen looked up. "Then let's attack it." His words were met with looks of shock. "I'm serious. It's coming for us. We have to fight it no matter what. Let's go forward full speed, hit it with everything we've got. You must have harpoons on board. It's a fish. Let's go fishing!" *The water will be so cool on my hot skin.*

"We have several harpoons," Kadana agreed. She frowned thoughtfully. "I've never gone whaling, but I've used the harpoons before against giant squid who've attacked my ship. No reason they wouldn't work against a leviathan. It's an Autumn Dweller — they don't like cold iron."

"Do you think we can kill something like that?" Shalonie asked worriedly.

Kadana shrugged. "Sounds like we don't have a choice. I've found that most things bleed when you stick 'em with a blade." The others all began talking at once, all filled with various suggestions of how they could arm the ship for battle.

I want to go swimming. Omen sighed as he staggered slowly to his feet, aided by Kyr's thin hands gripping his arm. *The water looks so cool.* He closed his hands over the railing.

"You is not swimming," Tormy purred toward him, rubbing his warm nose against Omen's neck. The cat's slow steady purr rumbled through his body, fortifying his shield. "You is wanting to cook us breakfasts, 'member, 'member?" the cat told him. "You is liking the cookings."

"I like cooking," Omen agreed. *I'm starting to sound like Kyr. I like green.*

"So we is going to the kitchen?" Tormy asked eagerly.

"You is cookings the breakfasts?"

"Yes, breakfast," Omen agreed, and he followed his cat toward the door to the lower deck.

Chapter 15: Hunt

DEV

The creature was gone. It had withdrawn its terrible song and with it, the decaying spirits of lost souls that had invaded their ship and gnawed at their sanity. It had fled from them because of whatever Omen had done.

It was over.

They were safe.

But now Omen and Kadana wanted to charge after it.

Hunt it.

Get it before it got them. *And that's assuming Omen is right and it really is coming for us. Why not just change course and flee? Far safer.*

Dev muttered a string of curses he'd known since his childhood in Revival. Curses he saved for moments like these.

"&%$#!" little Tyrin repeated, jumping from rigging block to rigging block as he followed Dev. "That is being very descriptive." Unabashed awe glittered in the cat's amber eyes as he studied Dev carefully. "I is not even knowing that a &%$# had a flying &*@. You is very good at the cursings, Dev."

He knew better than to encourage Tyrin's pertinacious line of questioning. "Where's Kyr?" he deflected, wondering why the creature was following him and not his master.

"Kyr is being in the galley. With Omen. They is cooking the breakfast. I is learning the cursings."

"Breakfast?"

"That is being the meal after the wakings up."

Pressing his lips together to keep from answering, Dev looked down to the main deck where all hands busied themselves with setting the ship back in order. Freed of the song's terrible compulsion, they worked quietly, seeming disoriented still.

Why would Omen be cooking now?

The sharp stink of the slushy muck that had dripped from the ghostly forms still lingered and assaulted Dev's nostrils as he climbed to the afterdeck.

Can't imagine anyone wants to eat with this stench everywhere.

Shalonie stood at the taffrail rounding the stern and stared out at the dark waves churning behind them. He couldn't hear her words, but her lips moved continuously. The mist was finally lifting, burning off as the sun rose in the far eastern sky.

Praying to her Sundragons, no doubt. They're not going to be any help out here. That's the problem with domestic deities. Bloody useless when you're away from home.

He decided not to disturb the girl's reverie, but instead made his way back to where Kadana had taken the helm. Three of the crew stood by Kadana's side, listening and nodding to a brisk catalog of orders. Dev heard them repeat the commands of how to position the ship's three harpoons.

Etorina, a young Corsair sailor, held a leather scroll up for Kadana's perusal.

Dev thought nothing of interrupting. "Lady Kadana—"

"Captain," Etorina corrected him as Kadana leaned into what seemed to be a nautical chart scratched into the flaking leather.

"*Captain*." Dev wasted no time."May I ask the wisdom of pursuing a mortiferous threat bent on eating all of our souls? Wouldn't it be more prudent to call ourselves lucky and run?"

Kadana threw him a quick glance, her eyes sparkling like green fire.

"I don't say this for myself." Dev cleared his throat. He knew he had to try to stop this folly. He also knew Kadana would never listen to him. *But if I don't try to stop her, I won't be able to report to Avarice that I tried to stop her.* "I say this for the sake of the families who would be . . . perturbed — your family, the Daenoths, the Corsairs, the Sundragons, Cerioth's brood — if something were to happen to their precious offspring."

"We're going after the Widow Maker. If Kyr is correct, and I believe he is, we have no other choice." Kadana no longer even glanced at him. "Go below deck and see to my grandson, Devastation Machelli."

Her mind's made up.

Dev gave a curt nod in Kadana's direction and retreated.

This is madness.

He passed Templar who was leaning against the mainmast in an entirely too casual manner. "Don't take it to heart," the prince said flippantly. "She wouldn't even talk to me this morning. Just had the first mate tell me to make myself useful."

Dev noted the sails, full and billowing despite the lack of wind. He also noted the periodic flurry of tiny gestures Templar directed at the sails and the slight sheen of sweat on the prince's brow. *Guess his experiment was successful. One bit of good news.*

"We all do what we can." Templar grinned. "Tell Omen

to save me some bacon."

"Bacon," Tyrin cried and leaped onto Dev's shoulder from above.

Should have been ready for that.

"Take me to bacon!" the little cat commanded. "Is I doing it right?" He addressed both Dev and Templar. "Grandma Kadana is saying, 'Go below deck and see to my grandson, Devastation Machelli.' And you is doing it." He nipped Dev's earlobe. "Is I saying it right? You is not going when I is saying it."

The needle-sharp bite grazed tender skin. *That little—* Briefly Dev considered dropping the kitten into the rainwater barrel.

"Perhaps you need to repeat his full name," Templar suggested, suppressing a laugh. "There's power in names."

"Go below deck and take me to bacon, Devastation Machelli," Tyrin tried again.

Biting back the words he would have liked to have flung at Templar's head along with his fist, Dev gave a sharp bow and proceeded below deck, the cat swaying on his shoulder as if he belonged there.

"I like fried fish." Dev heard Kyr say as he pushed past three youths waiting at the entrance of the galley. Each sailor held a wooden tray, ready to carry food items to the mess.

"But does it go with eggs?" Kyr's voice continued to be full of wonder. "Are they fish eggs?"

"No, Kyr, we're not having fish eggs," Omen said patiently as he lifted one cast iron pan from the hot stovetop and replaced it with another. "Fried fish and scrambled eggs. Chicken eggs. It's a breakfast they eat on the Corsair Isles. Arra sometimes makes it right on the beach over a fire." He poured a generous amount of oil into the hot pan. "I have to improvise."

While they had the help of a dishwasher, Dev noted the absence of the ship's cook.

Cupboards swung open, and jars slid from side to side but none fell out, held in place by the magical ship's many spells. The large pantry door knocked against the stove, and the fire elementals flickered to life in the lighting orbs as the grey haze of gloaming crushed the sunlight streaming in through the portholes.

Tormy sat pressed up into a corner of the galley, away from the stove, and allowed Kyr to flick pieces of crisp bacon directly into his mouth.

Nestled against the great cat, Kyr took the occasional bite for himself and continued to quiz Omen about his culinary creation.

Tyrin launched himself from Dev's shoulder and landed on Tormy's head. "Where is being my bacon?" the kitten asked Kyr sweetly and was immediately rewarded with a piece the size of his entire paw. Tyrin set to work with diligence and concentration.

"How are you cooking right now?" Dev sputtered. "I mean how . . . It's . . ." *If anything he should be resting. Fighting the Widow Maker took a lot out of him. He's going to have to be ready in case—*

"It's simple," Omen said as he deftly placed thin slices of prepared white fish into the pan, letting them sizzle. "Just a few spices and some flour. Enough to coat the fish very lightly. Then drop the slices in the oil. The oil has to be good and hot. As soon as it's gold on both sides, let it rest." He demonstrated by taking a perfectly golden slice from another pan and placing it on stretched-out butcher paper

215

on the counter.

Dev noted how calm Omen sounded. *As if he didn't just face a horde of ghosts and we weren't chasing after a leviathan. I don't understand these people.*

"That should do it," Omen directed at the cabin boys. "Bring the rest of it to the mess and then come back to clean up." He plated the sizzling fish on large platters alongside mounds of scrambled eggs.

One by one, the three boys hurriedly balanced their trays down the corridor, presumably to serve any of the crew who hadn't yet partaken of breakfast.

As Omen rinsed his hands, Dev noted a slight wobble to the young man's movements. *He's still having trouble.*

"I can smell them in the water — foul creature, stealing my souls," Kyr suddenly proclaimed, his voice distant and hollow. The pile of bacon had disappeared, Tormy and Tyrin looking contented and unconcerned.

"So soon? Best get to it," Omen said, determination in his face. "If Kyr's connected to the Widow Maker's mind again, we must be getting close."

"I'll crush them this time," Kyr continued, "and take them down to the bottom. I'll take all their souls."

A loud clatter sounded through the galley. The dish-washer, Kharakhian Dev guessed, had dropped a stack of tin plates. Her face was ashen.

"It's him!" the girl whispered in Kharakhian. "He *is* the Widow Maker. It's in his head."

Now it begins, the blame, Dev thought dispassionately.

"Don't worry." Omen moved closer, holding out a hand to calm her. "He's not the Widow Maker. He's just—"

"That boy will get us all killed!" The girl snatched a large knife from the counter and held it out toward Omen.

"He's cursed. That's how Urgolath is finding us!"

"He's not," Omen said gently. "He's just—"

"Cursed!" the girl shrieked. "He must be given to the Lord of the Sea—"

One smooth gesture brought Dev's blowgun from his sleeve to his lips. The dart stuck in the girl's neck, and she crumpled before she could finish her sentence.

Omen looked outraged as he quickly put together what the last seconds had garnered. "You can't just—"

"She's fine." Dev returned the reed to a small hidden pocket. "She'll barf for the next three days, but no permanent damage."

"She is one of—"

"She would have riled up the crew," Dev said, matter-of-fact. "They would have thrown Kyr overboard. I've seen it before. People in a mass are more horrible than people alone. Kadana's crew is scared kakless."

"Want the hearts and want the souls," Kyr muttered. "It's so lonely at the bottom of the cold, cold waters."

Determination swept over Omen's face. "Time to go."

Chapter 16: Tentacles

OMEN

He arrived on the main deck to changing weather, dark clouds rolling in, and plummeting temperature. Early light painted the world grey and blue, casting even the people around him in a steely, colorless palette.

"Above," Kyr blurted out. "It's above. All I have to do is reach out."

Omen's gaze flew up. But he saw nothing but sails and sky.

"Why aren't you armed?" Templar called out. The prince had slid into place next to Omen, bone blades drawn.

"I was cook—" Omen broke off hearing the ridiculousness of his own statement. He thought he caught a smug look on Dev's face.

Why aren't *I armed?* As if clamps had been taken off his thought processes, Omen reeled with the realization that the ghostly choir had reached into his mind and manipulated his thoughts. *They were trying to get me to jump. I wanted to go swimming,* he remembered. He glanced at Tormy who still searched the blackening sky. *Tormy told me to go below deck and cook breakfast. He saved me.*

"Has the Widow Maker been spotted?" Omen finished instead.

"No!" Templar stared out at the churning ocean. "But you can feel it, can't you?"

"Not far now!" Kyr screeched, the cat on his shoulder

218

one large ball of puffed up orange fur.

A turbulent buzz of energy shot through Omen and pinged back and forth from his feet to his scalp. His skin felt as if it were crawling with thousands of fire ants. "Not above!" he burst out, savagery sparked by the pain building in him. "It's below us!" He realized that Kyr was seeing through the Widow Maker's eyes. *We're above it.*

That very moment, the great ship jerked to one side, then to the other, making all but the cats lose their balance. Omen saw Shalonie and Kyr scramble back to their feet instantly, but something kept him pinned as he struggled to rise.

The silver embedded in the ship's hull sparked as the Ven'tarian vessel defended itself against the harassment.

"Something is trying to grab us from underneath!" Omen heard Kadana shout with a ragged voice.

"Drag them down into the waters deep," Kyr confirmed the creature's intention.

"There's nothing to hit!" Kadana thundered. "If we can't see it, we can't harpoon it. To the boats!"

In a mad scramble the crew raced to loosen the skiffs. Templar and Shalonie ran to join Kadana on the quarter-deck.

Omen curved his back like a cat as he tried to push himself up. It wasn't until Dev wrenched his shoulder back violently that Omen realized he hadn't moved at all, his hands and feet still planted on deck where he had fallen. *Can't leave.* He shook Dev's hand away and pressed his face to the wooden planks. At first he saw nothing, only the dark of the wood, but in a blink the molecules of brown scattered and his sight pierced the layers of the ship like arrows flying through fog.

He heard a deep growl coming from Tormy and felt the cat place himself next to his side, shielding his body from Dev.

"Back the &%$# off!" Tyrin screamed at the Machelli through the howl of a sudden gust and the nonsensical gibbering emanating from Kyr.

"I'm trying to get him up — to safety. He's sick!" Dev protested.

At the same time, Omen felt Templar's magic flow past him like a light breeze. *He's trying to fill the sails so we can get away,* Omen acknowledged distantly.

"Too late," Kyr cackled loudly, a mixture of glee and horror breaking his voice.

Just as Omen's vision escaped through the bottom of the cargo hold and shot through the seething waters, the ship dropped as if a hole had been cut into the ocean. *I'm having a psionic episode,* he realized dispassionately. It was something that commonly happened with children coming into their powers, but it hadn't happened to Omen in years.

Don't attack! His father's dire exhortation returned to him as if 7 were screaming his warning across the miles. *"The Widow Maker isn't human — it's ancient, and powerful, beyond anything you can imagine . . . You're no match for it."*

Desperate cries seared Omen's hearing. Through the jumble, he heard a heart-breaking yowl, "I is not swimming!" The ship lurched to the side, as something inexorably pulled it downward, trying to sink them.

You're not drowning my cat!

He cast his gaze about, frantic. His sight fell on one of the harpoons — a great spear of Ven'tarian design — abandoned by a sailor now clinging to a cargo net. *The Widow*

220

Maker is beneath us. They can't see anything to shoot at.

Fly, he commanded the harpoon with his mind. The weapon flung free of its casing. *Dive,* he guided the blade through the air and into the water, at no point certain what he was trying to accomplish.

With a sudden jolt, the Golden Voyage dropped below the surface of the water, rushing toward the bottom of the ocean as the long dark tentacles of the amorphous creature hauled them downward.

Somehow Omen remained in place, fixed to the deck despite the violent shudders shaking the ship. He glanced over his shoulder, sucking in a breath.

A tremendous white and silver bubble slid into place over the top of the highest masts, closing them in and protecting them from the dark waters.

More Ven'tarian magic! He had no time to marvel, but flipped his focus back down, looking through the ship as if it were made of glass. He gasped audibly at the size of the creature dragging them down.

Omen could almost make out the individual parts of the Widow Maker, a large dark body and hundreds of long whipping, suction-cupped limbs. *Like the sandlures — but bigger.*

His arms and chest still felt like they were on fire, but the rest of his body grew cold and numb. He became aware of being in two places at the same time, on the deck — stuck — and coursing through the sea, ramming toward the creature as if he were himself the harpoon.

Water trickled on the back of his neck.

"The Ven'tarian shield isn't holding," he heard Shalonie call out. "I can't—"

There it is. He saw what he hadn't known he was look-

221

ing for. Rippling through the darkest part of the creature, presumably the head, Omen caught flashes of bright blue and red sparks firing back and forth. The complex activity flashed in unidentifiable patterns as one burst connected to thousands of others, creating a code of trillions of combinations.

And he also saw the mighty harpoon, launched by his mind, pushed along by his psionics, rushing toward its inevitable target.

He was rushing toward the target.

There's your brain. Omen released a sharp blaze of psionic power into the end blade of the harpoon, sending it into the largest cluster of sparkling lights.

Agony lashed back at him as the tip of the spear tore through the core of Urgolath's brain. Omen snapped back to consciousness, fully aware that he was only a frail thing balancing on a wooden board in the middle of an ocean he did not understand. The realization drove the breath from his body, as if his lungs were squeezed by a giant's hand.

The tentacles shuddered and retracted, releasing the ship. The creature convulsed and spasmed, its countless amorphous limbs folding into its form like the legs of a dying bug. Blood gushed into the water, turning it red as the explosion of liquid rushed from the Widow Maker's brain. The last Omen saw of it through a shroud of his own tears was the immobile mass of the Widow Maker sinking down toward the ocean floor, dark and dead.

But wait, did one of the tentacles move? Can't be.

The Golden Voyage bobbed up to the surface like a cork that had been held under water momentarily. There was a crackling as the shield crumbled away in a sparkle of silver dust that covered the ship and crew like a dusting of snow.

There was complete silence.

Omen breathed deep. No longer glued to the deck he staggered to his feet. His vision had returned to normal, though he noted that everything looked more colorful, as if the saturation had been increased, making the blue of the sky bluer than he'd ever seen it before.

Tormy's orange fur shone like a flame. "Is you hungry, Omy?" the cat asked with an innocent smile.

"I could eat," Omen replied, locating his companions on the deck.

Liethan and Kadana stood together, shock plain on their faces, but shock mixed with inquisitive enthusiasm.

Dev was close too, standing protectively over Kyr who whispered and cooed as he petted Tyrin. Whiskers splayed, fur on end, the kitten seemed flustered but happy.

Templar and Shalonie were the first to move, as both of them made their way back to where Omen was standing.

"What did you—" Templar started as a cheer rose from the crew. They could see the mass of blood in the water and guessed at what happened. Somehow, someway, the creature had been harpooned.

"Back to work!" Omen heard Kadana shout.

"I harpooned it." Omen stumbled slightly as he took a step toward Templar. "I think . . ."

"Let's get you below," he heard Shalonie say. "Time to talk later."

"Is it gone, Kyr?" Another shiver flew through him as they headed for the main hatchway.

The boy gave him a wry smile but did not answer.

Chapter 17: Storm

SHALONIE

Shalonie had wanted desperately to hear Omen's explanation for the near sinking and impossible reemergence of the ship. But she could see the confusion in his eyes and thought it better he should rest before thinking on what he had done with the harpoon.

She was worried that things hadn't gone as well as they believed, but she had no intention of nagging Kadana. The crew was celebrating their narrow escape, and Kadana seemed content to set the course back to the port of Khreté, as was their original plan. The Ven'tarian ship had somehow protected them long enough for Omen to . . . do whatever it was he had done.

Exhausted, Shalonie briefly wished she were back at home in Melia, reading about instead of participating in adventures.

Don't be a hatchling, she scolded herself. She closed her eyes and repeated the Song of Melia in her mind until she fell asleep.

Hours later, the sound of a heavy thud woke Shalonie with a start, violent motion disorienting her as she realized with alarm that her bed was swinging so much that the outer frame had struck the wall of her cabin. Grabbing the sides of the frame, Shalonie braced herself, startled to realize that the entire room was swaying intensely as the ship rode up and down on the immense waves of the turbulent sea. Outside she could hear the roar of the wind and the crashing of water. Muffled caterwauling resounded beyond her door.

Heart pounding, Shalonie scrambled from the bed, barely catching herself as the rising swells made the floor unsteady beneath her feet. She stumbled toward the door. Pulling it open, she saw people hustling through the corridor, sailors yelling to each other to batten down the hatches as the unexpected storm rocked the Golden Voyage. The glowing orbs that lit the hallway flickered on and off, even the elementals inside reacting to the ferocious storm. They dimmed, casting the interior into gloom as the wind screamed past the vessel.

She spied Liethan Corsair and grabbed his arm as he ran past her door. "What's happening now?"

He grinned at her, his eyes burning with almost ecstatic light. "Storm," he exclaimed. "I love storms! You should see the wind!" He raced off in the direction of the ladder that led to the upper deck.

Maybe Kyr isn't the only crazy person on board. She stumbled after Liethan, deeply concerned. Based on what Kadana and Haptis had said earlier, she knew there shouldn't be any storm — especially not one this brutal.

Of course if the Corsair isn't worried, maybe this isn't as bad as it seems, she told herself in vain. She was slammed against the bulkhead as they pitched upward again. *Maybe now is a good time to try the stabilizing Cypher Rune.* She bit the inside of her lip. *If a ship with this much magic is getting tossed about like a toy, the storm has to be bad.*

She found Omen, Kyr and Tormy crowded in the doorway to the outer deck, Tyrin clutched tightly in Kyr's right hand. Shalonie noticed the boy was holding the hilt of a heavy sword in his left hand, the sheathed blade far too large for someone of his small frame to hold properly. It looked like he'd dragged it behind him when he'd followed Omen into the corridor. *Omen's sword.* She wondered what the boy was doing with it.

Shoving her way alongside Tormy, Shalonie tried to make out what was happening outside. The deck was fairly well-lit with glowing elemental orbs, though they were swinging wide on their hanging chains. Sailors fought hard to pull ropes and secure the sails that were fraying in the howling wind. The ocean itself was black and only occasionally could she see the silver gleam of water as the glowing lights caught on the surface just before a humongous wave swamped over the deck, sending anything unsecured sliding. The great bow of the Golden Voyage rose up against the black sky as lightning cracked, momentarily illuminating the monstrous swells all around.

Dragons of Melia protect us! Shalonie prayed silently. She caught hold of Tormy's fur to steady herself, the ship's erratic rise nearly throwing her down.

Omen reached out then and braced her, his face pinched with worry.

"Where did this come from?" Shalonie shouted to him over the wind's blare.

He shook his head. "No idea!" he shouted back. "Liethan doesn't seem worried. I'm sure it's fine!"

She wanted to agree — that if the Corsair boy wasn't frightened, everything was probably normal. But through the open doorway she could see the golden-haired boy running nimbly along the heaving deck, laughing while he helped the overwhelmed sailors secure the sails. The crew did not share his enjoyment.

"I think your friend's a bit loony!" she yelled back to Omen. They watched as Liethan clambered up the ropes around the mainmast to lash down a portion of the sail that had come undone in the wind. The towering mast seemed to oscillate with each heavy swell, but the Corsair cackled and whooped as if he were having the time of his life.

"I think you're right!" Omen no longer looked reassured.

"Do you see it, Omen!" Kyr exclaimed, pointing out at the deck. "The fish with swords!"

"There's no fish out there, Kyr!" Omen tried to shoo his brother back below deck.

Any fish would have the good sense to swim deep and avoid the waves, Shalonie couldn't help reasoning. Another surge washed over the bow, drenching the deck. A glint of light flashing on the surface of metal caught her eye, and she squinted to see through the darkness. "What's that man doing!" She gestured past Omen toward where a sea-drenched sailor seemed to be climbing over the railing, a long thin sword in his hand. *He's climbing onto the deck — not off.*

"It's a fish!" Kyr squawked. "Don't peel the potatoes. Use this." He dragged the huge sword forward and pushed it toward Omen, pressing it into his brother's hand. "It wants to burn your head. And I only had one lesson."

Omen took the sword wordlessly and turned toward the dripping sailor. The light from one of the swinging elemental orbs illuminated the stranger, and Shalonie gasped as she realized there was something truly wrong with the man. "He doesn't have legs!" she screeched, fear biting the back of her brain.

The undulating thing wasn't a man, nor was it a ghost. While the shape initially appeared to be the torso of a drenched man, strands of seaweed in his hair, one out-stretched arm holding a sword, it was instead a twisting mass of flesh — flowing, morphing, changing shape. It gripped a timeworn blade, bringing the weapon down hard against the deck. The broad blade scored a deep groove in the wooden surface.

"Widow Maker!" Outcries of terror rose from the crew even as the sailors pushed forward to meet their enemy with knives and swords.

The leviathan lives! She held back her own cry. *And it's found us again.*

Something gargantuan and terrible wound itself around the outer hull; hundreds of swaying tentacles, lashing in the wind, twisting and writhing, reached out to grasp the vessel. It was all part of one entity — from the ocean deep, it crawled and oozed onto the deck, and wrapped itself around the Golden Voyage in a tangle of moving flesh, pulling and dragging its hideous body upward. The numerous tentacles seemed to be wielding a strange preponderance of weapons — blades of all types which it used to slash and hack at the ropes holding the ship's contents secure.

Shalonie watched in horror as one of those blades came crashing down on a sailor, slicing him nearly in two before another twisting black rope of flesh wound around the bleeding man and lifted him away into the boiling sea.

"Templar! Get your swords!" Omen hollered down the corridor, as he took hold of the blade Kyr had shoved into his hand. "Kyr, stay here! Don't go outside, no matter what happens!" Omen raced forward, drawing the heavy blade from its sheath, and attacked the creature with undaunted fierceness.

Tormy took off after him, and Shalonie caught hold of Kyr as he stumbled, steadying him and herself both against the bulkhead. The boy, golden hair whipped about by blasts of wind, gripped an equally terrified Tyrin tightly to his chest, and they watched Omen and Tormy leap forward to attack one of the swaying tentacles about to pull another sailor to his death.

Shalonie spied Kadana, also armed with a large blade, rushing to aid them. She hacked at one of the tentacles that had wound itself around the mainsail mast.

A moment later Templar, armed with twin blades of white bone in either hand, raced past them toward the deck, leaping to join the battle. He bellowed into the wind, and a bolt of lightning whipped out from around his body, striking the tentacle on the mast, forcing it to uncoil. A forceful shudder ripped through the ship, and an ear-piercing shriek rose on the wind as some ancient, unseen mouth roared its displeasure. *Its voice sounds different — wounded. Omen must have damaged it badly with that harpoon. Maybe that's why it isn't trying to sing.*

Deep in her bones, Shalonie felt a beat pulsing through the deck, the spells that protected the vessel fighting back against the terrible force wrapping like vines around its frame. Over the front hull, above the railing, a colossal swelling body rose — the forbidding entirety of the creature, grotesquely swaying shapes and tendrils with a thousand eyes squirming from the ends of long stalks of ropey feelers, and a gaping maw filled with rows of serrated teeth. A hideous oozing scar marred the side of its shape, evidence of Omen's harpoon.

Scanning the surface of the deck with its clusters of glowing, writhing eyes, the Widow Maker aimed strikes and slashes downward with the sword-wielding tentacles at the three warriors cutting away at its flesh. While Kadana and Templar both moved with swift agility to avoid the strikes, Shalonie saw Omen brace himself for a clashing blow of blade against blade, holding back with inhuman strength a force that shook the entire ship.

The Widow Maker is going to rip us apart long before they can do any damage to it, Shalonie realized in a grim flash of insight. The creature was too big. *Their blades might cut it. But if a harpoon to the brain didn't kill it, what are swords going to do?* She saw Kadana sever one of the tentacles all the way through with a well-placed blow. *Templar's magic might burn it.* But she knew Urgolath could take the damage, every wounded tentacle replaced by ten more. *They can't stop it!*

She could feel the Golden Voyage's magic straining and pulsing as it fought back against the terrible force pulling it apart — the Ven'tarian ship would likely have defenses against such monstrosities, but it was doubtful that anyone on board knew how to activate them.

The silver on the outer hull. Her thoughts streamed freely, connecting rivulets of ideas into a rushing river. Her plan snapped into place. *I've been thinking about testing the silver hull's stabilizing spells. Why not use it as a weapon!* She recalled Kyr's words from days ago. "You'll need the one for the lightning."

"Kyr, you're a genius!" She nearly hugged the boy. "Now all I need is—"

Kyr held up his hand, holding out the hilt of one the small knives that were housed in the kitchen. "I kept it for you." His violet eyes illuminated in the lightning cracking beyond the doorway.

She beamed at him, taking hold of the blade. How he could have known to bring both Omen's sword and this knife for her, she didn't know, but she wasn't going to question her good fortune.

She grabbed hold of the edge of the doorway and pulled herself outside, bracing against the swells of the sea as the deck moved up and down. She stumbled forward, her bare feet sliding against the slick surface of the water-drenched deck, not far from where Omen, Templar and Kadana were cutting away at the massive tentacles. Sailors moved about at what seemed like a turtle's pace, desperate to secure the ship while dodging the terrible grasp of the creature.

Shalonie stifled a yelp as a man only a few feet from her was swept up by a ropey tentacle and lifted away into the darkness. She pushed on, terrified they wouldn't last much longer. *If the ship sinks, we're at the mercy of both the ocean and the Widow Maker, with no chance at all of defending ourselves. We'll die.*

Reaching the center point of the deck, she dropped to her knees, shivering and numb with cold as another brackish wave washed over her, nearly sending her sliding away toward the railing. She held on, scrambling to keep the knife firmly in her fist and frantically trying to calculate the shapes and symbols she would need.

Recall came easily to her, always had, her mind working with feverish speed as she pictured the shapes in her head. She tried to shut out the squall's racket, the terrified yawp of the sailors, the shrill of the creature trying to pull apart their floating world, the clash of swords and clamor of battle. She dug the knife blade into the surface of the deck and started carving. The forms came to her quickly, though carving accurately while the ship rose and fell violently up

231

and down was nearly impossible.

She scratched the first symbol, then the next, tuning all else out until she felt something cold and slimy wrap around her bare ankle, and she turned in horror to see one of those ropey tentacles twining its way up her leg. The crushing force of its grasp stopped the blood flow to her foot like a tourniquet. But before it could lift her away from the surface of the deck, an arrow pierced it, pinning it to the deck's surface. The tentacle released her at once, ripping itself away as it tore free of the arrow.

Ankle pulsing, Shalonie looked up to see Dev standing over her, a long recurve bow in his hand, another arrow already nocked and waiting.

"Will that help?" he shouted, motioning toward her carving with a sharp nod of his head.

"Yes!" she returned. "It'll keep the leviathan from ripping us apart!" *I hope!*

He shot another arrow into an approaching tentacle. "I'll cover you, keep going!"

Accepting his assurance, Shalonie turned her attention back to the deck and knife, carving the next symbol as swiftly as she could. She was vaguely aware of Omen, Templar, and Kadana responding to Dev's need for aid, moving to take up positions around her and allowing her to carve unhindered by the creature. At one point she became aware of the dripping wet form of Tormy bridging his furry body over her protectively.

She cut symbol after symbol into the surface of the deck, grimacing as she realized that the gush of water constantly running past her over the deck's surface was now tinged red with blood. She'd need power to activate the mark — lots of power. More than she was capable of summoning. She

232

knew magics unimagined to most people, but she herself wasn't particularly powerful.

I need a force to match the magics of the Ven'tarians themselves. They would have used one of the most powerful elementals they could capture to power such a thing, and I have nothing like that . . . wait . . . or a force of nature! she thought as she finished the last mark and looked up in frantic anticipation. "Omen!" She caught the young man's attention as he ducked past another flailing, sword-wielding tentacle. "Help me!"

"Go!" Kadana barked at her grandson, stepping in to take his place in the ring they'd formed around Shalonie. Templar, still lashing out with burning strands of lightning, expanded his web of spells to fill the gap around them. Dev, she could see, was now fighting with sword in hand. His bow was in the hands of Liethan Corsair who shot arrow after arrow at the gargantuan head of the Widow Maker which rose above them, maw opened as if prepared to swallow them whole. Tormy, the only steady form on the surface of the deck as he'd dug the claws of all four paws into the wood, continued to stand over Shalonie, bracing her against the elements, his ears pulled flat against his head, teeth bared as he hissed and yowled.

She grabbed Omen by the front of his tunic. "You need to activate the mark, aim a psionic blast at the surface, as strong as you can, as much power as you can summon! Use one of the Otharian Patterns — the strongest you know."

He looked momentarily shocked. "I'll blast a hole in the ship!"

She couldn't guess how powerful the Daenoths' psionics actually were, though she'd seen 7 do things that defied imagination. But she knew that this time, they'd need it all

233

— everything Omen could muster. "Not at the deck! Not at the creature!" She clenched her aching fists. "At the mark! Focus on my carving, aim for it! Trust me!"

It spoke volumes to her that they had all accepted her decisions without question, all of them moving to defend her while she carved — not one person questioning the wisdom of it. *Sheer insanity, desperation, or trust?* she wondered. Without hesitation, Omen motioned her to back away.

Shalonie caught hold of Tormy's fur and pulled herself back from the circular carving of archaic symbols she'd etched into the deck, her eyes moving frantically over each of them as she second-guessed herself, hoping her memory had not failed her, that her hands had been steady enough to carve the shapes accurately, that she'd calculated the equation properly. *I'm not creating my own magic,* she reminded herself. *I'm just trying to activate magical defenses already present.* She held her breath, imagining the defenses Ven'tarian shipwrights could have put in place. *Please work. Please work.*

"Do it!" she called to Omen. Instantly, she felt a pulsing wave of power emanate from the red-haired man gazing down at the marks upon the deck. *A force of nature.* The reaction was immediate; the marks flared with blinding light, a shock wave of force exploding outward, knocking her back against Tormy as the magic erupted out in all directions. The woven strands of silver that ribbed the outer hull flared to light, illuminating the ocean like a midnight sun, making the water roll and boil and hiss, burning and scorching everything it touched.

The leviathan wailed, the massive head arching back as the tentacles, wrapped in a death grip around the vessel, burned and charred. Spasms shook through the entire ship, and the tentacles whipped away, releasing them. The creature reared back, all but flinging itself into the ocean in an effort to get away from the burning light of the outer hull. It crashed down into the ocean, sending up an enormous swell of water that lifted the Golden Voyage high into the air and carried it away out across the turbulent surface. Urgolath disappeared back down into the black depths of the sea. Overhead lightning crashed, and the wind pushed them hard from the south.

"Omen!" Kadana grabbed for her grandson as he dropped to his knees, sword falling from his grip. Shalonie reached out to steady him, realizing with some remorse that the force of the backlash of power along the Cypher Rune had rebounded upon him, knocking him out.

Kadana caught him with one arm, sword still held in the other as she ordered, "Dev, get Omen and Shalonie down below deck!" The Machelli grabbed one of Omen's arms, slinging it over his shoulder, catching him around the waist.

"Templar, Liethan, help me finish securing the deck. We still have to get through this storm!" Kadana motioned toward some of the sailors still trying valiantly to hold their own against the wind and the waves.

One hand gripping tightly to Tormy's fur, Shalonie caught hold of Omen's other arm, slinging it over her shoulder as she and Dev made their way toward the interior doorway where Kyr was crouched, watching them, eyes wide. They dragged Omen to safety, while all around them the wind screamed with unbridled fury.

Chapter 18: Recovery

DEV

Dev had traded off with Shalonie, watching over Omen while Templar, Liethan, and Kadana had spent their time on deck, navigating through the storm, which raged on without mercy for days.

Omen slept like the dead, seemingly unconscious. They'd moved him into a hammock to avoid the possibility of him rolling out of the more comfortable bed. Tormy slept below him in a nest of pillows that had been set up as a giant cat bed.

To Dev's amusement, Kyr also slept on the cat bed, tucked under one of Tormy's heavy paws, the boy all but buried in the thick orange fur. Like Tormy, the boy never left Omen's side, though he appeared to draw more and more into himself as the hours progressed, tuning out the rest of them as if they didn't exist. Tyrin looked on with concern, periodically leaving the room and then running back in to give the boy updates about what was going on outside in the storm. And though Dev never heard Kyr respond, the cat blithely answered questions that were not asked, and expounded on points that were not queried. *Kyr is lost without Omen.*

Nearly three days later, Omen started showing signs of consciousness. Dev sat perched on the ledge of the single port window in Omen's room, looking out at the black sky and tumultuous sea. He'd been writing an update to Avarice, telling her of the events that had transpired, using

236

the journal she'd given to him before leaving Melia. For once Kyr was gone from the room, led away by Shalonie who had taken him and Tyrin to the galley for lunch — both the girl and the cat were concerned that Kyr was not eating and had insisted he join them. Pale and silent, the frail boy had followed them dutifully.

"How is everyone?" Omen's voice caught Dev's attention, and he looked up from his notebook to see Omen's strange multi-colored eyes watching him. One silver, one green — Dev had noticed the oddity the moment he'd met him, and had seen it as a peculiarity of his remarkable heritage.

"Your friends are all safe," Dev told him, guessing Omen's chief concern.

"And the crew?" Omen asked. His voice was weak, and there was a deep furrow between his eyes like someone suffering a deeply painful headache.

Dev quirked an eyebrow at that. This group of people — nobles all — continuously surprised him. *Haven't met a lot of nobles who'd ask after the crew.* "We lost four," he told him honestly. "Three in the battle, one the day after." The man in question had died early the previous morning. They'd already committed his body to the sea, Liethan Corsair offering up the prayers for the dead common on the Corsair Isles.

Omen frowned. "The day after?" He seemed to search for something. "What was his name?"

"Baruch," Dev said, remembering Liethan's prayer. "Your friend, Templar, tried to heal him. But Baruch had lost too much blood. He died in his sleep." That had surprised Dev; not that the sailor had died — the moment Dev had seen the major artery nicked, Dev had known Baruch was going to die. Even the healing potions Kadana stocked could not restore lost blood. Without the magic of a true healer, the man had been doomed.

What had surprised Dev was that Templar had tried to heal him at all — tried his best despite not being a proper healer. The Terizkandian prince was well-versed in all sorts of magics, and had some psionic means to manipulate flesh, but true healing was a specialty that came from a god's blessing alone, something Templar lacked. *And no wonder, Night Dweller that he is.*

Dev had been able to spot Night Dwellers ever since he'd learned as a child what exactly it meant to cross their path. He'd always considered the people of Terizkand mad for happily following a royal family tainted with Night-blood. *Twisted, dark, unmerciful — not one of them can be trusted.* He'd learned that the hard way. Befriending Night Dwellers never ended well. *Though I could say the same about the Dawn Children. They're as useless as the Night-blood are evil. Worse, really. At least I know exactly what to expect from a Night Dweller.*

Except that Templar had genuinely tried to heal the man — a virtual stranger to him. *And he was grieved when he failed.* Dev knew the difference between fake remorse and genuine grief, and the Terizkandian had shown honest remorse at the loss of a mortal life. Which didn't square well with what Dev knew of Night Dwellers, and he didn't like the unknown. It made his skin itch, and he found himself reaching for the pulse at his neck, using the slow steady beat to calm his nerves. His hand twitched — it was a habit he been trying to break. He didn't like having predictable tells.

Dev watched with curiosity as Omen began struggling to

extract himself from the swinging hammock despite being far too weak to rise. "Did he try—" he began, only to break off and sag weakly back down into the swinging mesh. "Of course he did . . . Templar doesn't give up."

Dev found himself biting back a stinging retort. *So loyal to his friends. Surprised Avarice hasn't taken steps to correct that weakness.* That she hadn't gave Dev pause. Avarice was not known for being trusting. *Maybe it's his father's influence.* Dev didn't know 7 well, but his one encounter with the man had left him with the understanding that there was nothing 7 wouldn't do to protect his family.

"What about the cats and Kyr?" Omen asked, his gaze on Tormy who was still sound asleep on his pile of pillows, the lack of twitching ears indicating that the giant feline was deeply asleep and not simply resting.

"Fine," Dev replied. "Tormy's just tired — the fight took a lot out of him, and he appears to be a bit of a worrier. Shalonie took Kyr and Tyrin to the galley — the boy's been here the entire time. Stopped talking when he realized you were unconscious, but the cats seem to think he's fine, so no one's too concerned."

Several emotions passed through Omen's features at that. He finally seemed to settle on unease. "He doesn't like to be left alone," Omen said softly. "He sometimes has a hard time figuring things out."

Figuring out what's real, he means. Dev had caught on to that early. *Mystic or not, the boy is insane. The kind of insane that needs a locked room and blind priestesses to pray over him.*

"Well, that and the fact that our dead crewmen appear to be talking to him," Dev quipped. "Avarice told me that if Kyr became nonverbal I should hand him a knife and a piece of wood and leave him alone. Seemed strange advice. I generally avoid giving sharp, pointy objects to crazy people, but I did as she suggested and it appeared to work. He's carving a rather remarkable replica of the ship."

Omen's features hardened. "Kyr is not crazy!"

Dev laughed out loud. "Omen, you're all crazy. Every last one of you, and for many more reasons than Kyr's weird talk. And I'm crazy for agreeing to come along with you. But there you have it. The world's full of crazy."

His laughter seemed to disarm Omen whose features smoothed out. "I suppose."

"You saved the ship," Dev said then, curious to see how he'd respond. He was beginning to suspect . . . *Ah yes, there it is.* Omen shook his head in denial. *Not going to take credit for it. So humble — wonder how long that will last.* Still it did appear to be genuine, but experience had taught Dev that sooner or later ego ruled supreme.

"Shalonie saved the ship," Omen stated flatly.

"She said you did," Dev replied.

"I merely supplied the power; she did all the work," Omen insisted. "I don't even understand how she did it!"

"No one does," Dev assured him. "She's tried to explain, but with the possible exception of Templar, none of us understood the explanation even after she repeated it several times. She even provided diagrams; didn't understand those either. Well . . . Tyrin claims he understood them perfectly, but I'm beginning to suspect he was having us on."

Omen smiled faintly, but Dev could see his migraine was growing worse, the furrow between his eyes deepening. "Can't figure out why I'm so tired," he murmured.

Dev scoffed. "According to Shalonie, the psionic blast you threw at the ship was about ten times more powerful than necessary. She thinks she might have over-calculated when she asked you to throw everything you had into it." If he was honest with himself, Dev found the whole scenario alarming.

Omen looked horrified. "Did I damage the ship?"

Dev shook his head. "No, she wasn't kidding when she implied that mark she carved could take it. Apparently all that residual power has pushed us weeks ahead of where we should be. We left the Widow Maker far behind us. We're well beyond its reach — assuming it's still alive. And we're nearly to port. If that whole heir to a throne thing doesn't work out, you have a future hiring yourself out as a means of propulsion. Can't imagine having that kind of power."

"Why do you say that? You're psionic." Omen's eyes narrowed. "You have a shield, a strong one. Noticed it the moment we met."

He doesn't get it, doesn't understand. Like a giant baby blundering through the world. Maybe that's why he's not afraid of a Night Dweller. Dev knew that his psionic shield, such as it was, wouldn't be any match for Omen — should he choose to dismantle it. 7 had scanned his mind as if his shield didn't even exist the moment Avarice had informed him he'd be traveling with Omen. *Were I not used to such abuse, I might even have feigned offense.*

He wondered how long it would be before Omen did something similar. *Wounded betrayal would probably play better with Omen, acting offended would likely make him feel justified,* Dev reasoned. Not that he cared of course — he had no secrets to hide.

Dev's skin began to itch again, and he shook off the sensation caused by his unease, smiling instead. "Not like yours. If I had the power to peel potatoes with my mind, I'd

241

take over the world."

Omen groaned and rolled his eyes. "Mégeira told you," he groused.

"Repeatedly," Dev agreed. "No doubt your mother will find the story just as amusing."

That caught his attention. "You're going to tell my mother?" He looked worried.

Dev smirked. "What part of reporting back to her in excruciating detail didn't you understand? I take my job very seriously. I have an excellent work ethic. And before you ask me not to tell her, I already told her." He held up the small leather-bound journal.

The blank look on Omen's face made it plain that he did not recognize the object.

"It's a magical bonding book," Dev clarified. "Avarice has a matching journal. Anything written in one book instantly shows up in the other."

Omen's lips twisted with distaste. "You're completely shameless," he muttered, starting to drift away again as there was little heat in his words.

"Completely," Dev agreed, amused. "It's one of the reasons Avarice likes me so much. You should get some sleep. It's going to take you a while to recover."

"I'm fine . . ." Omen slurred, as he was already nearly asleep. Then he fell silent.

Outside the storm was finally beginning to die down, the screaming wind settling into a hushed roar. *How does a storm rage over such distance?* Dev rolled his head to one side, then the other. *Who am I to ask?* He stared out the porthole, keeping his mind blank as he watched the endless waves.

When a wind-tossed Liethan Corsair entered the room a

242

half hour later, accompanied by the silent Kyr, the two of them were delighted to learn that Omen had briefly awoken. Kyr grinned lightheartedly before climbing again onto the pillows and snuggling against the still slumbering Tormy.

"Kadana wants to see you on deck," Liethan told Dev. "Go on. I'll watch Omen."

"The storm over?" Dev asked, rising from his perch by the window and shoving the small bonding book into the pouch at his belt. *Perhaps I should leave it lying around so Omen can read it — might prove entertaining.*

"The heavy wind and rain have passed." The Corsair boy looked bitterly disappointed, reinforcing Dev's certainty that everyone on board was mentally unbalanced. At least the crew hadn't shared in Liethan's enthusiasm for the rough weather, leading Dev to conclude that Liethan's storm madness was unique to him and not a congenital insanity shared by all Corsairs.

Dev made his way through the dimly lit corridor toward the upper deck. Though it was day, little sunlight cut through the grim clouds overhead; and while the rain had stopped, the driving wind still sprayed ocean water into the air, making the wood slick.

Blood's washed away, Dev noted on his way to the navigator's bridge. His gaze moved to where Shalonie had carved the mark — it still glowed with residual power. Considering the girl had carved it during a pitched battle, in the middle of a raging storm, on a ship being literally pulled apart by a leviathan, the work was remarkably well done — the complicated sigils crisp and clear. *Wonder what else she can do with those marks.*

"There you are, Machelli," Kadana greeted him as he

joined her, Templar, Haptis and Shalonie at the helm.

Using my last name . . . must be irritated. Dev smiled at her and nodded cordially to the yellow-eyed Night Dweller standing beside her. "Problems?" he asked pleasantly.

"I thought Avarice sent you to help with my little project with the Machelli Guild," Kadana started without preamble.

Though this was the first Dev had heard of any project she might have with the Machelli Guild in Kharakhan, he gave no indication of surprise. He smiled as if urging her to go on.

"Now I'm thinking you're here for a different reason, Machelli."

"Avarice sent me along to keep an eye on Omen and Kyr." Another half-truth — but Dev tended to avoid the truth whenever possible, on principle alone. Lies generally garnered far more information than the truth ever did. He was well aware that Avarice had sent him along solely because she didn't trust Indee or believe any part of the story the queen had told Omen. He knew as well as anyone that Omen hardly needed his protection. Avarice wanted information, not whatever fanciful tale might have been conjured for her naive son.

"Avarice sent you along because Indee is up to her usual games, and she wants a heads-up before things spiral into chaos," Kadana said bluntly, gaze sharpening as if daring Dev to deny it.

How refreshing! Dev thought with delight. He loved people like Kadana — blunt, straightforward, steadfast. He always knew exactly where he stood with people like that.

"Indee is married to Lord Sylvan," Shalonie began with a protest.

"Yes, yes." Kadana waved her off. "Fantastic lot, your

dragons, but let's not forget I've known Indee for decades. Fought in several wars at her side. I know when something has gone terribly wrong. We take this route to Kharakhan because it's calm and peaceful during the summer. Here it is not even Midsummer's Eve yet, and we just sailed through one of the worst storms I've seen in years. And we've been attacked by a creature that only roams the sea on Haunter's Eve — which is months from now."

"Wait a minute. The creature. What else do you know about it?" Templar asked as if a thunderbolt had reverberated in his head.

"I know it should never have been near Melia," Kadana said, a new edge of tension in her voice. "Every sailor knows of that creature. Every sailor knows to avoid it," Kadana said as if instructing an apprentice. "That it should have stalked us in the open sea — something is deadly wrong." Her extraordinarily green eyes bored into Dev and then Templar. "Which brings me to my question. What's this complicated quest of Omen's all about? No lies, boys."

"There's nothing complicated about it." Templar took a deep breath. "Indee's son King Khylar has been kidnapped by the Autumn Dwellers and taken into the Autumn Lands. We were sent to rescue him."

Shalonie's face twitched as if she were having a seizure. "Omen only said he wanted to go to the Mountain of Shadow!"

A curse sprang from Kadana's mouth. "Of course 7 and Avarice didn't mention—" She cut herself off, visibly reconsidering. "The Mountain of Shadow is the best way to get into the Autumn Lands. Especially since the Autumn Gate should be closed during summer."

"Which begs the question . . . How did the Autumn

Dwellers kidnap Khylar?" Shalonie's words spilled out quickly, her thoughts clearly galloping ahead. "Of course . . . that would explain . . ." Her voice trailed off as she seemed to turn her thoughts inward, her gaze growing distant.

"Explain what?" Kadana snapped her fingers, pulling Shalonie's attention back to the present.

Shalonie pulled herself together. "Assuming the Autumn Dwellers have somehow managed to open the Autumn Gate out of season, it would likely throw all the seasons off. Migratory creatures would be confused and creatures like Urgolath could be free to wander the mortal realm. The real problem would be if the Gates are actually still open."

"Meaning what?" Kadana put a hand to her head.

Shalonie shrugged helplessly. "The Gates aren't supposed to stay open. They're only supposed to open midseason for one night. They're also not supposed to open out of turn. The fact that one has opened means we can't assume it was promptly closed. Any manner of creature could be escaping from that world into ours."

"Why would they want to?" Templar protested. "We're not talking about the Night Lands. The Autumn Lands are not a prison. Its inhabitants chose to live there, they have no reason to escape. They're free to come and go as they please every equinox. Most choose not to because they have no interest in the mortal world."

"And they should have no reason to kidnap a king of a mortal kingdom, and yet they have," Shalonie reminded him. "We can't make assumptions. This also puts the Covenant of the Gods at risk — since it governs the workings of the Gates. If someone or something is willing to do that, we can't count on anything."

"Which means there's more going on here than Indee let on," Kadana agreed with Shalonie's assessment. She turned toward Templar, her face stern. "What exactly did Indee tell you?"

"Indee didn't tell me anything." Templar seemed more than willing to tell everything he knew. "Fog, her cat did. He came looking for Tormy to rescue Khylar. Omen went to talk to Indee."

"Alone?" Kadana pressed.

"Well, with Kyr and the cats." Templar reconsidered. "Yes, basically alone."

"Which is when Indee hexed Kyr. Didn't you notice the mark on his hand?" Dev threw in. He'd recognized the hex the moment he'd seen it — would have known what it was even if Avarice hadn't already explained the situation to him. He was surprised the Night Dweller hadn't noticed, since it certainly had to be a form of magic he'd studied or practiced. *Remarkably trusting, this lot. Blindly following Omen on some quest they know nothing about.* He watched Templar closely for a reaction.

"What hex mark?" Templar demanded, looking gut-punched.

Dev once again reassessed his opinion of the man. *He's actually worried.*

"On the back of his left hand," Dev explained. "She meant to hex Omen, but got Kyr instead. If Omen even hints that he's not going to fulfill the demands of the quest — rescue Khylar and return him to Kharakhan — the mark is triggered. That's why Omen won't explain — he's afraid of hurting Kyr."

Kadana blinked slowly as if trying to contain her reaction. "Now that sounds more like the Indee I know. She's remarkably efficient at getting her way."

"Efficient?" Templar protested.

"I'm sure Lady Kadana meant treacherous," Dev quipped. "She just didn't want to offend Shalonie."

Shalonie sniffed with annoyance but remained silent.

Kadana however nodded her head as if making a decision. "Regardless of what word you want to use, I know Indee. Whatever quest she's given Omen, she's determined that he will go through with it, and Omen is likely stuck because of the hex mark on Kyr." She pointed at Dev. "You're stuck because Avarice told you to go, and Omen's going to need you, Shalonie, to get into the Mountain of Shadow and more importantly get back out again, so you're committed as well." She glanced over at Templar. "And you and Liethan are the idiots who thought this would be fun, so you're stuck on principle alone."

"I would never abandon Omen," Templar objected, as if offended by the very thought. Something stirred in his yellow eyes. "What do you mean idiots?"

"Actually I think, Liethan is here because his cousin Tara Corsair, Khylar's soon-to-be bride, is also missing," Dev piped up. "Which makes Templar the only idiot."

"Your opinion is worth less than fleas on a cow's—" Templar started, aggressive and fired up, but Kadana cut him off.

"Regardless!" she stated conclusively. "We all go forward as planned. Omen and Kyr need us. And I hope Indee isn't getting us into another war."

"War? What war?" Shalonie said, deeply disturbed. But Kadana was already heading toward the wheel where Haptis was waiting to determine their new course. Shalonie followed after her, fists balled up with frustration.

Templar leaned heavily against the railing and folded his arms. After a moment, his face contorted with disgruntled mirth.

Bloody Night Dweller! Dev gave a curt bow and headed back below deck.

Chapter 19: Aftermath

OMEN

Omen leaned against Tormy as he stared out at the tumultuous ocean from the foredeck of the Golden Voyage. The waves writhed like an endless nest of baby vipers, making his stomach roll. He dug the fingers of his left hand into the downy fur behind Tormy's ear for comfort, both the cat's and his own. The giant cat curled around him and continued to doze in the sun.

Nearly a week had passed since the storm and the leviathan. Omen tried not to think of the gruesome creature, grateful it had sunken to the bottom of the ocean after the blast. He hoped it had been devoured by scores and scores of tiny fish.

Omen had missed most of the days and nights in restless sleep, his nightmares filled with the screams of the men they had not been able to save, his body attempting to restore itself after the harsh energy drain and the harrowing backlash of the psionic jolt.

Shalonie saved the ship and everyone on it. Just glad I could help. He rolled his head from side to side to release the built-up tension from sleeping in a confined space for nearly a week.

Sleep? More like forced hibernation: in his swaying den on the ocean sleeps Omen, the great dancing bear. His mind spun a theme to the ditty, but his imagination wandered off mid-composition to the traveling carnival he'd seen in the Melia market. "Remember the dancing bears,

250

Tormy?"

"I 'member 'member. They is being funny," the cat said, groggy and not opening his big amber eyes. "They is sleeping all winter long."

Omen halted briefly, an unpleasant thought forming in his mind about the seasons and how animals in nature were affected by them.

If the seasons are in upheaval . . . He stared at the petulant waters darkly. The waves were choppy but not violent. *How did Kyr know about the seasons?*

They said the initial storm had raged for three days straight with no break. Kadana and Haptis had fought to adjust the course to make an escape from the downpour.

When it had been her turn to oversee Omen's recovery, Shalonie had explained the details of their navigational efforts. He had listened, trying to make sense of it all as he lay in his hammock below deck, helpless and weak. Tormy never left his side, purring evenly to keep Omen relaxed and dozy.

He must have ducked out to eat when I was asleep. Must have, Omen thought but didn't remember ever not seeing the cat curled up within reach.

Omen had finally roused himself that morning, and he and Tormy had scrambled onto the deck before breakfast, looking for fresh air and conversation. Omen had leaned on the giant cat for balance as he'd put one wobbly foot in front of the other. His knees felt like overcooked noodles.

He'd quickly selected the foredeck, wanting to stay out of the way but still able to observe the sea. Omen was worn out by the effort of just climbing the stairs, but he enjoyed the cloudless sky, the salty air, and the energetic bustle on board. Watching the sailors going about their work, he spotted Tyrin climbing the rigging. Omen wasn't certain if he was trying to get a better view of their surroundings or chasing after the pint-sized monkey, who managed to keep himself well out of reach of the cats. Carrying a small bag filled with supplies, the little monkey scurried up to the crow's nest and the ginger-haired man on watch.

Looks like he got over his fall.

Templar had assured Omen that young Terald had been unhurt and had insisted on resuming his duties. Further, Templar went on, the group had decided to cease worrying about Tyrin going up and down the ropes.

"Couldn't stop the little bugger if we tried; besides he climbs nearly as well as that pet monkey," Templar had said. Omen had accepted Templar's words as metaphorical, but staring at the little monkey swinging from the crow's nest by his long fingers, Omen couldn't help feeling uneasy about Tyrin's escapades. The monkey held on with both hands and feet and his long prehensile tail. Tyrin just had his tiny claws.

Omen looked over at Dev who'd seated himself on the other side of Tormy, legs stretched out as he leaned against a wooden crate. He diligently wrote into the bonding book on his lap. *His turn to babysit, I guess.* Omen eyed the book with annoyance, wondering what Dev could be writing.

"Surely you've already told my mother everything there is to say," he groused. "You can't possibly have anything more to tell her."

Dev's lips twitched upward as he continued to write. "You are correct," he agreed mildly. "I don't think she'll ever use the term 'excruciating detail' around me again."

Omen blinked at him in shock. "You're purposely annoying my mother by writing nonsense to her?"

"Oh, we passed annoying days ago," Dev replied.

Omen was torn between amusement and alarm. "Generally people avoid annoying my mother."

"I did tell you, I'm very disobedient." Dev nodded firmly. "I can be quite difficult — she knew that when she hired me."

Omen clicked his tongue. *Have to admit that makes me feel a lot better about the spying.* He could imagine the look on his mother's face when Dev regaled her with the never-ending commentary supplied by Tormy and Tyrin.

Omen spotted Kadana crossing the deck at a brisk pace, and he waved toward his grandmother in greeting.

"You look like you could use this." She held out a small leather wineskin.

"Scales, no!" Omen shook himself, waking the giant cat again.

"Is we being there yet?" Tormy purred and chewed the air in an exaggerated yawn.

Omen patted the cat's furry shoulder. "Go back to your nap, Tormy."

"It'll be a few days yet, fuzz-face," Kadana said, scanning the horizon and the moderately turbulent sea, "before we hit the port of Khreté."

She loosened the cork of the wineskin. "After wrestling with Urgolath, we had to find a better crossing. Shalonie and Haptis plotted a new course for us." She placed the wineskin down on the deck within reach of Omen's hands. "You should take this. It's an herbal brew. Mégeira brewed it for you. She swears it will restore you."

Omen had his doubts. "Psionics zapped my energy. I'm not seasick or hungover."

"Mégeira grew up on Xelos." Kadana looked at him as if

she expected him to know what that meant. "It's the Island of Witches. The Corsairs gave Eradiadne and her coven a place to live after they were forcefully driven from Kharakhan."

Omen frowned. "I've met Eradiadne. She did crystal magic at the Winter Fest. Nice lady." He shook his head. "Why would someone want to hurt her?"

"Kharakhan is sick with magic," Kadana explained. "It is densely ensconced in some of the wildest magic in the world. Creatures, artifacts, people who wield magic, people who abuse their powers. That makes the regular population nervous. They are very superstitious."

"Like my mother?"

"Something like that."

"But you're a Kharakhian. Magic doesn't seem to bother you." He took the wineskin, uncorked it and sniffed at the contents.

Bergamot. Cedar. Black cherry. Pleasant. Doubt it'll do me any good though.

"Unlike so many of my friends and children, I have no magical talents," Kadana told him. "I came to terms with that a long time ago."

"How?" He couldn't imagine living without magic.

"I stuck a sword in a wizard who had been terrorizing my village," Kadana said nonchalantly. "If it bleeds, I can cut it down. Magic or no magic. That's all."

"What if you can't stick a sword in it?" Omen gestured to the fierce ocean beyond.

"Can't fight the seasons," Kadana mused, "even if they change on us. It's what seasons do — we're supposed to adapt. If summer decides to act like autumn, we will just pretend it's autumn." She gave him a meaningful look. "Unless there is something you want to tell me about the seasons that might shed some light on . . ."

"I don't know what I can safely say," he admitted, finally.

"Omen," she said his name with an edge, "I know Indee, and how her mind works. As long as you don't refuse your quest you should be fine speaking about it. Now, I understand the Autumn Gate is open."

Omen nodded sheepishly.

"So she hexed you — or rather Kyr — to force you to complete the quest no matter what," Kadana probed. "You have to rescue Khylar, who is in the Autumn Lands for some reason."

"And if Omen refuses, even merely says he won't, the hex activates," Dev volunteered, looking up from his bonding book.

"Hey!" Omen exclaimed in warning, worried that Dev's words might trigger the hex.

"The hex doesn't react to me — or anyone else. Only those of you who were in the room when it was cast — so you, Kyr and the cats," Dev pointed out. "As long as none of you refuse, you're fine — unless you take too long. That would probably be bad too."

Omen didn't understand. "And how do you . . ."

"I'm a Machelli," Dev answered. "We know about hexes."

"Machellis also know about all sorts of other things," Kadana added. "So tell us what you know about Khylar and the Autumn Lands."

"Indee's family on her mother's side is faerie from the Teyledrine Court," Dev swiftly supplied, as if he'd been waiting to be asked. "The current keeper of the Autumn

Gate is the king of the Teyledrine. That's how they were able to take Khylar through the Autumn Gate — but why they took him, I don't know. And we can't assume they're done with whatever they're doing — or that they closed the Gate behind them. It may stand open, letting—"

"Letting all manner of things into our world and elbowing aside the emissaries of summer." Kadana looked at Omen. "As Shalonie said, the Gates aren't supposed to stay open — only one night a season. And Autumn has some nasty inhabitants."

"I just have to make things . . ." Omen searched for the most innocuous word. "Right. I have to make things right."

Kadana laughed out loud. "That instinct isn't one you got from my family or your mother's lineage, and certainly not from that Night-dwelling god-creature Cerioth. Must be pure Daenoth." She leaned down and patted Tormy's head. "It suits you though. You and your cat could be heroes. I like the ring of that."

Omen didn't know if she was making fun of him.

"Will you help us?" he thought to ask.

"I think a little trouble is good for Indee, if I'm perfectly honest," Kadana said. "But, as is ever the case, her troubles spell far greater troubles for innocent folk who can't defend themselves." She glanced at Dev. "And that's why Avarice sent you along, to make sure this gets done expediently."

Dev's mouth twitched, ever non-committal. From some hidden pocket, the young man had dug out a large-toothed ivory comb, and he wordlessly busied himself working the knots out of Tormy's tail.

What exactly does she mean by expediently?

"We'll be in Khreté soon." Kadana looked back at her helmsman. "This might not sound like the most rational advice, but if you are going to go through with this — listen to Kyr. The next time Kyr says a fish has a sword, you can be damned certain that a fish is going to have a sword. The gods get cranky when we ignore the words of a prophet."

Omen gulped.

Kadana laughed again. "And no matter what happens don't take it all too seriously. If you forget to laugh, none of the work and sacrifice will have been worth it." She patted Tormy's head again and walked away.

Khreté.

He wondered what waited for them. Kharakhan had been a place of mystery to him. His parents had told him stories of the strange magic that infused the land, and the violence of the Kharakhians was legendary. How quickly would they get to the Mountain of Shadow? How much longer could Kyr stand the hex? And where was Khylar?

Omen had an irrational thought of wanting to punch Khylar in the face the moment he saw him. *"And that's for my brother and my friends!"* In his daydream, Khylar went down in one strike. The thought made him smile.

"Won't be long now." Templar had moved next to him at the railing.

"Never did ask." Omen realized that there were still a lot of unanswered questions. "Have you been to Kharakhan before?"

"A couple of times," Templar said with a smirk. "It's just full of unicorn poop and bad stew."

"Hope those are unrelated." Omen thought he heard Dev laugh at that.

"Unicorn &*%$!" Tyrin tittered from somewhere unseen.

"I was there for the coronation," Templar said quietly.

257

"Khylar's?"

"That must have been magnificent," Dev cut in.

"There were . . . complications." Templar grasped the rail with both hands and fell silent.

Aren't there always.

Omen stared at the waves parting before them, blues and greens topped with tiny whitecaps and caressed by the sparkling sun. He took in a deep lungful of fresh, salty air.

They would arrive in a new city, in a new land, on a new continent soon. Untold complications lay ahead. A spark of exhilaration ignited in Omen's stomach.

"I don't know what's coming," he said quietly to himself. "But with this group, it's bound to be fun."

Want More?

Follow Omen and the gang into Kharakhan and beyond as the tale unfolds in HOLLOW SEASON (Book 4).

❖

If you've enjoyed SUMMER'S FALL, please consider telling a friend, or leaving a review. Help us spread the world Of Cats and Dragons. And, as Tormy would say, that is being greatlynessness!

More OF CATS AND DRAGONS tidbits and artwork are waiting for you on our website:
OfCatsAndDragons.com.

Join our adventurers by signing up for the OF CATS AND DRAGONS Newsletter.

Audiobook Lovers! Listen to OF CATS AND DRAGONS on Audible.

Thank you!

Carol

The day our first book came out, I was diagnosed with cancer. A few months later it had reached stage 4 despite the treatment I was getting (ironically "radiation therapy"). I'm now in chemo, and it seems to be working to shrink the tumors. However, the entire thing has taken a horrific toll on my body. There is no way I would have been able to get through the last few months without the aid of a number people that I would dearly love to thank.

First and foremost, my parents: they have taken me into their home and have become my full-time caretakers. I honestly don't know what I would do without them. They have been so patient and loving, and have gone above the call of duty to keep me going day to day. They are genuinely beautiful people.

Next, I'd like to thank my siblings and I'm including Camilla in that number. Camilla has been so much a part of mine and my family's lives that we all consider her part of the family. Camilla, my younger sister and my older brother have taken turns flying across the country to stay with me and give my poor parents a bit of rest in their caretaker duties whenever possible. And my younger brother has taken it upon himself to pack up all my belongings in my home and put them all into storage for me so that I need not worry about my old house. The four of them have been a font of strength for me, and I cannot thank them enough for all they do. And let me add a thank you to the various spouses who have put up with the long absences of their partners.

I'd also like to thank my coworkers and students. They have all reached out to me in various ways and offered their prayers and support — one of my co-workers took over the task of making cat food for me (my cat is on a special diet). Another started a write-in campaign with my students. I received countless cards and letters from them that have touched my heart in ways I can't describe. They're all wonderful people.

And last, I'd like to thank the clergy members who have visited me, the numerous relatives, my beautiful nieces and nephew, and the total strangers who have offered to pray for me throughout this entire ordeal. I think I have people from every major faith praying for me all over the world. When you go through something like this, you really see what an amazing world we live in.

Camilla and I are going to keep writing Of Cats And Dragons as long as we can. We have so many stories to tell, and I'm going to fight with all I have in me to keep on telling them. And if I stumble along the way, I know Camilla will always be beside me to pick up the banner and keep going.

❖

Camilla

A lot of people stepped up when the unthinkable happened.

Carol's diagnosis came the day NIGHT'S GIFT was released, so we never even had a moment to celebrate that wasn't under the shadow of this horrible cancer. Since then, there have been many ups and downs (more downs than ups, if I am totally honest). But we've hung in there, and we've continued the series — which we love.

261

Carol has been strong and determined. She is the warrior I've always known her to be, but the enemy she is battling is fierce and powerful.

We are hopeful. But this is real and terrifying.

Some great friends came to my rescue these last months. I have experienced deep loss, but what looms here is beyond my ability to cope with all alone.

My husband, P.J., has been more than terrific: The long conversations about the meaning of it all. Taking care of things at home when I fly up north to spend time with Carol. And the insistence on the promise that, no matter what happens, I won't break. And on top of all of that, he continues to support our work — as an editor, a story doctor, and the exquisite narrator of our audiobooks. I could not do any of this without him.

Carol's parents and siblings, all of whom are incredible — I am so grateful and humbled that they consider me family.

Bonita, who understands and lifts me up, even when pushing the next werewolf book back causes her sleepless nights.

The Barry girls (though they are now also Campbells and Fraenkles), who are only a phone call away and have not forgotten our shared history.

Fran and Nicole, who are the best kind of friends in a crisis.

Andonia, who magically appeared the second she was needed, and who got me through a few very scary days with unwavering love and deep, deep faith.

And we want everyone to know that this is not the end OF CATS AND DRAGONS. After SUMMER'S FALL, Carol and I have two more complete books that are now being edited, and a handful of partially completed manuscripts. We also have over 250 story fragments, short stories, outlines, dialogues, and scenes. We have a timeline that reaches over generations in our story world. We have been working on the world OF CATS AND DRAGONS for over thirty years. There's a lot there. We have a plan.

I am deeply committed to sharing our stories because that is what I can do to honor our friendship. We love these characters so much, and since we made the decision to share them — that is what will happen.

There will be more Tormy. There will be more Omen. And Kyr. And Tyrin. There will be more. . .

❖

We also want to thank all of our friends who listened to the tale of the tale unfolding, and threw nothing but positive energy and love our way.

And a big thanks to Team Tormy and everyone who keeps asking, "What's next?"

About the authors

Carol E. Leever:

Carol E. Leever, a college professor, has been teaching Computer Science for many years. She programs computers for fun, but turns to writing and painting when she wants to give her brain a good work out.

An avid reader of science fiction and fantasy, she's also been published in the Sword and Sorceress anthologies, and has recently gotten into painting illustrations and book covers. A great lover of cats, she also manages to work her feline overlords into her writing, painting and programming classes often to the dismay of her students.

Camilla Ochlan:

Owner of a precariously untamed imagination and a scuffed set of polyhedral dice (which have gotten her in trouble more than once), Camilla writes fantasy and science fiction. Separate OF CATS AND DRAGONS, Camilla has written the urban fantasy WEREWOLF WHISPERER series (with Bonita Gutierrez), the mythpunk noir THE SEVENTH LANE and, in collaboration with her husband, written and produced a number of short films, including the suburban ghost story DOG BREATH and the recent 20/20 HINDSIGHT. An unapologetic dog lover and cat servant, Camilla lives in Los Angeles with her husband actor, audiobook narrator and dialect coach P.J. Ochlan, three sweet rescue dogs and a bright orange Abyssinian cat.

Get in touch

Visit our website at OfCatsAndDragons.com
Like us on Facebook @OfCatsAndDragons and join the
Friends Of Cats And Dragons Facebook group.
Find Carol:

caroleleever.deviantart.com

Find Camilla:

Twitter: @CamillaOchlan
Instagram: instagram.com/camillaochlan/
Blog: The Seething Brain

Or write to us at:
meow@ofcatsanddragons.com

42401541R00168

Made in the USA
Lexington, KY
16 June 2019